THE DARCY BENNET ARRANGEMENT

HARRIET KNOWLES

Copyright © 2017 by Harriet Knowles

All rights reserved.

This book is set in Regency England. It is written by an English author, using British English words and spelling.

Edited by JW Services

Proofreading by Mystique Editing

ISBN-13: 978-1548425180

ISBN-10: 1548425184

CHAPTER 1

*M*iss Elizabeth Bennet carried her basket through to the flower room in the gardens at Longbourn. It was almost full with the late lavender stems she'd picked, and she wanted to speak to Jane, who'd broken off the conversation and hurried into the room a few minutes earlier.

"Oh, Jane, what did I say that upset you so?" Elizabeth placed her basket on the old wooden table and reached for the twine to bunch up the lavender.

"Why, Lizzy, nothing at all." Jane had recovered her composure and smiled her usual serene smile at her sister. "I am quite happy, as you can see."

"Indeed, and I would not wish to continue the

conversation if you find it distressing." Elizabeth tied the lavender deftly, and hung the bunch from the hook where it would dry quickly in the breeze that blew through.

She reached for another length of twine. "But it is usual for us to talk of all sorts of things while we are without risk of being overheard."

Jane blushed a rosy pink and looked down. "I know, Lizzy. I just found it suddenly difficult, thinking of poor Lydia. I hope that she can be happy now that she is married, but now that we know the character of Mr. Wickham so much better, I fear for her future."

Elizabeth took a deep breath. She had not Jane's sweetness of nature, she knew that, but she would not wish to cause any distress to her sister. "I am sure she will be, Jane. You know Lydia pays no heed to the proprieties and she feels no shame or embarrassment for what she did." She looked over at Jane, who was gathering each stem very slowly and thoughtfully. "She is so happy at having married before all of us, and sees it as an absolute adventure. I do not believe she will regret her choice, and she sees nothing wrong with her actions."

She hung the next bunch up, thinking of her next words. "I think we are more unhappy than she is, for we know what it has cost her — and us

— in respectability, and how it has changed our own futures for the worse." And as she spoke, her own heart was heavy. She remembered her last sight of Mr. Darcy, how his concern for her had changed to an expressionless mask and how anxious he had seemed to escape from the room.

She sighed. She would never see him again, she knew that. And he would see to it that Mr. Bingley never saw Jane again, as well. Both of them were ruined, and although Lydia was now married, the scandal would be remembered by those who knew of it, and it would be whispered to new arrivals in the village. They would never escape it. They were without fortune and now without virtue. When Longbourn was gone, they would be obliged to seek work as governesses or companions. Their lives would be very different to what they had hoped.

"Don't be so downcast, Lizzy." Jane tried to cheer her up. "Let's talk of other things. You haven't told me everything about Hunsford and how Charlotte is finding married life."

She smiled over at her younger sister. "I'm sure you do not regret refusing the hand of our dear cousin, Mr. Collins."

"Indeed I do not." Elizabeth laughed. She put down the lavender and pushed back her hair.

"I could not abide another day in his

company, and when Lady Catherine de Bourgh tried to get Maria and I to stay those extra weeks, I nearly died."

Jane smiled reluctantly. "I remember your letter telling me of that. I cannot believe that Lady Catherine is the sort of person that you describe, you make her out to be so unpleasant. But you are a good judge of people and most observant, so I must believe you." She hung up her flowers.

"And what of Colonel Fitzwilliam? You have not described him in very great detail, other than he is Mr. Darcy's cousin. Is he like him?"

"Oh, no, Jane. The Colonel is a most amiable man, exceptionally pleasant company and most handsome. He is about thirty years old, I would say, and his manners are pleasant to experience. He makes me feel quite a lady." She stopped and swallowed. She would never meet him again, either, she was sure.

"So Lady Catherine must have had two sisters then, and Mr. Darcy is the son of one, and Colonel Fitzwilliam the son of the other?" Jane surmised.

"I think she must have had a brother." Elizabeth thought.

"For Colonel Fitzwilliam himself told me that, as the second son of an Earl, he would not be able to marry without a consideration of fortune. So

Lady Catherine's title is because she is the daughter of an Earl."

She smiled ruefully. "The aristocracy seems as much above the landed gentry as those gentlemen seem to feel themselves above us, who are descended, at least on one side, from *trade*." She laughed.

"I think they are all quite above themselves." She thought for a moment. "Except your Mr. Bingley. He is quite the most amiable and friendly man I have ever met, from any walk of life. But I cannot say the same for his sisters." She snipped the stems level.

"You cannot argue, Jane. You told me yourself that Miss Caroline Bingley was abominably rude to you in London when she did deign to visit, and I will not have you defending her." She waved the scissors at her sister.

"She feels herself so high above us, and yet their fortune is from trade, too!" she shook her head.

"I just wonder how Mr. Bingley and Mr. Darcy became such good friends. They are so different in their station and behaviour."

"It is true." Jane was no longer making any pretence of being busy with her hands. "But I am sorry to think ill of Miss Bingley. I am sure she feels it is for the best for her brother and therefore

I must believe that he cannot care for me in the way I had thought."

Elizabeth had nothing to do with her hands either, having finished all that was in her basket. She picked it up, and Jane's too, and placed them neatly on the shelf. "I am very ready for some tea," she said. "Let's go into the house and see what is afoot."

CHAPTER 2

The next morning, she was astonished to receive a letter. The direction was written in a young, unformed, but feminine hand, and she turned it over and over, puzzled. Looking at the seal, she saw a large, ornate letter P, and was puzzled anew.

She made her excuses to her family and went up to her room instead of the gardens, for the sky was heavy in expectation of rain. Sitting in the chair by the window, she broke the seal and began to read.

> *Dear Miss Bennet,*
> *I hope you don't mind me writing to you,*
>   *but as I do not know when we are*
>   *likely to meet again …*

Elizabeth frowned, she still didn't recognise the handwriting, and yet this young woman appeared to know her. She turned over the three closely written pages to look at the signature at the end

Your most affectionate friend,
Georgiana Darcy

She stared at the signature. It appeared that Mr. Darcy had not told his sister of the facts which had led to Elizabeth's precipitate departure from Derbyshire, or the girl would most certainly not have been permitted to write to her.

She turned back to the beginning of the letter and read it fully.

Dear Miss Bennet,
I hope you don't mind me writing to you,
but as I do not know when we are
likely to meet again, I wanted to keep
in touch by correspondence. I
remember most affectionately the
kindness which you showed me when
we met, and in particular when you
came to Pemberley with your aunt
and uncle.
I do not know the nature of the business

*which called you away so urgently,
but I know my brother was deeply
affected. He has gone away now with
our guests to London, and I am alone
here at Pemberley, with just my
governess and the servants.*

*It is a little lonely here, and it means I
think about you very much. You are
one of the few people who noticed
how difficult I find it to make
acquaintances into true friends and
you noticed it so soon that I am sure
you and I will be fast friends as soon
as we can meet again.*

Poor Georgiana, Elizabeth thought. It was certain that Mr. Darcy would stop the correspondence as soon as he knew about it, and would therefore need to vouchsafe the reasons for her own precipitate departure from Derbyshire. She sighed. The friendship had developed quickly on her side as well as that of Georgiana, she was a delightful young lady and Elizabeth knew that they would, in more encouraging circumstances, have had an intimate friendship, even perhaps as close as she was to Jane. She turned back to the letter.

> *I am most fortunate to be under the guardianship of my brother and Colonel Fitzwilliam, whom I understand you met at Rosings recently. They are the kindest of gentlemen and I could not wish for better to look after my interests. But sometimes I feel they protect me too much, and I am determined to write to them and ask if I may go to London too, for there is much to see and do there, even if the crowds sometimes intimidate me.*
>
> *You told me that you sometimes stay in London with your aunt and uncle, and I wonder if there is any likelihood of you being there soon. It would be wonderful to meet again.*

Elizabeth shook her head sadly. The letter was open and trusting and she would have been most pleased to have responded to the friendship it offered so disarmingly. But Mr. Darcy would stop any possibility of friendship with her. He would not want his sister's virtue tainted by friendship with any Bennet, and she needed somehow to let down Georgiana's expectations without shattering her fragile confidence and thinking that Elizabeth thought ill of her.

She folded the letter thoughtfully, wondering how and when she should respond.

A knock on the door drew her attention. "Come in," she called, and Jane entered.

"Lizzy, it is time for lunch, I was wondering what was in the letter that had caused you to forget the time."

Elizabeth smiled. "If it is time for lunch, then we will go down and I will tell you afterwards, for the telling now would make us both tardy, and for that, our mother will rebuke us most heartily."

Laughing together, they descended the stairs, and Elizabeth contemplated how fortunate she was to have a sister to whom she was so close.

❧

*B*ut the very next morning, she received yet another letter, this time from Aunt Gardiner. As the weather was more clement, Elizabeth took this letter out to the gardens and sat on a bench under the dappled light of the sun below the trees.

This was the answer to her letter asking why Mr. Darcy had been at Lydia's marriage, and why it seemed to be such a secret as Lydia was incapable of keeping. It was a bulky letter, comprising many sheets of writing paper, and Elizabeth felt quite ashamed of having demanded such attention from her aunt. But she also felt happy, because such a long letter would give her all the facts that she had assured herself she required.

> *My dear niece,*
> *I have just received your letter, and shall*
> > *devote this whole morning to*
> > *answering it, as I foresee that a little*
> > *writing will not comprise what I have*
> > *to tell you.*

Elizabeth smiled affectionately, and read the letter as fast as she could, finding herself both amazed and surprised at finding out that Mr. Darcy had, in fact, done all the discovering of where Lydia had been and had done all the bargaining and applied all the pressure to make the marriage go ahead, and had also borne all the costs. The only thing he had allowed Mr. Gardiner — no — insisted on, was that the credit all go to him. Mr. Darcy was not to appear involved at all.

She stopped, and stared at the clouds scudding past. Why would he have done what he did, if he had not wanted his own involvement to be known? She leafed through the pages again, looking for the relevant part.

> *The motive professed, was his conviction of its being owing to himself that Wickham's worthlessness had not been so well known, as to make it impossible for any young woman of character, to love or confide in him. He generously imputed the whole to his mistaken pride, and confessed that he had before thought it beneath him, to lay his private actions open to the world. His character was to speak for itself. He called it, therefore, his duty to step forward, and endeavour to remedy an evil, which had been brought on by himself.*

That, she supposed, would be believed as a reason, if anyone were to know, but she soon understood that Aunt Gardiner was imputing a whole different reason to his actions, and she blushed at the very thought as she read the final paragraphs of her aunt's letter.

> *Pray forgive me, if I have been very presuming, or at least do not punish*

me so far, as to exclude me from P. I
shall never be quite happy till I have
been all round the park. A low
phaeton, with a nice little pair of
ponies, would be the very thing.

No, her aunt was wrong. Mr. Darcy would never propose to her again. At Lambton, she had almost begun to hope, herself, that he might have forgiven her unpardonable rudeness when refusing him before. But now the disgrace of Lydia, and more so, the fact that she was now sister-in-law to the detested Mr. Wickham, would render the chance to be mistress of Pemberley utterly impossible.

No, she would explain to Jane what had happened, for her aunt had allowed that, but no one else must ever know the extent of their debt to Mr. Darcy.

CHAPTER 3

*H*is carriage bounced and rattled over the ill-made road into Kent. Fitzwilliam Darcy scowled. Why could not the local landowners keep this road better? He made sure all the roads on his estate were much better kept than this. And so close to London! It was insupportable.

"Come now, Darcy! I would have you be more cheerful, cousin." Colonel Fitzwilliam sat opposite him, amiable as ever. "We will have a chance to walk in the Park and eat from an excellent table."

Darcy just grunted. "Perhaps. But the company is not likely to be improved, and I find it most distasteful."

His cousin made a face. "I agree that Lady Catherine has no restraint in her conversation and that can make it hard to respond politely. However, it is necessary to make these occasional visits and perhaps Mrs. Collins' delightful friend might again be visiting them. That might improve your opinion of this visit."

"Perhaps." Mr. Darcy knew that Elizabeth would not be staying with Mrs. Collins. But he could not divulge the reason to his cousin, and so he would not mention it.

"But I hope that Lady Catherine does not invite the odious Mr. Collins to Rosings too often."

"I agree, he is not a happy addition to the dinner table." Colonel Fitzwilliam looked around. "We are nearly there. Let us make the most we can of the weekend. Then we will be free of it for another month."

Darcy grunted again. He knew his cousin would forgive his mood, it was always the same when they journeyed here.

At least it was the afternoon, and as soon as tea might be over, he would walk in the Park until dinner, and thus would pass the Friday.

He thought of the time he arrived and discovered that Miss Elizabeth Bennet was staying at Hunsford. It had discomposed him entirely, and speeded his discovery that his feelings for her were much stronger than he had previously allowed himself to think.

He groaned at the memory of his proposal to her, and her reply, *"had you behaved in a more gentle-man-like manner"* — the phrase which now burned nightly in his dreams. He had examined again and again his words to her and had mortified himself as he acknowledged the truth of her accusation.

"Cousin. *Cousin!*" Colonel Fitzwilliam's voice intruded upon his thoughts. "What is the matter, sir? You have become quite silent, even more than is usual for you."

Mr. Darcy pulled himself together. "I am sorry, Richard. I was thinking of another matter."

"That is very evident." The Colonel laughed. "I must advise you to be careful around our aunt, or you might find yourself agreeing to something you had not fully considered."

"That would be difficult indeed." Mr. Darcy swung down from the coach after his cousin, resolving to be more careful when letting his thoughts return to Miss Elizabeth Bennet.

He had been so surprised to see her at Pemberley and then delighted to find her attitude so apparently changed towards him, he had begun to hope against hope that she might one day accept him and he'd be able to forget those terrible days.

"You have forgotten yourself again, man!" The Colonel's voice was amused, and Darcy shook his head irritably.

"I must say again that you should be on your guard. The last occasion when I was here, when you were too occupied in Town to accompany me, Lady Catherine was talking at length that you had reached the right age to be settling into matrimony and how she longed to bring out her plans for your wedding to our cousin, Miss Anne."

"What?" Mr. Darcy started, and he felt his face suffuse with colour. "And you did not tell me before we arrived here?"

"Of course not. If I had, you would again have discovered urgent business that required you to stay in London, and my last visit alone was quite uncomfortable enough for me to need you here."

Darcy fell into step beside Fitzwilliam. "That is most unsporting of you, Richard. I am not happy with your reasoning."

"I am." The Colonel laughed. "Just be conscious of this fact; for once you say one word wrong, you will be obliged and have no escape."

"I think that you would do well to consider the option yourself, sir." Darcy continued the conversation in a lower voice as they mounted the steps.

"I have Pemberley and no need of Rosings. But you would do well to gain the estate yourself."

"No. You forget the requirement. Miss de Bourgh is our cousin and I feel most acutely for her, but I do not wish to make her my bride, even for Rosings."

"I thank you for the warning." Mr. Darcy knew the conversation was at an end as he heard his aunt's strident voice from the drawing room.

"Is that my nephews? I have been waiting for them to arrive for some time. I am not accustomed to tardiness, especially in the family."

The two men exchanged resigned looks and Darcy followed the other into the stifling presence of their aunt.

❧

*H*e kept a close check on his thoughts and his mind on all that was said during tea and over dinner and escaped to his room as soon as was reasonable.

Once there, he could stop and think clearly. He remembered the anger and incredulity when he had retired to this very bedchamber after Elizabeth had refused him. He shrugged in resignation. He now understood why she had done so, but the pain was still acute.

He'd sat there — at that very desk — and written to her. Then he'd waited in the grove to see her as she walked and he had given her the letter. His heart had broken when he'd walked away from her that day.

But now he had hope, hope that she might, in time, think differently about him. He was conscious of his defects and faults that she had pointed out with such acute observation and he'd worked hard to be more amiable and open.

And she had smiled at him as he talked to her aunt and uncle at Pemberley, she had not looked despisingly at him.

But his most recent memory of her was what pained him the most, the sight of her weeping over the ruin of her sister and knowing that she too, was tainted by those actions.

He had been unable to tell her that it made no difference to him at all, he had not yet been ready to make his offer to her. Instead he had determined to make everything right for her. That he could do, his money was able to buy much and he would not hesitate to relieve her pain.

He longed to travel back to Netherfield, to try and see her again, assure himself of her. But it was not right yet. Not until he was certain that Wickham and his bride had left Longbourn would he be able to go and find her.

He looked out into the darkness towards the parsonage at Hunsford. He could not imagine Mr. Collins would suffer any of his cousins to visit them now, however strong their friendship to his wife. But tomorrow he would ask the Colonel to call and check. The Collinses had not been at dinner, perhaps because Lady Catherine would not invite them if Elizabeth were there.

The slight hope helped him as he prepared for his repose. He would dream again of Miss Bennet, see her eyes laughing up at him, and wake hoping that she would soon be his.

CHAPTER 4

The next morning, he and his cousin walked in the Park, discussing the latest news from London, and from France. They were united of the opinion that Napoleon was still a present danger and Darcy was glad that he had not been obliged by circumstances into the army.

As they walked near the parsonage, he nodded towards it. "You should go and pay your respects, cousin. It might be that Mrs. Collins has her sister staying. You thought she was a sweet girl, I think."

Colonel Fitzwilliam frowned. "Well, I suppose I could. But she is not yet old enough to have formed a character that I could discern. She was frightened into silence by the atmosphere at Rosings."

"That is hardly surprising, sir. Many people

are taken that way."

The Colonel laughed. "Except your young friend, Miss Bennet. She was amazingly composed, and was delightful company."

"Indeed." Mr. Darcy could not let the conversation proceed. He did not want his cousin to form any opinion of his feelings. That would be insupportable if it got back to anyone who might provoke a conversation.

"Well, I will go and call on them, if you wish it." The Colonel was not reticent about any social requirement. "I presume you will not accompany me."

"That is correct. I will continue to walk and see you at lunch, perhaps."

The two men bowed and parted company.

Darcy was now free to allow his thoughts to wander in whichever direction they chose. And he found himself thinking of Miss Bennet. He was sure that she knew nothing of his involvement in the marriage of her sister to Wickham and he wished it to stay that way. However, he enjoyed thinking of her reaction to the letter from her uncle in which she would have received the news.

He was thus happily occupied until he saw Colonel Fitzwilliam striding towards him. He raised his hat, and the two men met and turned companionably back towards Rosings.

"They have no visitors, as you had supposed, Darcy." The Colonel didn't look at him directly. "But Mr. Collins was at pains to tell me why he was not prepared to accommodate any of his cousins in his home again. He went to great lengths to tell me a whole sorry story about the youngest Bennet girl. I found it most difficult to listen to, and in particular, his violent enjoyment of their downfall."

Mr. Darcy set his jaw. He must not make any comment that would involve him in this affair in his cousin's mind, but his rage at the apparent glee of Mr. Collins made him want to go and make that clergyman regret spreading the story. But he must be careful. He must control himself.

"Did he have no sensibility of how much that must have hurt Mrs. Collins? After all, she was a most intimate friend of Miss Elizabeth Bennet."

"No, I do not believe the man is capable of any consideration of another at all. Mrs. Collins seemed quite downcast."

"I am very sorry." Mr. Darcy walked on. He determined on one thing. If the Collinses came to dinner this weekend, he would discover urgent business in Town and cut the weekend short — before dinner.

*B*ut it was just the family again that evening, as they sat at the candlelit table. Lady Catherine de Bourgh sat, as always, at the head of the table and directed the conversation.

Mr. Darcy sat and thought — as he always did, that if someone had controlled that lady's behaviour and attitude many years ago, she might even have become a more pleasant companion. But it was too late now to do anything but oblige the lady and escape as soon as possible.

He watched his young cousin as she sat silently at the end of the table, her companion beside her, encouraging her to eat. He wondered how much of Anne's sickly ways were forced by her mother and whether she would have been different had she been able to visit other homes of the family when she was younger.

But there was no spark of life or vitality in her eyes, her vacant expression and constant illnesses were profoundly depressing to him. He felt acutely sorry for her.

She should have suitors and choices galore. An inheritance such as Rosings would normally have many, many young men visiting and vying for her hand in marriage.

He smiled at his thought. Even Wickham had

not attempted to try for the honour, despite visiting with him when they were younger.

He suddenly wondered if it had been in Wickham's mind to prevail upon the younger woman when her mother died. Lady Catherine would not countenance an approach from the son of a steward while she was alive.

But now he was married to Lydia Bennet, and all such possibilities were naught.

"Mr. Darcy! Mr. Darcy! I will not have such inattention at my table. I demand to know of what you were thinking, sir!" Lady Catherine's strident tone pulled him back to the present and he saw Colonel Fitzwilliam's warning glance.

He thought quickly. "I am most sorry, Lady Catherine. I was thinking of the news from France."

"Hmph! I do not think it is necessary to ponder on such things. You cannot change anything, and we are very safe here in Kent. You, young man, need to attend to what I am saying." She leaned forward in her seat.

"I was instructing you that you need to settle into matrimony, sir. It is time Pemberley had a mistress and that you secure your estate with an heir."

Darcy stared at her in astonishment. He had not thought she would be so open about the conversation in the presence of her daughter. But the older woman had no compunction in continuing.

"Rosings is also in need of securing into the next generation. It is time for you to fulfil your mother's most urgent wish and unite Rosings Park and Pemberley. We must formalise your engagement to my daughter."

He turned and looked at Anne. Her gaze was vacant and she stared into the distance. He wondered if she had even heard her mother's words.

"I think that is premature, Lady Catherine. I am not yet thirty years old, and I have a great deal of business to attend to."

The old lady drew herself up. "I am not accustomed to being refused, young man! Your mother would have been ashamed of you refusing to fulfil her wishes." She glared at him.

He could not help it, and the comparison between Anne and Elizabeth was too acute. He could not possibly consider marrying Anne.

If he could not marry Elizabeth, he would never marry. The realisation of this sudden knowledge stunned him for a moment. But he must be careful.

He shook his head and his aunt drew a deep breath. As her voice washed over him, he thought about how Elizabeth would react, could she be here and hear what was going on. He smiled as he imagined her face and her thoughts. She would not be afraid to say what she was thinking and he must not, either.

But he didn't want to cause Anne any pain, even though he wasn't sure what she thought about the situation.

He was drawn back to the present by a loud cough from the Colonel and as he glanced over, he saw his warning glance.

Looking over at his aunt, he saw a self-satisfied look on her face and wondered what he had missed. No, he must be absolutely clear.

"Lady Catherine, I am not yet ready to marry. I have Pemberley and I will always wish to live there. I do not want to leave Rosings empty, and I do not think it is right to unite the two estates." He drew a deep breath again.

"If you wish to unite the family, and ensure Rosings stays within it, you have a number of nephews, many of whom are in much greater need of Anne's fortune than I."

He waited for her anger to erupt. Perhaps he would be able to get away even tonight. No, it was too late, he must at least stay the night.

"You are most inattentive, you ungrateful nephew!" Lady Catherine stormed, and he sat impassively to let her express her displeasure and get used to his decision.

"How dare you insult my daughter? You have given no thought to her wishes and her feelings. And as for my own wishes …? I am most seriously displeased with you."

He thought with amusement how she gave no thought to his wishes or feelings on the matter.

"Madam, I have never received the slightest intimation from Miss de Bourgh that she has any feelings towards me at all. However, I am perfectly willing to discuss with her what she thinks the future might hold and whether I can assist her in any way for her future as mistress at Rosings."

Lady Catherine looked at him suspiciously. "Anne wishes to be betrothed to you, and married as soon as possible. Rosings is much more convenient for London than Pemberley is, and your sister would be able to take Pemberley when she marries."

He was unmoved. "I need to discuss the matter with Miss de Bourgh, but I assure you that my own mind is clear. I have communicated my reasons to you."

She glared at him, and then at her daughter. "We will have this conversation over coffee in the drawing room. Come, Anne." And she swept to her feet and the ladies withdrew.

CHAPTER 5

*T*he gentlemen stood as the ladies went out. Then they sat at the dining table as the doors were closed and the footman presented the port to Mr. Darcy as the senior gentleman present.

"Whew!" Colonel Fitzwilliam looked over expressively. "I think, Darcy, that this will continue to be an interesting evening."

"You might think so." Mr. Darcy was thinking hard. "I am determined to try and speak to Anne without the presence of her mother or her companion."

He turned to his cousin. "Have you ever had any sensible, serious conversation with her?"

"No." The Colonel looked thoughtful. "Do

you think she cannot make such decisions? No, I am sure she is able to think sensibly."

"Perhaps." Darcy sipped his port. "I wonder if she has been too long under the influence of her mother and if she has any wishes that we might discern as her own. We must find out, sir. It is, perhaps, our duty."

"I still feel that you are in some considerable danger of being outmanoeuvred by Lady Catherine." Colonel Fitzwilliam laughed across the table at him.

"I know that you are determined and single-minded, but she is a remarkable woman, and you do not have that killer instinct which I see so clearly in her. After all, her daughter would be best served by marriage within the family. Then she will be protected and can receive the security her mother craves for her."

"If you can see the advantage, I must say again that I wonder you do not step forward and make an offer. You have even more advantages than I, being of fully noble stock."

"You mock me, Darcy. The younger son of an Earl is more materially disadvantaged than a landed gentleman. You know that."

"All the more reason to aspire to a young lady with great fortune to inherit." Darcy poured himself another glass of port.

"If you drink that whole glass before going through to the ladies, I am convinced that you will be obliged to Anne by the end of the evening." Colonel Fitzwilliam leaned forward and removed the glass from Darcy's fingers.

"I am protecting you, although I know you seek solace from its contents."

Darcy glanced at him. "Thank you. But, apart from the actual lady concerned, why would you not want Rosings? It is a gracious estate."

"Indeed. But I am a soldier by profession. My life is not mine to promise, not until I am too old for battle. If I should die in France, then what would become of her? He shook his head. "No, Lady Catherine would not countenance it."

"You hold up a straw man, Richard, and you know it. You could quite easily buy out your commission if you were to marry her." He narrowed his eyes.

"No, I think that you have quite another direction in mind." He was rewarded for his perspicacity by a change in the colour of the other man's face.

"So, I am right, am I? And when might I be able to congratulate you and know which fortunate young lady has secured your affections?"

The other man shook his head. "You are too precipitate, man. It is much too early for you to know anything. But I promise you will be the first to know, if all goes well."

And Darcy had to be content with that. "So. If I cannot have another drink, we might as well go through and incur more of Lady Catherine's displeasure. What say you?"

"I concur, my cousin." The Colonel stood up and they prepared to join the ladies.

~

*I*n vain did Lady Catherine rage at her two nephews. Mr. Darcy was quite implacable.

"Madam, Colonel Fitzwilliam and myself will talk to Miss de Bourgh in the morning. We will speak to her together and ascertain her desires and how we can assist her. The weather is fine and settled and we will sit in the small summer house which is warm in the sun and is also in full view of you in the house, so that the proprieties can be observed."

"That is insupportable! Anne requires my presence to explain her wishes, and they concur most completely with mine!"

Mr. Darcy glanced over at his young cousin. He thought he could detect a flicker of resentment in her eyes. Perhaps she was not insensible of what was happening after all. He turned back to his aunt.

"Lady Catherine, I have stated what we intend to do tomorrow. Let us change the subject." His eyes lit on the piano in the alcove. It was a pity there was no one to play, and he remembered Miss Elizabeth Bennet teasing him as he stood beside the instrument.

Colonel Fitzwilliam gave another warning cough, and Darcy sighed, and turned to him.

"Thank you." He was a good friend.

"It is a pity we have not enough for a hand of cards. I think I might retire early and attend to some correspondence."

"You will remain here, sir, and attend to your family duties!" Lady Catherine was not going to give in.

He bowed to her. "I am happy to wait upon your conversation, madam, provided we do not return to the conversation just concluded."

She glared at him, but he sat unmoved. If she wanted to be miserable, then that was her choice. But he must remain on his guard and try not to let himself think of Elizabeth.

There were several minutes of silence. The old lady sat with her lips pressed together angrily, before finally caving in. She loved the sound of her own voice too much to sit in silence.

"Well, Mr. Darcy. Since you disapprove of my conversation, let us hear yours."

He kept his face impassive. "Of course." His manners could be impeccable when he tried. "I think that the roses this year have been exceptionally good, and the rose garden here at Rosings Park is one of the finest I have seen anywhere." He was then able to sit back when Lady Catherine seized on the topic.

"Of course! I had Humphry Repton himself come and landscape the entire park. You know of him, I am sure." She shook her head in her earnestness.

"He designed the estates of the Dukes of Portland and Bedford. I visited them to inspect his work before engaging him." She leaned forward, and her hat wobbled slightly.

"I was most insistent about the roses in particular." She stared at him, daring him to contradict her.

He bowed, smiling. "That is very evident, Lady Catherine. The scent is most pleasing, especially at dusk."

"And all of it could be yours." She stared at him resentfully.

"We have finished that conversation, madam." He rose to his feet.

"If you will excuse me, I have several letters to write." He was absolutely determined not to reward her bad manners any longer. It might be too late, but he would not now let her win all the battles.

The Colonel had risen too, and they both bowed at Cousin Anne, before bowing to Lady Catherine, who seemed quite unable to answer what she would see as such calculated defiance.

As the men climbed the stairs to their rooms, the Colonel looked at his cousin with puzzlement.

"I am at a loss, Darcy, to understand why you have suddenly decided to stand up to our aunt in such a firm manner." His quizzical expression made Mr. Darcy chuckle.

"I have decided that Miss de Bourgh has probably taken as much disdain as she has any right to expect. If Lady Catherine is determined to run my life too, she will find that she has stirred up trouble in places she does not expect."

The Colonel shrugged. "Well, I am with you, whatever you say. We have the responsibility, perhaps, of seeing our cousin settled in life, even if neither of us intend to marry her."

"Indeed. A responsibility much like my sister,

37

although there we have the formal guardianship in place."

He received no answer to that, and later found himself puzzled by it. But at that instant, he was thinking of the letter he would write to Charles Bingley, suggesting he open Netherfield, so the moment passed.

CHAPTER 6

"*L*izzy! Lizzy!" Kitty's voice rang out over the gardens, and Elizabeth glanced at Jane, her eyebrows raised. The sisters were sitting in the afternoon sunshine, reading, and Kitty's interruption was most unexpected.

"Kitty!" Elizabeth rose to meet her. "I thought you were visiting Aunt Phillips in Meryton this afternoon?"

"I was." Kitty reached her sisters, bouncing with excitement. "But there is much talk in Meryton that Mr. Bingley is to return to Netherfield with a shooting party." She was quite breathless with running.

"Aunt Phillips heard it from the butcher, who has received such a large order that he has had to send to town urgently for some more cuts." She gazed eagerly at her sister, who raised her eyebrows.

"That is indeed a surprise, Kitty. I was quite of the opinion that Mr. Bingley would not return and soon give up the rental." Elizabeth smiled.

"I think you must tell Mama. She will be in a flutter of excitement."

"Oh, yes! I will!" Kitty ran back towards the house.

Elizabeth turned to Jane, who had stayed with her head studiously bent over her book.

"Well, Jane?"

Jane looked up. Her cheeks were pink, and she seemed to be struggling to keep her serene, untroubled expression, but Elizabeth could tell her excitement.

"It is no good pretending to be unmoved, Jane. I can see the brightness in your eyes."

"You are mistaken, Lizzy." Jane carefully closed her book. "If it is a shooting party, the men will be much engaged with it and may not even bring the ladies with them."

"Oh, I hope you are wrong, dear Jane. I believe Mr. Bingley will call as soon as he arrives here." Elizabeth longed to see her sister's happiness restored. But her heart was heavy. Would Mr. Darcy permit him to renew his friendship with

Jane after Lydia's ruin? She could not allow herself to truly believe it.

"I wonder when the gentlemen will arrive?" Jane was obviously more concerned than she was trying to show. "If the butcher has such an urgent order, then perhaps it means they are arriving within the day." She looked suddenly flustered.

"But we have been hiding here rather too much, perhaps. We do not know how those in Meryton feel about our disgrace. Perhaps they will convey our reclusiveness to those at Netherfield, who will then feel that we do not wish to be disturbed."

"I am convinced that if Mr. Bingley wishes to call, he will pay no regard to the tattle of idle people, Jane." Elizabeth leaned towards her sister. "Let us wait calmly on events, so that no one knows of any internal anxieties we may harbour." Her own heart twisted. Did this mean that she would see Mr. Darcy again? Would he risk coming to Netherfield, knowing that he might see Elizabeth?

Her heart told her no. She had seen how anxious he was to leave her presence that morning in Lambton, and nothing had changed since. Oh, following her marriage, Lydia's ruin was now merely a disgrace. But when combined with the gulf between their stations in life, that which he had made so clear to her that day of his proposal, she could see no prospect that she would ever be accepted again.

She turned back to her book, to hide the tears that started to her eyes. He had seemed so different in Derbyshire. So much so, that she had convinced herself that his proud demeanour and the arrogant words he had spoken were but an error in her memory.

However, his manner when she had described Lydia's flight to London with Mr. Wickham had killed all hope within her. Slowly she put her book down, and sighed.

"I think I will go to my room, Jane. I have a slight headache, so that sitting in the sunlight is no longer agreeable."

"Of course. I will return to the house as well. I do hope you feel better later, Lizzy." She tucked her arm possessively into Elizabeth's and they went back to the house.

"Lizzy!" Mr. Bennet had seen the sisters walking in from the garden. "Why not come and sit with me in the library to read? The sun is at an uncomfortable angle for reading out of doors now."

"Thank you, Father, but I was intending to go upstairs for a short while. I have a slight headache which I hope will soon be relieved, and then perhaps I may join you as you have requested." Elizabeth turned her bonnet in her hands, hoping he would not insist on her joining him.

"Oh, very well, my dear. But do not suppose there is any quiet to be had upstairs. Your mother has obviously had some news which must be vouchsafed at a high volume."

"Why, yes, Father." Elizabeth smiled. "Kitty brought the news from Aunt Phillips. It appears Mr. Bingley is reopening Netherfield Hall for a shooting party."

Mr. Bennet turned away. "Oh, is that all? I would have hoped something more interesting than that would transpire, judging from the scale of the noise emanating from your mother's room."

Elizabeth smiled. "Thank you, Father." She turned and went up the stairs to her room, making sure her mother did not see her as she went.

She dropped into the chair in front of the glass, examining herself gloomily in the reflection.

Since she had come home from Derbyshire, everything had seemed small and petty and unending. While Lydia had been missing and her father and uncle away searching for her, there had been some excitement and anxieties to discuss. But then the matter had been resolved as far as it could be, and now Elizabeth was faced with the prospect of endless days, all unchanged.

Local news; local social events when they dared show their faces again. Idle talk about eligible men and whatever fortune they might have. She was sick of it all, sick of the boredom of it. She had, for a few wonderful days, seen that there might be another way to live, another way comprising a large house, space to get away from the constant presence of others, large gardens and woods in which to walk and take pleasure. Wealth enough to travel and see wonders, an extensive library of books containing enough information to interest her for a lifetime. And Mr. Darcy.

But she had to forget all that, forget that she might once have been mistress of Pemberley.

Mr. Darcy wanted her no more. She had to accept that, and she also knew that she might never meet another man who could please her mind and heart as he did.

And after Lydia's transgressions, she might never receive an offer of marriage again. She was without fortune — fifty pounds a year was not enough to keep her — and she was now without virtue, thanks to the ruin brought upon the family.

She did not know what she was to do. The one thing she knew was that she did not wish to stay at

Longbourn, stay living the same life as she'd lived before, when now there was no end in sight to it.

But what else was there for her? She had thought, a few months ago, that she would map out a course of study for herself, using the books in her father's library, which was adequate for that purpose. She had thought it would provide her with a diversion from the shallow interests of most of the family.

But now, she could not force herself to be interested in this proposal at all. She felt as if she was staring down a long road devoid of all interest. If it had not been that Jane was with her, she thought she could not bear another day.

Perhaps she could visit the Gardiners in Cheapside. London had more to do, she could always persuade her aunt to visit museums and art galleries. She smiled at her reflection. It might be difficult to explain to Georgiana why she was in London but could not see her.

In any event, she could do nothing until the situation at Netherfield was clearer. Jane needed her while they did not know why Mr. Bingley was down. And she would still need her if he didn't call. In that instance it might be better if Jane came to London too. Yes, that would be good.

CHAPTER 7

*A*t last, he and Colonel Fitzwilliam were sitting in his coach as they made their way back to town. It had been an interminable couple of days.

Lady Catherine had still talked endlessly of his duty, his betrayal of his mother's wishes, despite realising that at any such comment he would remove himself from the room with icy politeness.

So she had contented herself with sharp, pointed remarks, lying in wait until they had just sat at table, or when he had just come in from a walk.

But she must know now that he had no intention of marrying her daughter, and neither man had told her what they had talked about to Anne that morning as they sat in the summer house.

Lady Catherine was enraged, but had the sense to realise that she must not become estranged from him. If he still visited, then she could still have hope that she could wear him down and bring him around to her way of thinking.

Mr. Darcy smiled out at the countryside. Her mind was so transparent, he knew exactly what she thought.

But it had been exhausting. Now her plans were in the open, she would not rest until he had capitulated.

"Richard, my friend. I think that next month, I might prevail upon you to attend our aunt without me. I might need the extra weeks to gird my strength for a visit the month following."

The Colonel laughed comfortably. His legs were stretched across the carriage, resting on the seat opposite. His hat tipped rakishly over his face, he had nearly been asleep.

"I think you presume upon my friendship too much to expect me to go alone."

"I do not expect it, but I do beg your favour." Mr. Darcy smiled. His cousin was a very good friend, loyal and amiable. Bingley was another such, and he valued their friendship very highly.

He wondered who Richard was thinking of when he had declined to think about marrying

Cousin Anne. He hoped it was a good and gentle lady, who would bring him happiness and fortune.

And thus his mind turned to Bingley. Now there was a good man who loved a beautiful young woman — a real lady — and he had, entirely without justification, prevented that engagement, such an engagement as would have made his friend blissfully happy.

It was all the fault of his abominable pride, his arrogance. He had learned that lesson at the hands of Miss Elizabeth Bennet, when he had arrived to propose marriage to her, arrogantly assuming she would accept him, because of his superiority and wealth.

He had learned his lesson with the painful humility of that memory. Daily he had tried to think of how she would have expected a gentleman to act. Daily he had rehearsed the words in his mind and hoped he might yet still gain her regard and her love.

Their unexpected meeting at Pemberley had at first given him great hope, but on that last morning when he had chanced upon her in such distress, his heart had broken anew.

In all her distress and anguish, she had not turned to him, had not asked for his help.

She had turned away from him, waiting for her aunt and uncle. She had acknowledged her ruin, acknowledged that she would not be able to visit Georgiana again, and had said goodbye with a finality which had frozen his own expression as he tried not to cause her any further distress.

He had spent time and money with abandon in his determination to alleviate — at least somewhat — the ruin which had been caused by Wickham and that empty-headed sister of hers, and had procured for her the very best outcome he felt possible.

But he dared not go back to Elizabeth until he knew for certain that Wickham and his new wife were out of Longbourn — out of Hertfordshire altogether. Perhaps she would still not wish to see him. She must view with pain the company of anyone who knew of her downfall.

He clenched his jaw, he must have her. He loved her, wanted to afford her every protection against circumstances that he could.

"You're quite in a dream again, Darcy." Colonel Fitzwilliam's voice stirred him back to the present.

"I do not know the cause of your inattention, but it has almost cost you your freedom." His cousin smirked.

"I would caution you against predatory ladies, of which there must be many."

Mr. Darcy yawned and stretched. "You are

right, Richard. I must again express my thanks for your protection against the wiles of Lady Catherine." He sat up.

"But perhaps we should take the privacy this journey affords us to discuss what we are obliged to do for Miss de Bourgh?"

The Colonel sighed and sat up straighter.

"You are correct, sir. And yet I find myself at a loss regarding our next actions. We are agreed that the lady would benefit from a few weeks in London when there are ladies at our establishments to receive her, but if we extend an invitation, her mother will insist on attending, should she even permit her daughter to do so, a consent which is, perhaps, unlikely."

Mr. Darcy frowned thoughtfully. "You are correct, Richard. And yet I cannot think of how to help her without removing her from the presence of Lady Catherine."

His cousin glanced over at him. "You were surprised, I think, to find the young lady quite sensible and pleased to talk without fear of interruption."

"I was indeed," acknowledged Darcy, with a nod. "But it merely serves to behoove us to ensure that her unhappiness is not prolonged."

"I fear there is not much that we can achieve

while Lady Catherine remains so completely in control of Rosings and everyone within it."

Darcy sighed. "You might be right, Richard. But I am sorry that I now know of Miss de Bourgh's awareness of her unhappy situation. I will have to do something."

~

*A*fter passing the Earl's London establishment so that his cousin might get home, Mr. Darcy was very content to finally arrive at his own London house.

He strode into the hall, and handed his hat and coat to the footman.

"Thank you, Jamieson." He walked into the drawing room, noting the stack of correspondence on the writing desk. He stood, leafing through the letters, until he saw Georgiana's handwriting. He smiled, and took that letter to his favourite armchair beside the fire.

> *My dear brother,*
> *I am hoping this letter finds you well on*
> *your return from Rosings, but I know*
> *that you do not enjoy those visits and*
> *regard them as a duty to be borne. At*
> *least Cousin Richard was with you*

and I know that you are good
friends.
I am writing, however, to ask if I may be
permitted to visit you in London? It is
very lonely here without you or other
visitors, and I know that you have
business in town and cannot return
here for some time.
I know Richard's sisters are also in town,
and I would be able to visit galleries
and museums with them, in pursuit
of my education.
Please say I might come and join you.
Your loving sister,
Georgiana

Mr. Darcy folded the letter with a grimace. Of course Georgiana must come if she was that lonely. But he had intended to follow Bingley to Netherfield the very next day.

He had to explain to him why he had discouraged the alliance with the oldest Bennet girl, and, if he was honest with himself, he wanted to see Miss Elizabeth Bennet too.

He folded up the letter and tapped the edge of the sheets thoughtfully on his desk. He must reply at once, but he could not let her stay here alone without …

∾

*H*e jumped to his feet and went to the hall. "Jamieson, please arrange for my carriage at once. I will not be gone long and will return for dinner." He went back into the drawing room and stood before the fire, waiting.

When his carriage was ready, he drove round to the Earl's residence again and, on admittance, was pleased to see Richard hurrying into the hall, surprised amusement on his face.

"Darcy! That was not long. I wonder what news brings you here so soon after we parted?"

The men moved into the drawing room, and Mr. Darcy was obliged to make polite conversation for a moment with Richard's brother, the Earl of Matlock, and the Countess, who questioned him closely on the situation at Rosings.

Fortunately it was only a few minutes before they were able to withdraw to the library and he passed Richard the letter from Georgiana and waited while his friend read it.

Colonel Fitzwilliam looked up. "I see you must have an objection, or you would have written with your consent without such urgent reference to me."

Mr. Darcy glanced at him, rather taken aback at the tight control in his friend's voice. But he decided not to draw attention to it, and smiled grimly.

"I had arranged to go down to Netherfield with Bingley for a shooting party. I wrote to him from Rosings, asking him to open up the house again for me."

Richard threw back his head and laughed. "And do you want to take Georgiana with you?"

"No!" Darcy was shocked at the thought.

"Well, I could, of course. But I would rather she does not have to deal with Miss Bingley. Even I find that lady's pride and pointed comments quite hard to take, and poor Georgiana was rather hurt when that lady referred to Wickham during their visit to Pemberley a month or so back."

The Colonel's face darkened with anger. "Then she must not go." He looked again at the letter.

"I do not like to think of her lonely so far away. Perhaps you had better not go to Hertford-shire, Darcy."

"I must go, although I can be here when Georgiana arrives for a few days, and then I can limit my stays there to no more than a few days at a time." He looked his cousin in the eye.

"I came here to ask if you were staying in London and will be able to look after her for me on the days when I am away."

"Indeed, I fail to see what the attraction of Netherfield is, but if you wish it so, then I will happily take on the care of Georgiana."

Darcy was pleased to see his cousin's manner noticeably improve. In fact he was positively jovial.

"Thank you, Richard. I know that she feels very safe when you are with her or within call."

He was surprised to see his cousin look slightly embarrassed, but he was too engaged with planning his next few days to pay much heed.

He bowed. "Thank you for agreeing. I will return home and write to Georgiana immediately."

The Colonel bowed in return. "It will be a pleasure, Darcy." He smiled.

"I wish she could befriend Cousin Anne without having to face Lady Catherine. That might help Anne a great deal."

"I agree. But it is not currently likely to happen." Darcy took his leave and the carriage rattled around the few streets between their establishments.

CHAPTER 8

*E*lizabeth and Jane strolled along the edge of the woodland, looking out over the fields between them and the town. Jane sighed.

"I do miss walking into Meryton. Perhaps soon I will stop thinking that everyone is talking about us and enjoying our downfall. Then I will be able to go and see Aunt Phillips and catch up with all the news."

Elizabeth was happy that she had persuaded Jane out for a walk, even though she still refused to go into Meryton. She understood why her sister felt too shamed and embarrassed, and while she herself cared much less what the local busybodies thought, she would not let anyone stop her walking out in the countryside where she would not meet anyone. She was happy Jane was now proving that she would, on occasion, agree to go with her.

She smiled at the horizon. She would still often go out alone. She would walk until she knew herself unobserved and then she would run and jump, her appetite for movement undiminished since her childhood. She needed to walk and run so that she had the fortitude to continue being polite and interested in the day-to-day lives of people whose interests seemed so bland and insipid.

But this was her life now, she had little chance of ever leaving it.

But she must not think of that, her mind was much occupied with Jane and her sister's hopes. It seemed they were to be dashed, the party had arrived at Netherfield some days ago, volleys of shots were to be heard each morning, and Kitty brought back news from Meryton of the orders placed at the greengrocer and the butcher.

But no gentleman had ridden over to visit, Mr. Bingley was conspicuous by his absence and Jane became paler and more unhappy each day.

"He does not care for me as I had thought, Lizzy. That much is obvious. But I shall not think of it any more. I shall be myself again and you are not to worry."

But Elizabeth was not going to let the thoughts

go. She wanted her sister's happiness above all else. The only reason she had done nothing was that she could not think of anything to do that could bring about that happiness. She tucked her arm into her sister's.

"Come on, let's go home. It is getting colder and you are not used to walking so far."

Jane did not demur and the two sisters walked back towards Longbourn. As they turned in the driveway, they were astonished to see two saddled horses being held by a groom.

Immediately, Elizabeth's heart went to her throat and she swallowed. Who would be visiting on horseback? She could only think of the days Mr. Darcy and Mr. Bingley had come to call.

A slight moan from Jane told her that Jane's thoughts were in accord with hers, and when the housekeeper came to the front door, beckoning urgently, Elizabeth nearly turned tail and ran.

She stopped and took a very deep breath. Then she turned to Jane. "You look wonderful, Jane. Let's go and see who is calling."

She held her head high and walked in with Jane.

"Quickly, Miss Bennet, quickly! Your mother is quite displeased that you were not here when the gentlemen arrived!" The housekeeper turned to the sitting room door.

"Wait! Hill, please tell us who has called?"

"Why, Mr. Darcy and Mr. Bingley, Miss Elizabeth. They have been here some time."

Elizabeth felt quite faint. How nearly they had missed seeing them. But she could not make out at all that they were here. She had been so certain that Mr. Darcy at the least, would never choose to see her again.

As Hill opened the door, the first sight was Mr. Darcy standing by the window. He was facing her and his expression was grave. Having been by the window, he would have seen them arrive at the door, and she wondered whether he had seen how discomposed she was.

"Come in at once, Jane! And you, Lizzy!" her mother's voice was strident and hectoring "Mr. Bingley and Mr. Darcy have been waiting some time for you. It was most thoughtless of you to have gone out for so long a walk."

Mr. Bingley had leapt to his feet when they entered. Mr. Darcy was already standing, and both men bowed.

Jane and Elizabeth curtsied and then took their seats. Mr. Bingley sat down again, leaning forward, his expression open and eager to please.

"I am so sorry that you had to wait so long, Mr. Bingley! But Jane is here now." Mrs. Bennet's voice was honeyed and dripping with her attempt to act as she thought the higher classes did.

Elizabeth tried not to look too embarrassed. She could not prevent a glance to the tall, handsome man standing by the window, and she wasn't prepared for the fluttering feeling in her throat. His gaze was on her, and she thought she could detect sympathy behind his steady eyes.

She dropped her gaze at once, listening to her mother sending Kitty to order tea. She was once again embarrassed at her mother's voice, at her obvious eagerness to push her visitors into matrimony, merely because they were rich.

She forced herself to stop her fingers twisting in her lap. Mr. Darcy had been right when he wrote to her after she had rejected his proposal. The words were still seared in her memory.

The situation of your mother's family, though objectionable, was nothing in comparison of that total want of propriety so frequently, so almost uniformly betrayed by herself, by your three younger sisters, and occasionally even by your father.

He was right. It had hurt her, and offended her — but he was right. It still hurt her.

She loved her family, but her mother did embarrass her, and she didn't know how she could bear it through the visit. It was strained and embarrassing, with long silences, which were scarcely less embarrassing than her mother's attempts at conversation.

Elizabeth was obliged to try and keep the atmosphere from congealing completely. Jane seemed completely oblivious to anything except the fact that Mr. Bingley had braved the company and was sitting there, unable to take his eyes off her. Kitty was tongue-tied at the gentlemen's presence and Mary was her usual silent, disapproving self.

Elizabeth glanced despairingly at Mr. Darcy, then turned to Mr. Bingley.

"Has Miss Bingley accompanied you to Netherfield, Mr. Bingley?"

He jumped and dragged his gaze from Jane. "Why, yes, we hope to be here for some weeks." He glanced at his friend at the window. "Yes, some weeks, I hope."

She was mightily relieved when the two men finally rode away. Her heart was hopeful, now that Mr. Darcy had called, when she'd thought he'd never seek her out again. But the actual visit had been most uncomfortable to everyone.

But she was delighted for Jane, even though her sister said that she would not allow herself to become fond of Mr. Bingley again, she could not let him toy with her heart once more.

"Oh, Jane!" Elizabeth hugged her. "You only have to look at him to realise he has never stopped loving you."

She took her leave and went to her room. The only question in her mind was why the gentlemen had called, when their disgrace could never be alleviated.

CHAPTER 9

The next day, Elizabeth and Jane were sitting at their needlework during the afternoon, when the sound of horses' hooves on the drive made them raise their heads.

Despite the embarrassment of the previous day, the gentlemen were back for another measure of the same. Elizabeth's heart warmed. And her heart began to beat faster. Was Mr. Darcy visiting her, or only supporting his friend? And had he now withdrawn his objections to that friend's alliance with Jane? It must be so, or they would not toy with such discomfort as they found here.

For the afternoon proved just as uncomfortable as the previous day. Elizabeth ventured a little conversation, but the presence of her mother's ill-considered remarks were just as mortifying to her daughters, and it was not long before the gentlemen had drunk their tea and bowed their goodbyes.

Two days later, they were back again. Still Mrs. Bennet sat there, like some controlling creature, and there was no opportunity to converse or discover the intentions of the men.

That evening, Elizabeth sat on Jane's bed, watching as she brushed out her hair.

"I think if Mama does not leave us alone soon, she will frighten the gentlemen away, which is not at all what she would like."

"But what is to be done?" asked Jane despairingly. "We cannot tell Mama what her actions are doing, but you are right, Mr. Bingley and Mr. Darcy will not keep visiting when this is what transpires."

Elizabeth pondered for a few moments. "Do you like Mr. Bingley enough to risk a little discomfort?"

Jane put down her hairbrush and turned to face her. "You must know the answer to that, Lizzy. You have been watching us these last few days."

"Of course I have." Elizabeth smiled gently at her sister.

"I wish to suggest that tomorrow in the morning we walk into Meryton. Kitty seems to find it not so terrible, and we might hear news of a dance at the assembly, where you can meet Mr. Bingley and dance without Mama's close attention."

Jane blushed a little. "Perhaps you are right, Lizzy. We should not hide away here. After all, we are not the ones who have sinned." She brightened.

"Yes, let us do that in the morning. It is a good thought."

～

*T*he next morning, the two sisters walked the mile to Meryton. Jane was obviously anxious and Elizabeth talked of inconsequential matters to occupy her mind. As they entered the town, they received a few sidelong glances from some of the townspeople, and Jane tugged at her sister's elbow.

"We should go, Lizzy," she murmured.

"We are going to visit Aunt Phillips," Elizabeth said firmly. "She will be offended if we have come to town and we do not call."

"Oh, yes, you are right. Dear Aunt Phillips,

she has been good to keep calling on us these last weeks."

They were warmly welcomed by their aunt and sat down to hear all the local news.

"And I heard the gentlemen have called on you! Kitty told me yesterday. I think that is quite encouraging, girls. Do you agree?"

"Oh, yes, thank you, aunt. It is a great comfort." Elizabeth assured her.

"But of course, we have seen them each day here in Meryton." Aunt Phillips continued, reaching for her teacup.

"Oh!" Jane could not help a gasp.

"Oh, yes!" Aunt Phillips was really pleased to have them as an audience.

"They ride in on their fine horses in the afternoon, then stop and look around the main street for some minutes before they ride off towards Longbourn." She nodded so violently, all her curls wobbled.

Elizabeth glanced at Jane and smiled slowly. This might be their chance to get Jane to meet with Mr. Bingley without her mother being present.

She changed the subject and they talked of other matters before bidding Aunt Phillips goodbye and they then turned for home.

"So." Elizabeth glanced at Jane. "I think we need to visit Meryton more often, particularly at three in the afternoon." She smiled as Jane went pink.

"Oh, Lizzy! How can we do that?" Jane sounded distressed. "You know Mama is insisting we are at home at that hour in case the gentlemen appear to visit us."

Elizabeth shook back her hair. "I think we can be thought to be in the gardens. After all, no one will come to find us, because Mr. Bingley and Mr. Darcy will not arrive, for they will be talking to us in Meryton."

Jane smiled. "You think of everything, Lizzy. Should we return here today after lunch, or tomorrow?"

Elizabeth stopped and looked at her. "Today, to be sure. I cannot bear another uncomfortable visit. If Mama says another word about five thousand a year, I think I might suffer her hysterics myself!"

Jane laughed, and the two sisters walked back arm in arm.

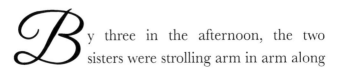

By three in the afternoon, the two sisters were strolling arm in arm along the Meryton road, as if they had nothing else on their mind than a pleasant stroll.

Then Jane's hand closed on Elizabeth's arm. A single gentleman was sitting on a horse at the other end of the road. Elizabeth felt an acute sense of disappointment.

"It is Mr. Bingley!" Jane's whisper was frantic. "What do I say to him?"

"Whatever you wish, without Mama here!" Elizabeth teased her, but her own heart was heavy. Where was Mr. Darcy?

She walked on, listening to Jane's rapid breathing beside her. As they came towards the great oak tree at the centre of the street, the horseman spurred his horse and it walked towards them, tail swishing.

"Miss Bennet! And Miss Elizabeth Bennet!" Mr. Bingley sounded disbelieving and delighted at the same time. He dismounted, and bowed deeply. They curtsied in reply.

"Good afternoon, Mr. Bingley. It was such a pleasant afternoon, we decided to walk into Meryton." Elizabeth broke the uncomfortable silence when Jane seemed too tongue-tied. "But if you will excuse me, I need to look at some of the linens in the milliners. I promised Kitty I would find out if the new colours have arrived from Town." She curtsied and stepped the few paces to the milliner's window. There she stood with her back to the couple, as if totally absorbed in the display. She would not turn around, she would not.

However, she could not help but focus occasionally in the reflection of them in the window glass. She was delighted when they began conversing seriously, and when Mr. Bingley indicated the bench under the oak and they sat together to talk, Elizabeth silently hugged herself with joy.

It seemed a long time, and Elizabeth was heartily sick of the contents of the shop display, when finally, Mr. Bingley stood up, helped Jane to her feet and they walked towards her.

Jane was smiling so joyfully, Elizabeth knew that her own heart's desire for Jane's happiness must be about to come true.

"Oh, Lizzy! Mr. Bingley says I might tell you while we all walk together back to Longbourn." Jane embraced her sister, while Mr. Bingley stood back slightly, holding his horse and looking faintly embarrassed.

They all turned and began to walk back towards Longbourn.

"Mr. Bingley is going to walk back with us and is going to speak to Father and ask him for his consent to our marriage!"

"Oh Jane, I am so pleased for you." Elizabeth wanted to embrace her sister and press her for all the details. But they were in public and Mr. Bingley was with them, so she held onto her decorum, and just squeezed her sister's hand tightly.

She turned to Mr. Bingley and curtsied. "Mr. Bingley, may I offer my congratulations? I cannot think of anyone who will be able to make you any happier, or who cares so deeply for you."

He beamed and bowed to her.

"Indeed, Miss Elizabeth Bennet. I concur with your feelings most wholeheartedly. I hope that I might make your sister as happy as I am at this moment." He smiled at Jane, who dropped her eyes, barely able to contain her joy.

"I hope Father is able to receive you today." She sounded a little anxious.

"Of course he will be." Elizabeth laughed. "Indeed, I am more concerned at Mama's reaction, which will be very loud. I hope you are feeling strong, Mr. Bingley."

He bowed again. "I think I can surmount any obstacle today, and I am most grateful to you for accompanying your sister to Meryton this afternoon and giving us a little privacy to talk."

Elizabeth laughed and they all three walked with a spring in their steps towards Longbourn,

Mr. Bingley's horse following obediently on a loose rein.

"And is Mr. Darcy no longer at Netherfield, Mr. Bingley?" Elizabeth could not contain the question any longer.

Mr. Bingley was as eager to please as ever. "He was most ready to come this afternoon, Miss Bennet, and then return to London later to meet Miss Darcy when she arrives there from Pemberley. But something occurred that necessitated him leaving during the morning." He hesitated. "I think he was sorry to leave so early."

Elizabeth listened to him with mixed feelings. By saying that Mr. Darcy had been sorry not to visit Longbourn — was that because he wished to see her? Or was Mr. Bingley being polite?

And he had gone to London to meet Georgiana. He would not be able to return if his younger sister was in Town. But she could not acknowledge this to Mr. Bingley. Even Jane had no idea as to her feelings for Mr. Darcy. She hadn't seen what he was like when at home at Pemberley, his open and friendly demeanour towards Aunt and Uncle Gardiner. Neither did she appreciate quite as much as Elizabeth the enormity of his generosity towards them when he gave freely of his time and money to rescue them from ruin after Lydia's elopement.

She looked out at the hills as they walked, feeling rather lonely. Jane and Mr. Bingley had eyes for no one else. She clasped her hands behind her and sighed. She must think only of her sister's happiness. That would raise her spirits, she knew.

CHAPTER 10

*M*r. Darcy handed his coat and hat to the manservant. "Thank you, Jamieson." He had no politeness to spare today, and he hurried through to the library, glancing at the clock as he passed.

Georgiana would not arrive until this evening, escorted by her governess and two manservants. He needn't have come to London this early, missing the chance to see Elizabeth again, to torture himself with the sight of her, unable to make any personal conversation while her dreadful mother was presiding over them.

He threw himself on the couch, his mind seeing her guarded face, looking over at him, conscious of the embarrassment they both felt at her mother's comments.

And today might be the day they could have met in Meryton. The younger Bennet girl — Catherine — she had seen them waiting in the town before riding on to Longbourn. Surely she would have mentioned it?

No, he wished he had stayed until later in the day at Netherfield, but Miss Caroline Bingley had forced his hand. Ever since he'd arrived last week, tormented by the pursuit of Lady Catherine to marry her daughter, Miss Bingley had taken up the pursuit.

While she hadn't known of his anger at Lady Catherine, it seemed she had decided that it was time she made her move and secure his hand in matrimony.

He knew, of course, that was her intention, but by ignoring her as far as possible, he'd hoped that his disinterest had been obvious without losing the friendship of her brother.

He could never marry Caroline Bingley. Even if he'd never met Miss Elizabeth Bennet, he could never marry her. Quite disregarding her unsuitable background, it was impossible to imagine her at Pemberley, impossible to imagine her befriending Georgiana. Most of all, it was impossible to even think of having any sort of comfortable home with Miss Bingley in it.

He didn't envy Bingley having to make a

home for her, and if he had been in that position, he would most assuredly do something about it.

But she had made his life miserable for those few days. The only reason to stay were their rides to Meryton. Even the discomfort of sitting in the small parlour at Longbourn with the whole female contingent of Bennets, was better than Netherfield with Caroline Bingley there.

He had no idea how he was to change her attitude towards him, how to make her realise she would never be his wife.

At least here in London, he was safe. He relaxed back into the seat. But Elizabeth wasn't here. He knew that he would go back. Like a moth to a flame, he could not stay away.

He closed his eyes, he could rest until Georgiana arrived. Elizabeth's face swam into view, and he groaned and sat up. He would write to her, pour out his feelings for her. Like the many other letters he'd written, he would burn it afterwards. But while writing, he would be more content.

> *My dearest Elizabeth,*
> *You would have been most amused to see*
> *me this morning at breakfast. Miss*
> *Caroline Bingley came into the room*
> *and sat opposite me. At every*
> *moment possible, she engaged me in*

*conversation. She gave me smiles,
she gave me many sultry glances.
She gave me many, many opinions,
and most of all she pursued me
again and again for my approval,
my smile and my ardour. That she
can never have, will never get
from me.*

*Oh, Elizabeth, my dearest love, how am I
to convince her I want you to be my
wife? Only you.*

*All the way into London this morning I
was berating myself for running
away from Netherfield. Today might
have been the day we would meet you
in Meryton. Away from your family,
I would hope that Mr. Bingley might
propose to your beloved sister and I
would be pleased to see your joy at
her happiness.*

*And, of course, in my dreams I often
revisit my proposal to you. This time
I am more careful, I am a gentleman,
and I am successful at winning you.
Soon we are married and I am the
happiest man alive.*

He stopped and read back the words he'd

written. If only he could go back in time he would do things so very differently.

The sound of horses and coach wheels outside, the shouts of men and a bustling noise drew him back to the present. He glanced at the clock, but the dusk drawing in meant he didn't need to. Georgiana had arrived. Hastily, he gathered the sheets of notepaper, and thrust them into the fire, watching them burn with an ache in his heart that he might never yet get to write them to Elizabeth and be in a position to send them to her.

Angrily, he seized the poker and stirred the embers until no single word remained on an uncharred fragment. Then he turned and hurried from the room.

~

*W*aiting on the steps as Georgiana descended from the coach, he felt so proud of her. She had grown into a lovely young woman with poise and character. She needed companionship and friendship to draw her out of herself and to gain confidence. His mind turned once again to Elizabeth. If she became his wife, she would be of great assistance to his sister.

A passing coach didn't even draw his eye, until

he saw two faces at the window. He wondered who they were, then dismissed them from his mind.

He approached his sister and bowed. She curtsied back and he bent over her hand before walking up the steps with her into the house.

"I hope you are not too fatigued from your journey, my dear sister?"

"Oh, no. We stopped at lunchtime each day and I took a short walk before continuing. It seems to help." She looked around. "But I am happy to be here. Although ..." she looked anxious. "I had not realised that you had planned to be away from London. I am sorry to have curtailed your plans."

"Do not be concerned in the slightest, Georgiana. I have come to a satisfactory plan and Colonel Fitzwilliam will look after you. I believe the family have considered many outings that you might enjoy with them, and the Countess is relying on you to entertain the children."

He was surprised to see that her face was pink and she could not look him in the eyes when she replied.

"It all sounds as if you have taken great care to ensure I very much enjoy my time here, dear Fitzwilliam. Thank you."

He studied her thoughtfully. "If you would rather I did not return to Netherfield, you have only to say so, my sister, and I will remain in London."

His heart sank as he said it, but she shook her head. "I am most happy with your arrangements, sir. I will be well looked-after and have a lot to occupy myself with. You are not to worry at all."

He frowned, was all well? "If you are sure?"

"Of course." She was earnest in her insistence, and he wondered if he could be there tomorrow afternoon for the ride into Meryton. But what should he do about Miss Bingley?

"Cousin Richard is joining us for dinner tonight, Georgiana. I have not invited anyone else, for I thought you might be fatigued."

He definitely saw her blush when he said that. Something was amiss. Perhaps he should ask Richard, after all, he shared the guardianship of her.

But his mind was back on Elizabeth. He must do something, his life, his business interests — he could concentrate on nothing while he didn't know if he could gain her as his.

CHAPTER 11

*A*s they sat over dinner, he found himself holding two conversations. Georgiana was quiet and, unusually for her, shy with the Colonel. She answered questions on her studies readily enough, however, and seemed excited about the plans for the weekend — a visit to some great botanical gardens and a tropical glasshouse.

Finally, Georgiana left the men to go to the drawing room for coffee while the men stayed for the port. They would not wait more than a few minutes, because Georgiana was alone, but the Colonel took the opportunity to ask if he'd had a letter from Lady Catherine.

"No." Darcy shook his head. "Have you?"

"Yes." The Colonel laughed. "I am instructed to persuade you of your duty to our great family heritage and to ensure you visit next month with me and that you *will* propose to Miss de Bourgh." He looked at Darcy. "I do suggest, cousin, that you think long and hard about matrimony. You will never be free of pursuit by ladies or their mothers while you remain eligible in their minds."

Darcy groaned and put his head in his hands. "Do not remind me. Miss Caroline Bingley has spent the last two days in heavy pursuit of me. You are correct, of course, but the time is not yet right. I do not see what else I can do."

"I can only suggest that you are very careful then, my cousin. We are friends, so I hope you will not take this amiss. You will be ensnared by fair means or foul. Someone will attempt to compromise you. Or you will find yourself obliged another way." His seriousness startled Darcy. He had not considered the risks and thought back to the previous day at Netherfield.

Miss Bingley had come into the library when he was reading and had turned to close the door. He hadn't even thought about it, but had opened the great doors out to the terrace and stood outside to speak to her. There were many gardeners around, working in the extensive grounds, and then he had walked with her around to the main entrance and had joined Bingley in the drawing room.

He turned to his cousin. "I thank you for the warning, Richard. I will be very careful."

The Colonel nodded gravely. "Let us join Miss Darcy."

They sat quietly as she played for them a little, and Darcy's mind was far away. After the warning he'd received, he had no illusions that Miss Bingley was determined to marry him. Lady Catherine was also determined in her own way. Anne de Bourgh would marry him if he asked her, but only because she was influenced by her mother, not because she loved him.

He knew Miss Bingley didn't love him, she loved only herself — and his position as a landed gentleman, along with his wealth.

He scowled, and heard Georgiana's playing hesitate. He startled and saw her looking at him fearfully.

"I'm sorry, Georgiana, my mind was else-where. Did you say something?"

She shook her head. "No. But I was watching you and I thought you were not pleased with me."

He could almost feel his cousin's warning glance, he was so used to them by now.

"No, my dear sister. Your playing is delightful, as always. Your music allows me to get lost in my thoughts — and it is my fault if my thoughts are displeasing to me."

He forced himself to concentrate on his sister and their guest for the rest of the evening.

~

*T*he following morning, he was sitting with Georgiana in the morning room, the spring sunlight lifting the blossom on the trees outside. She was sitting with her needlework and he was reading in the companionable silence.

A footman knocked on the door, presenting a visiting card to Georgiana.

"Thank you," she whispered, as the man waited for her reply. Then she looked at Darcy.

"I think I might say I am not at home, Fitzwilliam. I do not feel able to entertain a lady."

He went over to her and she gave him the visiting card.

Lady Sarah Laurents.

He was puzzled. He knew of the family, of course, but had never met them, and knew nothing of the lady.

"I quite understand if you decide that, Georgiana. We do not know the family, and it seems most odd that she is calling." He hesitated.

"But I confess myself curious as to why she is here." He drew up a chair alongside her.

"Would you feel able to accept her call if I promise to stay with you? I would very much like to get a feel of why she is here and then I will make some enquiries. I will not permit her to demand any assurances or a return visit."

Georgiana looked up at him. "If you wish it, then of course I will accept, my brother. But I thought I must make a return call, that is why I was anxious."

Mr. Darcy shook his head. "You are not of age, and you do not have an older female relative to accompany you. It would be most improper to allow you to go alone and is one of the reasons I am curious as to the real reason for her visit."

"Then I will accept." Georgiana stood up and turned to the footman.

"Please show Lady Sarah in and ask the housekeeper to serve tea."

Darcy smiled to himself and moved the chair away from Georgiana's place. The visitor would not be able to crowd her.

He moved over to a corner of the room and settled down with his book. Georgiana glanced at him and he winked at her with a smile, and was rewarded when she relaxed a little.

As the visitor swept into the room, Darcy and

Georgiana both stood. The woman was around thirty years of age and magnificently dressed. She bowed her head haughtily at Georgiana's curtsy and looked curiously around the room.

"Oh, you must be Mr. Darcy! I am delighted to make your acquaintance." She extended her hand haughtily.

He kept his expression neutral as he moved forward and kissed her hand, then he indicated the chair facing Georgiana and retreated to the corner, taking up his book.

Lady Sarah Laurents was obviously well-practiced in the social arts. Within a very few minutes she had swivelled in her chair and, although she was talking to Georgiana, she was asking questions that would necessitate him being brought into the conversation.

"And, of course, you must come to the ball we are holding in London." She looked archly at Mr. Darcy.

"You must make sure your brother accompanies you, Miss Darcy. There is always a great shortage of eligible men."

Her motive for calling was thus made very clear. Mr. Darcy was enraged for his sister. Her flushed cheeks and frozen expression showed she knew that Lady Sarah was not wanting her as a friend at all.

He rose to his feet. "Thank you so much for calling on my sister, Lady Sarah. I apologise that she does not have an older female relative to accompany her on a return call, and I have a full diary of events for her while she is in London. It has been most kind of you." He bowed, and the requirements of politeness compelled her to stand and curtsy back.

"I hope in the future that I might continue the acquaintance." She spoke to Georgiana, but her eyes were on him.

He clenched his jaw, he would not say anything he might regret later. But her behaviour here, joined to what he knew of the family, had convinced him that the Laurents were not a family of whom he wished closer acquaintance.

They escorted Lady Sarah to the door and turned back to the morning room.

"I am sorry, Georgiana, that your first caller was such a woman. There are many friendlier whom you will enjoy getting to know." He touched her shoulder. "But not that family."

"Who are they, Fitzwilliam? I have not heard their name before."

"They are from an old French family who betrayed their country in the past. They weaselled their way into the favour of the old king and he made the man an Earl. Now they live off the title and think themselves above ordinary people." Darcy's voice was bitter. Some of the greatest titles of the land were falling into the hands of people unworthy to hold the name.

Georgiana frowned thoughtfully. "It seemed obvious to me, brother, that she is attempting to seek your favour and a proposal."

She looked up at him. "And you told me about Lady Catherine's attempts at the weekend to ensure your betrothal."

"It is nothing for you to concern yourself about, dear sister." He bowed her to her chair, and took the one so recently vacated by their unwelcome visitor.

"Oh, I think it is, Fitzwilliam. I would not like to see you obliged to marry someone you did not care for, or whom I would find it difficult to be friends with."

"I will be very careful, Georgiana."

She poured a cup of tea and handed it to him. "I think you need to consider marriage, but not to anyone who is pursuing you so violently."

He raised his eyebrows. "And do you have anyone in mind — not that I agree with your premise?"

She looked up at him from under her eyelashes. "I could be great friends with Miss Elizabeth Bennet."

His heart nearly stopped, and the cup rattled in the saucer. He took a sip of the tea to gather his composure again.

"I think this conversation has run its course, Georgiana."

She looked down. "I spoke carelessly. I am sorry."

"It is not your fault. I should not have encouraged it to continue."

CHAPTER 12

The next morning, he ate breakfast with Georgiana. The Countess and her children were calling for Georgiana, along with Colonel Fitzwilliam, and they were travelling to Kew Park to admire the new landscaping.

Darcy was leaving for Netherfield, and his heart was in turmoil. He enjoyed visiting his friend very much, but the presence of Miss Bingley was making this much more uncomfortable. Whatever the discomfort, however, he could not stay away. Longbourn and Miss Elizabeth Bennet were nearby.

A footman brought in some letters, and he glanced through them, picking out the one in Bingley's hand.

He skimmed the letter fast. "Oh, that is good news!"

"What is?" Georgiana looked up from her perusal of the letter she had received.

"I have heard from Mr. Bingley. He and Miss Jane Bennet are engaged. Mr. and Mrs. Bennet have agreed, and all are very pleased."

"Oh, that is wonderful news! They must be so happy." She grinned mischievously.

"My letter is from Miss Caroline Bingley. She also gives me the news, but her happiness is rather more muted than I expect her brother's is."

He raised his eyebrows. "Why would she not want her brother to be happy?"

"You are silly. She wanted him to marry me!" Georgiana was obviously not discomposed by the news, so he was content to assume she had not fancied herself in love there.

"You are very young to be considering marriage, Georgiana."

He was surprised when she coloured and looked down. Something was amiss, and he needed to know what it was. Perhaps Richard knew. He would ask him when he next saw him.

Georgiana gathered her composure. "She also says that she hopes we might still one day be sisters. I do not think she imagines that I tell you about my letters, but she is most certainly another lady in pursuit of you. Dear Fitzwilliam, do not be compromised to her. I could not bear it."

"I am very conscious of the matter. Please do not be concerned."

❦

*L*ater that morning he sat in his coach as it rattled towards Netherfield. It seemed that all forces were conspiring to force his hand to matrimony and he was not yet sure enough of his proposal to Elizabeth. He could not bear the thought that she might refuse him again. It might mean he could never again see her, speak to her, listen to her conversation, take delight in those eyes sparkling with mischief as she teased him.

He jerked to awareness. He must be careful not to think of her too much, must not afford Miss Caroline Bingley the opportunity to take advantage of him.

He was very sorry he'd not been there on that day Bingley had proposed to Jane. Her sister Elizabeth would have been there and he wondered what she had made of his own absence. Had it distressed her?

She'd been reticent and quiet during those excruciating visits to her home. But then, so had he. The presence of Mrs. Bennet had not been helpful.

But Elizabeth had seemed so much changed when he'd seen her at Pemberley, and she had approved of it. She was relaxed in the presence of her aunt and uncle in a way she wasn't with her own family, and her eyes had had a luminous light in them that had given him hope.

But that hope had been dashed when she turned away from him in her distress over the letters about Lydia, and since then he'd had no chance to speak to her alone.

His whole instinct was to take matters slowly, to begin anew, to meet her, talk to her, to show her that his first proposal was best forgotten. But now these women were all pursuing him and he felt under such pressure as he'd never imagined.

He leaned out of the window. With a little luck, he'd be in time for a late lunch and then he hoped he and Bingley could ride into Meryton again. Perhaps the two Miss Bennets would be there.

*A*s the coach drew to a halt outside the steps of Netherfield, he was dismayed to see Miss Bingley come out to greet him. Reluctantly, he climbed the steps and bowed to her.

She curtsied to him and her smile was triumphant.

"Well, Mr. Darcy, you have returned! I am so pleased to see you. We can have a quiet lunch together as my brother is out for the day!" she tucked her arm into his and walked close to him into the hall.

"Where is Mr. Bingley?" he asked as he handed his coat and hat to the housekeeper.

Miss Bingley pouted at him. "What does it matter? We can have a private little lunch and talk about it all."

Mr. Darcy halted and looked at the housekeeper.

She hesitated and curtsied. "Mr. Bingley is visiting at Longbourn for the day, sir. We are expecting him back before dinner, though. He was not expecting you until then."

He stepped away from Miss Bingley. "Thank you. I will require a horse, I have business to attend to."

He turned and went to the door. He was sure Miss Bingley would have much to complain about, and he was being really rather rude. But he was very conscious now of his position. He could not abide it if he became compromised, he would not risk anything for that.

As he hurried down the steps to wait for the horse, he realised that even a meal safely in the dining room, in the presence of the servants, was a risk in itself. It merely needed Miss Bingley to say he had proposed to her. He shuddered. He must do something very soon, whether he was ready or not.

A footman hurried down the steps to return him his coat and hat. He nodded his thanks and mounted the horse that the groom brought around from the stable.

He need not have hurried from London. If Bingley was ensconced at Longbourn for the day, then Miss Elizabeth Bennet would be there too. He did not see how he could intrude.

He turned away from the direction of Meryton. He would ride out in a different direction and see what was to be seen. He would not return until Bingley was home.

A few miles across the country he found a small inn. He sat on the horse contemplating it for a while, smiling wryly at himself. Less than a year ago, he'd have considered it much below him to enter, to eat there, and to mix with country people.

But he'd found out that country people were

not as odious as he had thought, and today he was quite at ease about stopping for lunch.

He walked the horse forward and gave the reins to an ostler who hurried forward. "Thank you. Feed and water for him, please." The man tipped his cap and led the horse away.

Darcy ducked his head under the low entrance to the bar and ordered a private room and writing paper until lunch was ready.

He sat at the table, looking out of the small, low window. The notepaper was in front of him, but he didn't write anything, even though he wanted to write again to Elizabeth. Instead, he let his mind wander, safe from any interruption.

He made a good lunch and then he was on his way again. He turned up into the hills and woods, skirting in a circle to ensure he was back at Netherfield in time for dinner. For an hour, he sat on the top of the hills, staring out over the landscape that had formed Elizabeth's love of the outdoors. He longed to show her his favourite parts of Derbyshire.

He must propose to her soon, he must. And yet, he was not ready, he was not sure she had quite forgiven him yet for his disastrous attempt at Rosings. He dropped his head and stared at his hands. He had been so arrogant. He could scarce believe it now.

But he had changed. His love for her had helped him see himself through her eyes and he hadn't liked what he had seen.

But now, when he really needed her acceptance, he wasn't sure, wasn't convinced that he could offer her what she wanted. But he must try.

He pushed himself to his feet. He would find a suitable track and have a good gallop. That would give his mind and body some rest.

CHAPTER 13

*I*t was almost dinnertime when he returned to the house. As he trotted in, he saw Bingley's coach by the door, the horses tossing their heads. So his friend was only just home.

He handed over his horse. "Give him a good cool down, man." The groom nodded and Darcy smiled at him. "Thank you."

"Thank *you*, sir." The groom seemed surprised at being spoken to civilly.

Darcy turned and climbed the steps. Bingley was waiting for him, still in his coat. Dressed in his best, his eyes still held a sense of disbelief, but his newfound confidence was obvious.

"Congratulations, man!" Mr. Darcy slapped

him on the back. "I knew you'd gain her acceptance."

"Thank you, Darcy. I am still hardly believing it." He looked at the horse being led away. "But where have you been? You arrived early?"

Mr. Darcy nodded. "I thought it best not to stay here when you were out. I will explain as soon as we might be alone."

Bingley glanced at him. "We will do that now. I would not care for the thought that you did not feel at home here."

They walked into the house and handed their coats and hats over to the footmen. Miss Bingley appeared from the drawing room.

"Welcome back, Mr. Darcy." She gave him a winning smile. "And Charles." She nodded to her brother. "We might have drinks in the drawing room and hear all your news."

"We will join you in a few minutes, Caroline." Mr. Bingley showed uncharacteristic firmness. "Mr. Darcy and I have a business matter to discuss first." He bowed at his sister, who curtsied back, looking rather taken aback.

Mr. Darcy hid a smile as he followed Bingley into the library. His host turned and firmly closed the door and they went to the huge fireplace at the far end of the room.

Mr. Bingley flung himself into one of the huge armchairs there.

"I cannot thank you enough, Darcy, for encouraging me to offer marriage to my dear Miss Bennet. I am a different man."

Mr. Darcy nodded gravely. "It is obvious, Charles. I am delighted to see you so happy. And Miss Bennet is a charming young lady who will be the perfect wife for you."

Bingley sat forward. "Thank you. I am convinced you are correct." His smile vanished.

"But I wish to know what problem you found such that you felt you could not stay here this morning when you arrived."

Darcy went to the window and looked out. "I am more than five years older than you, Charles. It seems that many ladies have suddenly decided that means I am in urgent need of a wife." He turned and looked at his friend.

"I have told you in my letters of the weekend I spent at Rosings, avoiding Lady Catherine's determination to attach me to her daughter." He began pacing around the room.

"And only yesterday, in London, a young woman, Lady Sarah Laurents, called on Georgiana, without the slightest provocation. It was quite obvious to me that it was me she was interested in, me that she was pursuing, through making an acquaintance with my sister." He sat in the chair opposite his friend.

"And, I can scarcely say this to you, my friend, but I value your friendship highly. You must have seen that your sister aspires to wed me. Her attentions are frequent and her looks burning." He dropped his gaze.

"I cannot. Charles, I am sorry, but I cannot marry your sister, much though the uniting of our families would be pleasant for both of us."

"My dear Darcy, I would not dream of allowing you to marry Caroline. I can see that you would never be happy. She does not suit you at all." Mr. Bingley seemed agitated. He stood up and moved closer to him.

Darcy stood as well, and the two men leaned against the fireplace.

"But Miss Bingley does not agree, Charles. Several times, including this morning, she attempted to place me in a difficult position. I would not wish to be compromised."

"I am dismayed." Mr. Bingley looked out over the room. "Perhaps I should send her to London, here she is without female companionship, although if I wish to invite Miss Bennet, I would need her presence."

"No." Mr. Darcy went to the window.

"You need her here if, as you say, you might

wish to entertain Miss Bennet. I must be careful. But you needed to know so that if you find I follow you every moment, you might understand." He smiled back at his friend.

Bingley threw back his head and laughed heartily. "I understand, my friend."

Darcy turned again. "But if you would not be offended to hear this, it might be as well if you make alternative provision for your sister before you bring your bride here to Netherfield. I believe she might find it quite difficult to become truly mistress of this house."

Bingley joined him. "I am not offended, my friend. And I will do as you counsel. But what can I do now to ease your discomfort during your visit here?"

Mr. Darcy shook his head. He could not ask his friend to speak to Miss Bingley. And he could not imagine speaking to her himself, either. "I do not know, Charles. I really do not know."

"I hope *you* will not be offended either, dear friend." Mr. Bingley sounded a little nervous.

"But if you are thinking at all of matrimony, the problem might then be solved rather well. I would wish you all the joy that I feel myself."

Darcy could feel his own embarrassment. "I will confess I am. But I am not ready yet, and I do not feel the young lady concerned is perhaps prepared to consent."

"If I am correct in my thinking, then I would respectfully disagree with you there, Darcy."

Mr. Darcy glanced quickly at Mr. Bingley. Had his actions been that obvious? He wondered if Elizabeth Bennet knew he still loved her?

He shook his head. "I do not feel your confidence, sir." He moved towards the door. "Perhaps we have been here too long. We must join your sister at dinner."

Bingley joined him. "Indeed. But do not be too long about the business, Darcy. I think your problems cannot be solved any other way."

CHAPTER 14

*I*n his rooms later that night, Mr. Darcy felt acutely that he was overconcerned as he locked his bedroom door.

Dinner had been difficult. He had tried very hard not to be rude, but to also ensure he gave Miss Bingley not the slightest encouragement of any interest on his part. But she was a determined lady and not inclined to take any sort of intimation of something she didn't wish to hear.

He was glad when they tarried long over the port, and when they finally went through to the drawing room after dinner, he bowed politely to Miss Bingley and asked if she would play for them.

"Of course, sir, if you ask it." There were bright spots of colour in her cheeks and he thought she was angry at having been left alone so long. He could not find it within himself to be sorry about that, but as he sat down to listen, he thought of Elizabeth.

She would probably have felt rather sorry for Caroline, he thought, and so he tried to feel some sympathy too. But he could not. He remembered her cutting and hurtful remarks about Elizabeth after she had visited Pemberley with her aunt and uncle for dinner, that last night he'd seen her relaxed and happy.

No, let Miss Bingley feel angry with him, he would not be concerned for her. If she were not the sister of his best friend, he would not be concerned if he never saw her again.

He did not stay downstairs long, but stood up after she had played for a few minutes. "Please excuse me, I have correspondence to attend to in my room." He bowed to Miss Bingley, who curtsied back, looking rather displeased.

He nodded at Bingley, and took the stairs two at a time.

It was a relief to be in his rooms. He looked out into the darkness and sighed. Thankfully, it would soon be time to retire for the night. But he had time to write to Georgiana, and ask how she had enjoyed her day out today.

He sat at the writing desk and pulled a sheet of notepaper towards him.

~

*T*hat night, he hardly slept. Every time he fell into sleep, he would jerk awake, imagining Miss Caroline Bingley standing over him, wearing little but a triumphant smile.

After the third such awakening, he got up and poured himself a glass of water from the carafe. As he listened, he was certain he could hear the creaking of floorboards in the hallway outside.

He stilled, tense. After a few more moments he relaxed again. He must not let his fears overcome him. He wished to be here, near Miss Elizabeth Bennet. He would just have to accept that Miss Bingley was in this house, and make her understand somehow that she would never be his wife.

But how he would do that, he did not know.

~

*H*e had to marry, he knew that now. He would never be rid of ladies pursuing him until he did. He dropped into a chair, rubbing his hands through his hair. He was under no illusion that they desired him. They only wanted his money, his position, his estate.

There was only one woman he knew of who cared nothing for his money, and that was Miss Elizabeth Bennet.

He rubbed his face. But she thought nothing of him, either. He was under no apprehension that she thought his company desirable, he still remembered her stinging refusal of his proposal.

He climbed back into bed, exhaustion making the chill of the room uncomfortable.

But perhaps he could persuade her to accept him. She needed the security he could offer, if he could but make the offer to her in a way that was acceptable.

He turned over. She had liked Pemberley, she had said so, and that helped him a little.

Slowly, he relaxed, thinking of Elizabeth.

As he began to sleep, he was surrounded by Lady Catherine, Anne de Bourgh, Lady Sarah Laurents and Miss Caroline Bingley, and he jerked awake again.

It was going to be a very long night.

*H*e descended the stairs the next morning, rather short of temper, and was not pleased when he saw Miss Bingley waiting in the hall. Thankfully, her brother was also there, smiling anxiously up at him.

He bowed to Miss Bingley. "Good morning, madam." Without waiting for a reply, he turned to his friend.

"Good morning, Charles. The weather looks set fair today."

"Oh, yes! Indeed it looks like a lovely day for a walk." Miss Bingley spoke before her brother could utter a sound. She tucked her arm possessively into his and said. "I have taken the liberty of ordering extra dishes for breakfast. I know you gentlemen have hearty appetites!" she accompanied her words with a girlish laugh, to the astonishment of both men.

Mr. Darcy could not think of a single thing to say, but as soon as he'd walked into the dining room, he removed his arm and walked around to the other side of the table, leaving Mr. Bingley to assist her to her seat.

She didn't seem to take any sort of intimation of her impropriety from the men's grave faces, but pouted across the table at him.

"I declare it is too nice a day to remain

indoors. Don't you agree, Mr. Darcy? I think we should take the opportunity to walk in the countryside today." She looked at him in bright expectation.

He could not understand why she was suddenly so forward in soliciting his attention. Then he wondered if Mr. Bingley had remarked on his aunt's attempts to assure his betrothal to Anne. Yes, that must be it.

"I declare, Mr. Darcy, you are not listening." Miss Bingley's complaining voice was the last straw.

He must do this today. He must do this now.

He had barely eaten anything, but he put down his knife and fork and stood up.

"Excuse me. You will forgive me." He stepped towards the door. "Excuse me." He hurried out.

He would go now. Right this minute. He needed help, and it was hard to admit that, but he could think of no one else but Elizabeth. Elizabeth would help him.

The steward hurried up and Darcy ordered a horse. He strode up and down the hall, waiting. No, he could not go alone. He went back into the dining room.

"Charles. May I request your assistance in this matter?"

Bingley looked startled. He glanced at his sister. "Of course, Darcy. Now?"

Mr. Darcy nodded. "Now. Please." He turned on his heel and went back to the hall, hearing Bingley making his apologies to Miss Bingley.

When the steward returned, he asked for Bingley's horse to be got ready as well, and then he was joined by his friend and they hurried down the steps.

"So, what is this urgent business, Darcy?" Bingley asked as the groom assisted him to mount his horse, circling around in anticipation of a good gallop.

"I wish to speak to Miss Elizabeth Bennet. I would ask you to assist me in asking her to walk with us, and her sister."

"I do not object to that, Darcy. But it is full early." Bingley glanced at the sky.

"I am sure they will be ready to receive guests. If not, we can wait." Mr. Darcy spurred his horse and they trotted away from Netherfield.

CHAPTER 15

*E*lizabeth tried hard to appear as usual that morning as the family sat over breakfast. But she felt despondent.

Of course she was delighted to see Jane sitting there so radiant, her happiness overflowing on the rest of the table.

Even her mother was smiling and being extra nice to Jane. She hadn't even mentioned Lydia yet.

Elizabeth moodily stabbed at the bacon, and pretended to eat with enjoyment. She could not show her dissatisfaction with her life, not while Jane was still so excited over her new status.

But yesterday had been back to her usual routine, with the extra loss of her sister's company and confidence. Mr. Bingley had spent the day with the family, all previous discomfort apparently forgotten, Mrs. Bennet able to allow the couple to walk in the garden unescorted.

Elizabeth had picked flowers alone, arranged them for the table alone. She'd sat under a tree and read for a while and had stared into the distance. Jane's forthcoming alliance with Mr. Bingley had, perhaps, improved her own prospects, her ruin now did not seem quite such an obstacle to her future chance of marriage.

But she found herself thinking often of Mr. Darcy. Her future still seemed dull and unchanging, because now she didn't feel that she wanted to marry a man of suitable station in life, for whom she could only imagine affection at best. All she wanted was to marry Mr. Darcy.

She found him fascinating, the way his eyes rested on her across a room, his grave conversations, the almost imperceptible smile when she teased him gently.

But he was gone to London to be with his sister. And it was right that he should be with her, he had his family duty and Georgiana shouldn't be lonely.

And her life was here. Day after day of insipid, dull conversation with her mother and sisters. Day after day of local gossip, local affairs and endless needlework and artistic projects. She was so bored with them all. It was insufferable. And soon Jane would be gone to her own life and her own household.

Of course, she would be able to visit and stay often with her sister once she was mistress of Netherfield, but the mere thought of Miss Bingley and her barbed comments was able to take all the joy out of those thoughts.

She sighed again, then looked around quickly. She didn't want her family to see her unhappy mood. But they hadn't noticed. No one expected 'dear Lizzy' to be anything but cheerful and helpful. Only Jane knew of her secret hopes and fears, but Jane was caught up in her own thoughts now, and that was as it should be.

There was a slight disturbance as they heard the sound of horses on the gravelled drive. Kitty leaped to her feet and hurried to the window.

"It is Mr. Bingley and Mr. Darcy!" she exclaimed. "Why are they so early?"

"Oh, Jane!" Mrs. Bennet dabbed at her mouth with her napkin. "Mr. Bingley cannot stay away from you for long!" she laughed coarsely. "We must hasten the arrangements for your wedding!"

Elizabeth felt embarrassed at her mother's dreadful words. But she could not also hide from herself her excitement at Mr. Darcy's presence. He didn't need to accompany Mr. Bingley, not now that her future brother-in-law was so welcome. Maybe he had indeed come to see her.

She put down her knife and fork, unable to even pretend to eat. She looked over at Jane, who was flushed and smiling happily. Her own heart warmed at the sight. Anything was worth suffering for Jane's happiness.

The housekeeper opened the door. "Mr. Darcy and Mr. Bingley, sir."

"Thank you, Hill." Mr. Bennet rose to his feet. "Good morning Mr. Darcy, Mr. Bingley. Let us set extra places. You might join us for breakfast?"

Elizabeth glanced at Mr. Darcy. Did he look slightly concerned by the offer?

Mr. Bingley bowed. "No. Thank you, we have breakfasted. With your permission, we might wait in the parlour until Miss Bennet and Miss Elizabeth Bennet have finished their meal?"

"Of course, of course!" Mrs. Bennet could hardly contain herself. "Let me take you there." She turned back to the table. "Hurry along, girls! You have taken quite long enough!"

Elizabeth looked over at Jane, who was looking quite flustered. "Do not rush, Jane." She smiled. "If the gentlemen are so enthusiastic to see us, they might wait a while longer!"

She turned to her father. "Would you excuse

us, please, Papa? We should go upstairs and compose ourselves."

"Yes, of course, Lizzy. I know you will look after your sister." Mr. Bennet tipped his face for the affectionate kiss Elizabeth dropped on his forehead.

❧

*I*t was not long before the two couples were beginning to walk slowly along the road to Meryton. Jane and Mr. Bingley walked slightly ahead, and Elizabeth stepped lightly alongside Mr. Darcy who looked grave and taciturn. She thought he also looked very tired and her heart twisted in sympathy for him. She wondered what was troubling him.

"Mr. Bingley said you had gone to London because Miss Darcy was arriving, Mr. Darcy. Have you left her alone there?"

He turned to her. She thought he looked dreadfully haggard. "My cousin, Colonel Fitzwilliam, has undertaken to be responsible for her for a few days. But I must soon return."

"I hope she is well."

"Indeed. She will be happier in London while I am down from Pemberley."

Elizabeth nodded, remembering the letter

Georgiana had written to her. "I liked her very well."

He gave a slight smile. "I think the feeling was mutual."

She glanced up. If he was talking to her, perhaps he would not be against their friendship. But there was another matter on her mind.

"Mr. Darcy, I am thankful to have the opportunity to speak to you. You must allow me to thank you for the very great debt I — and my family — owe to you for your actions in ensuring the marriage of my poor sister, Lydia."

He looked as if he wished to speak, but she hurried on.

"Please let me finish, sir. I know you did not wish us to know of your involvement, but Lydia let the secret slip and I demanded of Aunt Gardiner that she tell me the rest." She took a few more steps and then stopped.

"We are so much in your debt, sir. I cannot conceive how we could ever repay you." She smiled slightly. "And I also believe you have facilitated the engagement of my sister and your friend. For that too, I am forever in your debt."

He bowed gravely. "I did not do these things in expectation of repayment, Miss Bennet. But I am happy that I could do them. You and Miss

Bennet did not deserve the blow that life dealt to you, so I am satisfied that I was able to help."

They walked on after the other couple.

"But it seems to me that you are troubled, too, Mr. Darcy. Are business matters difficult?"

"You are very observant, Miss Bennet." His voice was still grave, and he seemed weary.

"I am sorry to see you so tired." She stopped talking, perhaps he needed silent company. They walked on for some time.

Then he turned to her. "I came to you today because I wish to ask for your help, Miss Bennet. But I am at a loss to explain it."

CHAPTER 16

*S*he walked on. In what possible way could he need her help? Her heart sank. She had hoped, somehow, for a protestation of love. But it seemed she wasn't going to get it.

"Mr. Darcy, I have already told you that I know of the debt my family owes you. If there is any way — any way at all, in which to repay you in even the smallest measure, I will, of course, do all in my power to help you."

They walked on, more slowly than before. He seemed completely at a loss as to how to begin, and the silence stretched out. Finally, he sighed.

"Miss Bennet, I am finding certain aspects of my life rather difficult at present. I am twenty-eight years old now, and, due to the good fortune of my birth, I have wealth enough." He could not meet her eyes. "I am being — pursued, I suppose is the word — by several women intent on matrimony. I believe they are intent on my fortune, not me." He stopped and took a deep breath. "I have been able to think of no way of stopping that."

Elizabeth stared at the couple now many yards in front of them. This was nothing she could ever have imagined hearing.

"Well, sir." She tried not to sound too tart. "I might suggest that you choose one of them and once you are married, you will be safe from pursuit."

He stopped and turned to face her. "I have only met one woman in my life whom I am certain has no interest in my fortune, and that is you." His face was pale and serious.

"But, during this long night, I have taken heart in the fact that you seemed to like Pemberley very well when you visited it and that has encouraged me to come here today to ask for your help."

Her heart was hammering. Was he going to propose? Was he going to repeat his protestations of desire and love that he had told her when he first proposed at Rosings? She could not imagine it to be so, his words did not seem a precursor to that.

He was standing too close to her for her to be able to think clearly.

"I … I am afraid I do not understand you, sir."

"I know. I am sorry that I am not being clearer, Miss Bennet. But I am asking you to help me, to agree to an — arrangement so that you will marry me, so that you might become Mrs. Darcy and mistress of Pemberley. Thus you can assist me to avoid the unwanted attentions of these other women who are after my fortune and their happiness, regardless of my feelings and that of my sister."

Elizabeth stared up at him, astonished. Here there were no protestations of love, no regard for her feelings, no acknowledgement that this was a lifetime decision for both of them.

"Do you mean, sir, that you wish us to marry in order to prevent the unwanted attentions of other ladies?"

He nodded. "I do."

"You mentioned your sister, Mr. Darcy. What are her thoughts on this *arrangement*?" She was disappointed in Georgiana.

"She does not know I am here and we have not discussed it. I merely meant that you and she were on the way to becoming friends, that you like her for who she is, not because you see your way through her to me."

She turned and walked on and he fell into step beside her, his tension apparent to her.

She could not do this. A loveless marriage arrangement, purely for his convenience and comfort, was insupportable.

She could do this. She loved him, even if he could not see that. Surely, if she were by his side, she could make him love her again?

She could not do this. How could she persuade her father that she'd married for love, if she had not?

She could do this. Despite Lydia's marriage, she was still ruined. Perhaps she might never get another offer. She knew she could never love another man now she had met Mr. Darcy.

Her mind was in turmoil. She thought of Pemberley, a large, gracious home. She thought of Georgiana, who would make a delightful sister-in-law. She thought of Longbourn and how it would be after Jane was married and gone.

But most of all, she thought of Mr. Darcy. His grave, dark eyes. His expression when he looked at her. His handsome features and tall frame. Her heart constricted in excitement. What would it be like to be married to him? She shivered in excitement.

CHAPTER 17

$\mathcal{H}$e walked silently beside her. His heart was heavy. He had put the whole matter before her, told her everything. Except that he still loved her. He didn't think she wanted to hear about that, he still felt pain at her words last time —

From the first moment I may almost say, of my acquaintance with you, your manners impressing me with the fullest belief of your arrogance, your conceit, and your selfish disdain of the feelings of others, were such as to form that groundwork of disapprobation, on which succeeding events have built so immoveable a dislike...

He shuddered.

… so immoveable a dislike …

No, she would refuse. He was hoping for something impossible. And now she had the means by which to laugh at him.

He was almost ready to doff his hat to her and walk away, so full of chagrin was he at his foolish error to even ask her this. No amount of pursuit by other ladies was as bad as the loss of hope of winning Miss Elizabeth Bennet. He was almost startled when she spoke.

"How good an actor are you, sir?" She almost sounded mischievous, and certainly did not sound offended.

"What?"

"Everyone will be expecting us to announce our engagement because of love, sir. I have made it clear to all my family and friends that I have no intention of marrying for convenience or security."

His heart sank. She was going to refuse him, and if he professed love now, she would wonder if it was just a lie, because his other reasons had not worked on her.

He scrambled to keep the conversation going. "I do not have a reputation for showing emotion. However, I believe I might perform what would be expected of me, were we to be in love. Would you be able to?"

He saw her wince, and wondered how he had hurt her. He wanted to apologise, wanted to assure her of his love. But it was not the right moment, must not be thought of, and he held his feelings in check.

She looked up at him and her eyes were very serious.

"I am most deeply in your debt, sir. My whole family are. I … am not persuaded that your idea is the right way for you to become free of being chased by fortune-hunters, but if you think it is the right thing to do, then I will agree to your suggestion."

She gave a very slight smile.

"It will astonish my family. And I am just as certain that yours will be most displeased."

His heart was pounding. She had said yes! He kept a firm hold on his behaviour, and merely smiled. "I do believe you are correct, Miss Bennet."

He bowed over her hand. "I am most, most … grateful to you, and I promise you I will ensure your happiness and well-being to the utmost of all I am and all I have."

They turned and began to walk towards Mr. Bingley and Jane in front of them. They had seemed to notice nothing of the drama that had played out behind them, they were so enamoured each with the other.

Their route had skirted Meryton and circled around so that they were now approaching Longbourn again.

He could barely contain himself, he wanted to shout out to the world that she had accepted his proposal, she had agreed to be his wife. But he had to control his feelings, had to walk calmly beside her, back to her home.

But at least he could imagine the future now, could dream of being a man she could learn to love, and he would have the woman he loved beside him.

CHAPTER 18

They arrived back at Longbourn. Elizabeth could hardly understand how Jane would not notice the change in her; she felt her agreement must be so obvious to anyone who even looked at her.

It was going to be hard to act as if she were in love with him, and not show to him that she actually was. She didn't want him to know that she loved him, he must be dismayed by such emotion, he would not think she would be keeping to the agreement they had made.

As they went into the hall, he bent his head towards her and whispered to her.

"I will go and see your father now, with your consent?"

It was her final chance to change her mind.

She stiffened, she would not be that sort of person. She smiled up at him.

"Of course. I will act my part." Her heart was hammering with his nearness. She realised that as an engaged couple, they would have more time together. She hoped she could keep her composure.

~

*S*he sat in the parlour with her family. Mr. Bingley had pride of place and was the centre of Mrs. Bennet's attention. Elizabeth was very pleased about it, and she sat and listened, smiling at Jane when her sister looked over at her.

She caught Mr. Bingley's glance occasionally. Perhaps he was wondering where Mr. Darcy had gone to? She wondered how much he knew of what his friend had proposed. Would he know it was just an arrangement? Or would they need to keep up the act with him? She didn't know.

She had no opportunity to say anything, her mother was still loudly talking about wedding plans with Jane and Mr. Bingley, and she didn't know what to say anyway.

Then her father was coming into the room, and he made his way across the small, crowded room towards her.

"Well, Lizzy, will you come into my library for a few moments, please?"

She nodded obediently, and followed him quietly, aware of the sudden silence in the room as she left it. She bit her lip, was this going to be the hardest part?

Mr. Darcy was waiting in the hall. He gave her a slight smile as she followed her father.

Mr. Bennet shut the library door and turned to her. Fortunately he remembered himself and that Mr. Darcy was waiting outside, and kept his voice down.

"Lizzy, I think you must have lost your mind. You dislike Mr. Darcy so much. You find him proud and arrogant, you have said as much very often. And now he tells me that you have accepted his proposal of marriage!"

He sat down in the chair opposite the one she had sat in to stop herself falling into. "Dear Lizzy, has he forced you to accept him, has he told you that you will never get another suitable proposal, following Lydia's disgrace?"

Elizabeth's eyes filled with tears. "No, Father, he has not." She was happy her father did not know of Mr. Darcy's part in Lydia's marriage, or he would know that she was doing this to partially repay the debt the family owed. "No, Father," she repeated. "I love him very much and I have accepted his offer. Please consent to our engagement."

"Oh, I have consented. Mr. Darcy is not the sort of man I can refuse anything. But Lizzy, if you don't want this, I can tell him to leave now and I will protect you from him. I want you to be happy."

"I am happy, Papa. I have accepted Mr. Darcy's proposal, and I want to marry him."

Mr. Bennet stood up. "Then I give you my blessing, my dear Lizzy." He looked tired, as if he suddenly realised what Longbourn would be like without his two favourite daughters.

When she opened the door, Mr. Darcy was still standing where he had been, his body radiating tension. She smiled at him, and her father beside her was beaming too. She saw him relax, and he looked at her with the warm regard that she had seen him bestow on her at Pemberley. She had wanted to see it again so much, but now she knew that he was acting, the look tore through her.

He gave her a quizzical look. "Did you tell the rest of your family, Miss Bennet?"

She shook her head. "The opportunity did not arise in those few minutes, sir."

She dreaded telling her mother, and the reaction that would seem so inappropriate. But, despondently, she realised that a secret engagement was not the sort that would help his problems. She stood up straighter and took his arm. He must be dreading this part, too, and she wanted to help him.

"Go on with you both, then." Mr. Bennet hurried back into his library. He, at least, had no intention of helping them, and Elizabeth felt again a slight irritation for his habit of retreating from situations he did not like.

But this was now, and she was glad she had Mr. Darcy with her. He bent his head — so achingly close to her — and whispered, "I can act the part you need me to, and I am sure that you can do this too."

She stiffened, he did not know that this was doubly hard for her. She must pretend to her family that she was in love — but this part could be easy, for she was. The hard part was that she must not do it so well as to give him cause to think that she did.

"I am ready." She looked up at him; she must lighten the atmosphere. "I hope you are prepared for my mother's reaction."

His appreciative smile raised her spirits, and they entered the parlour, the sudden silence making her hesitate. Mr. Darcy squeezed her arm very slightly. She could do this.

She smiled over at Jane. "I hope I am not

being too unfeeling in encroaching upon your happiness by telling you of my own news, dear Jane."

Her sister rose to her feet, a disbelieving look in her eyes. She had guessed. But she could not say what she felt, the gentlemen were there.

"Lizzy, is it true?" she looked from her sister to Mr. Darcy and her gaze flew back to Elizabeth. "I can't believe it!" she came forward to embrace her sister. Then there was no need to say anything else, for Mrs. Bennet was there, her cries of delight and triumph washing over them.

It was fully ten minutes before Mr. Bingley could make it over to them to bow over Elizabeth's hand and offer his congratulations, and Elizabeth felt both men were probably finding the atmosphere rather overwhelming.

She turned to Jane. "Shall we all take a walk in the gardens? It seems a pity to waste this fine weather."

∼

"Thank you for your thoughtfulness in suggesting this walk." Mr. Darcy strolled contentedly beside her. "Your mother may now take time to compose herself from the excitement."

"Yes," Elizabeth said. "I am sure that she will wish to settle her mind to wedding plans." And as she said it, she wondered at her feeling of acceptance that her wedding day would not be the day she had dreamed of, but rather an occasion to be endured.

But she was doing this at Mr. Darcy's wish, and if this was the only way in which she could be with him, then that was what she would do.

"Are you unhappy, Elizabeth? I would not make you continue with this if it will cause you distress."

She shook her head and made herself smile at him. "No, sir. I understand completely what you have asked of me and I am content with my agreement." She must think of what she was gaining here. She had been despairing of her dislike of the endless life here at Longbourn, which would be made worse when Jane married and moved out.

Now she had the opportunity to make a new life at Pemberley. She had a new opportunity to travel and explore and learn new things, unhampered by concerns of cost. And Georgiana would be a good friend to her.

She smiled. "I am looking forward to renewing my acquaintance with Georgiana."

He relaxed and smiled. "I will write today with

our news, and I can imagine her delight when she reads of it."

Elizabeth walked on beside him. "Might I also be permitted to write to her?"

He stopped. "Of course you may. She will be most happy to correspond with you."

She nodded and they strolled on into the shade of the trees. His answer told her that Georgiana had not told him that she was writing to Elizabeth when she sent her letter the previous week, saying how lonely she was.

Mr. Darcy drew her to a halt. "I will leave you now, and return to Netherfield with Mr. Bingley." He hesitated. "Would you and your sister do us the honour of dining at Netherfield this evening? I will send a coach for you."

She smiled. "We would be delighted, sir. I am sure Jane will have no objection."

He nodded gravely. "I have one concern, though. I would wish to prepare you that Miss Caroline Bingley might decide to remain in her rooms and not join us for dinner." He looked slightly uncomfortable. "I would not wish you to think her very uncivil."

Elizabeth had a sudden vision of Mr. Darcy having spent the last few days being pursued by Miss Bingley around Netherfield. She smothered her amusement, it would not be right to show anything other than sympathy.

"I understand, Mr. Darcy. I think your news this morning might seem quite a blow to her, and I would not wish her to feel uncomfortable. However, if she does join the table as hostess, I will try not to make her feel uneasy in any way."

He bowed. "Thank you for your understanding." He looked at his friend and her sister. "We will go to them and suggest our plan."

CHAPTER 19

*E*lizabeth smoothed down her dress. She knew it didn't compare in any way to the beautiful gowns that Caroline Bingley wore, but it was her best, and she felt more confident when she was wearing it.

She pushed away the thought that, despite that lady's fine gowns, she was the one who had won Mr. Darcy's proposal, and it was to escape the pursuit of Miss Bingley among others. It was an unworthy thought and she felt rather ashamed of it. She would be pleasant to Miss Bingley.

Jane came into her room. "Oh, Lizzy! I am so happy. I cannot tell you how happy I am." Even in her simple dress, her joy made her beauty extra luminous.

Elizabeth smiled. "You look so beautiful. No

wonder Mr. Bingley cannot take his eyes from you."

Jane blushed. "But I can take my eyes from him long enough to look at you, Lizzy." Her smile vanished. "I am excited for your betrothal, and you looked happy downstairs this morning. But …" She tipped her head on one side. "I am concerned. You seem happy and yet I feel there is sadness in you, too." She embraced her sister.

"Are you happy, dear Lizzy? I cannot bear it if you think you have made a mistake that you cannot escape from."

Elizabeth knew that this was her hardest task, convincing her sister that her marriage was with love on both sides. "Jane, I am very, very happy. My sadness is for two things only, firstly that Netherfield and Pemberley are so far distant from each other that you and I shall be compelled to conduct our intimacy via correspondence, and secondly, for Papa. He will miss us both very much."

Her sister looked thoughtful. "I understand. You are right, Lizzy. I had been concerned that you might feel you had to accept a proposal you did not wish for because of — our trouble."

Elizabeth pushed aside a grimace. If she was careful, she could be truthful and also allay Jane's fears. "Dearest Jane. I love Mr. Darcy so very much. I cannot imagine ever loving another."

Her sincerity seemed to reassure her sister.

"I am so happy for you, Lizzy. Now I will enjoy the evening." She tucked her arm into Elizabeth's. "Let's go down and wait for the coach."

They sat quietly in the parlour while Mrs. Bennet fussed around them.

"And Mr. Bennet will see the parson. We must arrange the banns to be read." A sudden thought seemed to strike her. "Oh! But of course, such rich gentlemen, you must be married by special licence. Of course you will. Special licences — they cost five pounds, you know!" she sat back, delighted at the elevation to the landed gentry of her daughters.

Elizabeth smiled. She didn't care what her mother decided on, she knew Mr. Darcy would ensure that things were done as he wished them to be.

The sound of the coach turning into the drive brought the speculation to an end. Mrs. Bennet came out to the coach with them.

"You must ask Mr. Darcy about the special licence, Lizzy. It's important to do things right, you know! Ten thousand a year! Ten thousand!" She could be heard making her gleeful comments to herself as they settled themselves into the coach.

Mr. Bennet put his head in the coach doorway. "I know you are far too sensible to say any such thing to your intended, aren't you Jane, Lizzy? Let them sort these things out in their own time."

Elizabeth smiled at him. "Yes, Papa, we understand."

~

Now the coach was approaching the imposing entrance at Netherfield. Jane looked a little anxious.

"I am concerned at Miss Bingley's reception of us, Lizzy. I don't know if you recall, but she seemed very settled on becoming Mrs. Darcy." She looked anxiously at Elizabeth.

"Do not be concerned, Jane." Elizabeth looked out of the coach window, smiling. "I am in good humour tonight. Nothing Miss Bingley says will induce me to be anything but perfectly kind and amiable towards her."

Jane looked relieved of her anxiety and they watched as Mr. Bingley and Mr. Darcy came down the steps to meet them.

The footmen jumped down from the coach and lowered the step as Jane sat forward. Mr.

Bingley hurried forwards and gave her his hand and assisted her down.

Mr. Darcy stepped forward and extended his hand to assist Elizabeth. As she rested her hand on his for support, Elizabeth felt a shock of excitement down her arm as their hands touched, and her heart beat fast. Would he have noticed?

He bowed and raised her hand to his lips. Her heart beat even faster, and she had to hide a gasp. Heat flooded through her as he kissed her hand.

"I'm so happy you have arrived, Miss Bennet." And he turned and walked beside her up the steps to the house.

As the two couples entered the hall, she looked around. The housekeeper and several footmen were there to take their coats, but their hostess wasn't present.

"I am exceedingly sorry, but my sister is indisposed," Mr. Bingley said. "She begs your forgiveness that she is staying in her room this evening."

Jane looked distressed. "Oh, I am so sorry! Perhaps we ought not to stay?" She looked over at Elizabeth.

"Please stay, Miss Bennet." Mr. Bingley looked concerned. "She said to me most particularly that she hoped her indisposition did not curtail your enjoyment of the evening."

Elizabeth glanced at Mr. Darcy. He looked as

impassive as he often did, but she could sense his discomfort. She wondered if Miss Caroline Bingley had made a scene.

"I think that is most gracious of her." Elizabeth touched her sister's shoulder. "We might send a note over tomorrow to thank her for her generosity."

Jane looked reassured. "That is a good idea, Lizzy." And she seemed much happier as she allowed herself to be led into the drawing room.

They sat down close enough for conversation, but the two couples just far enough apart to allow small private conversations too.

"Thank you for your generous words, Miss Bennet." Mr. Darcy's voice was low. "I hope Miss Bingley does not take many days before she receives you. The longer she does not, the harder it will be for her."

"I would not wish that, sir." Elizabeth thought a few moments. "Perhaps if she tells you she is finding it difficult, we could contrive a brief greeting at some public event and then an invitation to tea at someone else's home." She looked at him. "We would need only stay a few moments, and that might ease her mind."

"You are most thoughtful." He regarded her carefully. "Particularly because I feel that Miss

Bingley was sometimes not quite so considerate to the feelings of you and your sister."

"She must feel herself grievously used, sir." Elizabeth shook her head. "I do not believe that she ever considered that she would fail to win your favour. Now, all hope is lost. I feel for her."

He sat quietly opposite her. After a few moments, he stirred. "Now I feel exceedingly guilty for causing such distress."

"Do not, sir. When I have been here before and I was watching you, I did not see you give her any signal that she was in your favour. You are not obliged in any way."

She stopped then, not knowing whether she should speak all her thoughts.

He smiled. "Pray continue, Miss Bennet."

She smiled back, a little uncertainly. "If you feel that you are obliged to her, I could say that …"

He held up his hand. "Please don't say that, Miss Bennet. Please." He glanced over at the other couple before dropping his voice further. "If you wish to withdraw from our arrangement, then I would not stand in your way. But I will never, *never* offer marriage to Miss Bingley."

Elizabeth looked up at him. "Do you wish me to withdraw, Mr. Darcy?" Her heart was breaking.

He shook his head. "I do not. But I am cognisant of the enormity of what you have agreed to, and I would not be surprised if you wished to relinquish it, having had a few hours to think about it."

She dropped her gaze to her hands in her lap. "I do not wish to withdraw, sir. But if ever you wished to be free, I will not stand in your way."

His voice sounded husky. "You are most generous of thought, madam. I believe I have made the best choice."

There was a smile in his tone and she looked up, startled. He was smiling too.

"Let us choose a happier topic, Miss Bennet. I would wish to know how you would like to spend your time when you arrive at Pemberley."

She could feel her eyes shining. "I remember Derbyshire with such pleasure, Mr. Darcy. It is most beautiful."

"I will enjoy showing you my favourite views." He sat back, more relaxed now.

CHAPTER 20

*W*hen dinner was called, the two couples went through and made an enjoyable meal. Without seeming to be a conscious thought, the men seemed to defer to Jane as the future hostess at Netherfield, and Elizabeth caught the odd glance between Mr. Darcy and his friend.

She smiled to herself as she returned her attention to her plate. Jane was creating the good impression that Elizabeth had known she would.

At the end of the meal, the ladies retired to the drawing room, leaving the men to their port. But as they were guests alone, it was only a few moments before the men rejoined them.

They sat around the fireplace, and sipped their coffee. Elizabeth wondered if they might ask her to play for them, but soon discovered that was far from their intentions.

"It is perhaps good that we are alone this evening," Mr. Darcy said gravely to them. "I must tell you that I cannot leave Georgiana alone for too long, so I must return to London shortly."

Elizabeth's heart sank, but she was quickly diverted when he continued.

"We were thinking that if we could perhaps arrange for you both to stay with your aunt and uncle for a few weeks, then Mr. Bingley would travel to London with me and stay at my establishment."

Elizabeth glanced at Jane. Her eyes were shining and she seemed pleased with the suggestion. Elizabeth smiled. She was certainly not averse to staying in Cheapside.

"It would enable us to visit some galleries and shows. You would also be able to renew your acquaintance with Georgiana." Mr. Darcy's voice was compelling, but when he continued, Elizabeth thought he sounded a little more hesitant.

"I would also hope that you might permit Georgiana to feel herself useful in accompanying you to purchase suitable gowns and wedding clothes."

Elizabeth hesitated. "I would hope that would be permitted. I would find more enjoyment if our mother did not wish to travel to Cheapside with us. She might wish to if she felt that wedding clothes were the reason for our trip."

"Oh." Both men frowned.

Elizabeth wondered if they felt she should exert herself to tell her mother to stay away.

"Sir, my sister and I would very much like to come to London." She flashed a smile at Jane. "I know Miss Darcy would also enjoy meeting Jane. Perhaps we can begin to arrange wedding clothes in consultation with our mother here before we travel to London."

"Please do not be at all concerned, Miss Elizabeth." Mr. Darcy bowed slightly. "I am sure something can be devised." He looked at Mr. Bingley. "Perhaps I should travel back to be with Georgiana, and I will send a recommended seamstress down to Longbourn. When the work is underway and you are no longer needed here, Mr. Bingley could escort you both to London and we might further our plans from then."

"Oh, that would be wonderful, Mr. Darcy." Jane found her voice and was smiling delightedly. "Imagine, Lizzy, having dresses designed and made for us!"

Elizabeth smiled at her sister's excitement. "Indeed, I can imagine the feeling."

"Then that is settled." Mr. Bingley seemed

pleased. "And while he is in London, Mr. Darcy will arrange an audience for himself and me at Lambeth Palace to gain permission from the Archbishop to marry by special licence."

Elizabeth and Jane smiled at each other, remembering their father's words. When Elizabeth glanced around she saw Mr. Darcy's eyes on her, an enigmatic look in his eyes.

"Then it is all settled."

~

*W*ith all the excitement of a top-class French seamstress and her assistants attending Longbourn, sewing and fitting a full trousseau for her and for Jane, the next two weeks seemed to go very fast.

Elizabeth felt rather sad, for Mr. Darcy had left for London the morning after they had dined at Netherfield, and it was Mr. Bingley who appeared alone each day to dine with the family. He and Jane were obviously so much in love, and Elizabeth was full of regret that her own arrangement meant that she could not be like that.

Jane was apologetic. "I am so sorry, Lizzy. I can see that you are missing Mr. Darcy very much, and it is selfish of me to expect you to watch Charles and me together."

"Don't be silly, Jane." Elizabeth reassured her. "I love to see you so happy."

One day she spoke to them both as they walked in the gardens. "Mr. Bingley, I am conscious of the fact that we have not seen Miss Bingley recently. I know that our news has been doubly difficult for her, but it will be important that social relationships are maintained for her own well-being." She looked at Jane. "I was thinking that perhaps it might be easier for her if Jane and I call one morning for tea while Mr. Darcy is away?"

Mr. Bingley beamed. "That is a good idea, Miss Bennet. Might you be spared from your fittings perhaps tomorrow? Mr. Darcy is travelling down for dinner on Friday night, but will then return to London the following day. It would be excellent if Miss Bingley has met you for tea the day before."

Jane looked at Elizabeth. "I wonder if the fittings will be over with by Saturday so that we could all travel to London together?"

Elizabeth shook her head. "I think it might be a few more days than that, Jane. Mama is enjoying herself quite too much to allow this time to end."

"Well, I think we might need to put the idea of the end date in her mind, perhaps."

Elizabeth looked at Jane with surprise. Her sister was becoming more confident in expressing herself each day, and choosing what she wanted, rather than fitting around other people's wishes. She wondered how they could do this.

"Perhaps … I think we could say that since most of the work is completed, we should send Madame Benoit and her assistants back to their own shop to continue with the detailed embroidery there." She smiled. "I think Father will be heartily pleased to have his home back to its usual calm."

"Oh, yes! Poor Papa." Jane seemed to remember her father's feelings.

Mr. Bingley bowed. "That might be settled, then. And you will call on my sister in the morning? And join us for dinner on Friday?"

Elizabeth curtsied. "Of course. Thank you, sir." She smiled at Jane and went back to the house.

"Lizzy! Lizzy!" her mother's voice assailed her as soon as she entered. "Come and see this wonderful stitching. It is so high-class. I'm going to speak to your father again. I must have a gown that is equal to my daughters, I must."

"Coming, Mama." Elizabeth sighed. As she admired the delicate flowers stitched over the shoulder of her gown, she spoke to her mother.

"Jane and I will be going to London on Saturday with Mr. Bingley and Mr. Darcy, who is coming down from London to accompany us. Madame Benoit will be able to return to London and finish our trousseaux there."

Her mother stared at her. "But how will we know they are to be finished right? And who will chaperone you on the journey?"

Elizabeth sighed inwardly. "Miss Bingley will be travelling with us, Mama. And the dresses are beautiful. Madame produces quality work. You can see that."

She admired the stitching again. White stitching on white silk, it was almost a pity that it could not be seen from a distance.

"Excuse me, Mama." She went to her room to write to Aunt Gardiner and tell her that she and Jane would be arriving on Saturday, and how much she was looking forward to seeing her.

CHAPTER 21

M r. Darcy sat in the coach as it rattled towards Netherfield. He was more anxious to see Elizabeth again than he wanted to admit even to himself.

He preferred Pemberley to London, of course. But there was much to occupy him in London, especially with Georgiana there to accompany him. He had been pleased to see that she seemed radiantly happy at his establishment and that Richard had ensured she did not dine alone when he himself was absent.

She had chattered happily about the Earl's young children and the places the Countess had taken her to. Most of all, he was content that she seemed genuinely happy that he had proposed to Elizabeth Bennet.

"Lady Sarah hasn't been back after the visit when you were here, dear brother," she said over tea. "But I've had two or three callers that I've declined to see, like you said. Colonel Fitzwilliam agreed with you. But I am happy that you're now engaged. Now no one can compromise you."

He smiled. "I am very happy too."

He wrote short letters to Elizabeth every two or three days, as would be expected of a man in his position. How he wished he could write of his love and passion for her. But he must not. He was so fortunate that she had agreed to this arrangement and he had no right to force himself on her, to ask more of her than she might wish.

Perhaps, if he was very lucky, she would come to accept his protestations of love and he could hope perhaps that she might, in time, return his love.

"You are deep in your own thoughts, Fitzwilliam!" Georgiana teased him, and he started.

"I am sorry, Georgiana. It is a bad habit of mine and you must stop me when I lose concentration."

"Do you wish to go back to Netherfield? I am quite all right here, Colonel Fitzwilliam is quite able to ensure my safety."

"No, Georgiana, it would be most uncivil of

me to allow you to come here because you were lonely at Pemberley, and then to leave you here alone."

"I would not have asked if I had known your heart was in Hertfordshire." She smiled at him with a teasing look and he chuckled. She was growing into a delightful young woman.

~

*B*ut now the two weeks were over, and he was on his way back to dine at Netherfield. He hoped most heartily that it would not be long before Elizabeth and her sister could travel to their aunt and uncle in London, it would be very much easier to learn to enjoy each other's company without her mother's constant presence.

As the coach drew to a halt outside Netherfield, he saw Bingley on the top step, waiting for him. He hurried up towards him.

"Hello, Charles, how is everything?"

"It is well, nothing of note has happened, although there is much excitement at Longbourn and the wedding clothes are being much admired." He laughed. "I have not seen so much of Miss Bennet as I would have liked, for Mr. Bennet and I have been rather driven from the house. He has spent some time in the library here, exploring the books."

"That wouldn't have taken him too long, surely?"

"That is not kind, Darcy. You know I am not nearly so much of a reader as you are." Mr. Bingley didn't take offence, he was too used to his friend's manner.

Darcy grunted and the two men entered the house and turned towards the library to continue their conversation.

He thought, rather belatedly, of his friend's sister and wondered what sort of reception he would receive at her hands.

"And, er … how is Miss Bingley?" he asked cautiously.

Mr. Bingley glanced at him. "She has been very quiet, generally. But your Miss Elizabeth Bennet was very kind and thoughtful. She and Jane called on her yesterday for tea with my approval, so that has made it a little easier for her. I hope she will be able to face you and join us for dinner."

Mr. Darcy bowed. "I will do my best to put her at her ease." It was a difficult position for his friend to be in, and he was grateful that he had not allowed it to spoil their friendship.

"Do you think it would be a good idea to ride

over to Longbourn and tell Miss Bennet I have returned?"

Mr. Bingley laughed. "They know you are returning today, and they are coming to dinner this evening. I am sending the carriage for them. So you should remain here." He stopped smiling. "We should go through to the drawing room and have tea with my sister. She should meet you before our guests arrive."

Mr. Darcy nodded. He remembered how she had looked disbelievingly at him when Bingley had told her of his engagement to Elizabeth, how she had choked out brief congratulations and then hurriedly excused herself.

This might be difficult, but it had to be borne. They went through to the drawing room. In the doorway, he stopped and bowed to Miss Bingley, who stood and curtsied in return.

"Good afternoon, Miss Bingley," he said gravely.

"Good afternoon, Mr. Darcy," she replied, equally briefly.

He smiled. "May we join you for tea?"

"Of course." She indicated the sofa and he quietly sat down as she poured and handed him the cup.

He waited for her to begin a conversation, but after a few moments, he decided that he needed to make the first move. "Georgiana sends her very best wishes, Miss Bingley. She is enjoying being in London." He smiled. "She particularly enjoyed the gardens at Kew Park, it is apparently a fine sight."

"She must be quite grown up now." Miss Bingley returned politely. But she hadn't changed, he was almost pleased to find, when she added, "You will soon be trying to find her a suitable husband." She shot a look of dislike at her brother.

Mr. Darcy recalled that she had harboured hopes that Charles would marry Georgiana and propel the family up the suitability ladder. He pushed aside the memory of her barbed comments to Elizabeth and tried to feel charitable towards her.

"Georgiana is only sixteen years old. There is plenty of time to find someone who would be the right match for her." As he said it, he wished he hadn't. He'd left themselves wide open to a remark that both he and Bingley had married beneath them.

But surprisingly, she stayed silent. They sat for some time over their tea and then he excused himself and went up to his rooms. He was glad that the first meeting was over, he knew that she'd want to stay on cordial terms, the pull of being able to continue to visit Pemberley would not allow her to cause any break in relations. But it was difficult.

Arrangement or not, he would not allow Elizabeth to be the butt of any rude or hurtful remarks. He still felt a deep chagrin from saying that she only looked tolerable the first time he had set eyes on her, and that she had forgiven him for that — and much worse at Rosings — made him want to make everything right for her in the future.

CHAPTER 22

*T*he coach was spacious, but even so, for five people it was reasonably crowded. Elizabeth was glad it was only twenty-four miles to Cheapside, as she sat staring out of the window. Miss Bingley sat on her right, and held the gentlemen in continuous conversation, while Jane on her left listened and smiled serenely.

Elizabeth hadn't much of a view from the middle seat, but it would have to do. She was acutely conscious of Mr. Darcy's gaze upon her, as she had been at dinner last night. She hoped that a few meetings in London might help to take the strangeness of their relationship away somewhat.

It was hard to try not to listen to Miss Bingley's conversation, and some of her comments penetrated.

"And, of course we must all go to the opera. It will be so good for dear Georgiana's education, and I expect Miss Bennet and Miss Eliza will find the novelty of the experience most diverting."

Elizabeth stared ever more fiercely out of the window. She kept repeating the same mantra in her mind that had worked the previous evening. *I'm the one that Mr. Darcy chose, not her. He chose me.* That helped a great deal, and she was gratified that both gentlemen ignored Miss Bingley much of the time, only answering when politeness compelled them.

Despite the fact that she would have to say farewell to Mr. Darcy until the next day, Elizabeth was very happy when they reached Cheapside. She was even more pleased that Miss Bingley was going to stay for the time being with her sister Mrs. Hurst. Aunt and Uncle Gardiner appeared at the door and she climbed out stiffly after Jane, Mr. Darcy's touch burning as he assisted her.

He bowed politely and asked after the family, but declined to stop for tea, pleading that he wished not to keep Georgiana waiting for them, instead promising to bring Georgiana with him the next day.

He bowed over Elizabeth's hand, holding it to his lips a fraction longer than she was comfortable with.

Jane introduced Mr. Bingley to Mr. and Mrs. Gardiner and Miss Bingley nodded at them from the coach. She had made it quite clear on her previous visit how much she disdained Cheapside, and was doubtless exceedingly angry at her brother for being so pleasant to them.

As the coach rattled away, Elizabeth followed Jane into the house, where they were assailed by the four lively children. She laughed as she fended them off, making her way to the nearest chair and collapsing into it with a sigh.

"Dear Aunt Gardiner, thank you so much for letting us visit you. You have no idea how much I have been looking forward to coming here."

"I agree, aunt." Jane's voice echoed her sentiments.

Mrs. Gardiner laughed. "The time before getting married is always exhausting and stressful, I can assure you both. No matter how happy you are."

Elizabeth laughed dutifully alongside Jane, but her heart was heavy. She should be pleased at seeing Mr. Darcy again, she'd missed him when he'd been away, but having to pretend she was so happy at their forthcoming wedding, having to hide her love from him, yet still appear to be in love to her friends and family, was proving to be more tiring than she could possibly have imagined.

She didn't regret her agreement, not for one moment, but she was sad at the subterfuge that they were playing on those around them. Most of all, she regretted that she couldn't tell him of her regard for him, and her knowledge that he no longer loved her. He wanted a wife — someone who would prevent the inconvenience of being pursued and trapped by a woman not of his choosing.

She climbed to her feet. "I'm so sorry, aunt. Would you be offended if I went upstairs and rested for a short while?"

"Of course not, Lizzy." Aunt Gardiner placidly continued to pour the tea. "Would you like tea brought up to you?"

"No, thank you." Elizabeth smiled tiredly. "I will not be too long, I am sure." She curtsied to Mr. Gardiner and went up to the guest room she always stayed in whenever in London.

She slipped her shoes off and unpinned her hair. Still fully-dressed, she lay on the bed and drew a light blanket over her. She lay quiet, her eyes closed, her mind full of Mr. Darcy. Could she really do this?

As she began to doze, she knew she had no choice. Of course, she could break off their engagement, but she would not do that to him unless he asked her to. He, of course, would not be able to discontinue the arrangement without a terrible scandal.

No, in only ten days' time, she would be Mrs. Darcy, for good or ill. In one week, they would return to Longbourn, and she and Jane would be married in the small parish church. After that, she would do whatever Mr. Darcy had planned for her. They would live at Pemberley, and she would spend the season in London if he wished her to, or not, if that was his wish.

She felt rather sick. Did she really know him well enough to trust that he would do the best for her?

She wiped her face with the back of her hand, and wondered when the tears had started. She blinked hard. She must remember what she had been feeling in the days before his proposal. She had felt trapped at Longbourn. She did what her father decided was the best thing for her, and she could only do what was considered proper for an unmarried young lady of limited means. She remembered feeling a sense of freedom when she knew that she had the opportunity to learn new things and new places. The chance to travel, to practice her languages, to read new books, to make a friend of Georgiana.

No, she must remember these things, and be calm. It was the right opportunity for her, and she loved him, even if he could not love her in return.

Thus reassured, she dozed for a while, hoping to feel better.

❦

The following morning, the two gentlemen returned with Georgiana. Mrs. Gardiner was her usual gracious self, calm and serene. She was obviously delighted at the engagement of her two favourite nieces, especially to such eligible men, and her welcoming nature provided a relaxed atmosphere.

Elizabeth was pleased to see Mr. Darcy seem less stern, he even smiled slightly as the youngest Gardiner child ran in to show his mother a drawing.

"Mrs. Gardiner, I am hoping very much that we will have the honour of welcoming you and your family to Pemberley in the summer." He sipped his tea. "I know how much you enjoy Derbyshire."

Mrs. Gardiner glanced at Elizabeth. "You remember very well, Mr. Darcy. We would be delighted to see you then, and also enjoy your beautiful home."

Elizabeth was reassured that she was doing the right thing. She remembered her aunt's words as they approached Pemberley last summer, that a lady might be prepared to put up with a great deal to be mistress of Pemberley.

She smiled to herself. She would indeed put up with a formal marriage arrangement to see again the pleasure in her beloved aunt's face that she might visit Pemberley.

She sensed Mr. Darcy's eyes on her again and she glanced at him. His gaze was warm and she felt herself blush.

Her aunt must have caught sight of her confusion, for she stood up. "It is a fine morning. Perhaps Jane and Lizzy would care to show you the gardens here? They do not, of course, compare with Pemberley, but we are pleased with them, and I have, this last year, planted new roses from France."

Both men rose when she did.

Mr. Bingley bowed. "What a splendid suggestion. We would be delighted, wouldn't we, Darcy?"

Elizabeth rose in acquiescence. Soon they were all strolling around the lawns, watching the children listening to their governess reading them a story under a great oak tree.

"So, the wedding is only just over a week

away." Mrs. Gardiner was in a conversational mood. "How much remains of the preparations?"

"I am no longer sure, aunt." Elizabeth laughed. "I know the gowns are nearly completed, and our trousseaux are also nearly ready." She looked at Jane. "Mama is ready, I think, with the wedding breakfasts. I am not sure of anything else."

Mr. Darcy bowed. "Mr. Bingley and I have arranged everything else with Mr. Bennet. I believe nothing is amiss, madam."

"Oh, please do not be offended with my questions!" Mrs. Gardiner laughed. "I merely wondered if there was anything I could offer to show my happiness that both my nieces are to be so happily wed."

He bowed to her. "I took no offence, madam. And I am delighted that you are pleased."

CHAPTER 23

*T*he week flew by. Two days before the wedding, Jane and Elizabeth travelled back to Longbourn, this time with the Gardiners.

Jane was almost silent with acute nerves, but Elizabeth felt very calm. She wondered if she would feel different if she were marrying someone who loved her and whom she could love openly. But she would never know. She just wished the wedding over, and then she could be herself once they were alone on the way to Pemberley.

"Are you travelling back to Pemberley immediately, Lizzy?" her aunt must be thinking the same sorts of things as she was.

"I believe so, aunt." She smiled.

"So Georgiana will be travelling with you?"

"Oh, I had not thought of that." How had she

not even thought of it? "I would think that would be correct."

Her aunt gave her a sharp glance. It seemed that Elizabeth was not keeping her face as impassive as she had thought.

She forced a smile. "Georgiana is a sweet girl and we are already good friends." She squeezed Jane's hand.

"And it is going to be easier for you too, isn't it, Jane, now that we know Miss Bingley is going to stay with her sister in London after the wedding?"

Jane turned and smiled at Elizabeth. "Oh, yes. I confess I was concerned that Miss Bingley might be distressed if she felt I wanted to be mistress of Netherfield."

Elizabeth sighed inside. "You always think of other people before yourself, Jane. You will be mistress of Netherfield once you are Mrs. Bingley, will you not?"

"Of course, but I must never forget that Miss Bingley has been most generous in keeping house for her brother these past years."

"Of course." Elizabeth did not wish to argue with her sister. "But the one thing I am sad about is that you will be so far away. I will miss you so much, dear Jane. You must promise to visit us very often."

"We will." Jane smiled. "It is well that Mr.

Bingley and Mr. Darcy are such good friends. There will be no difficulty in mutual visits."

~

*A*nd then it was her wedding morning. Elizabeth wondered what had happened to the previous two days, they had flown past in such a blur, and here she was, being dressed in her wedding gown by the newly-arrived Madame Benoit and her assistant, who'd already dressed Jane.

Her sister stood in the doorway, her face pale but determined. "Oh, Lizzy, you look so beautiful."

"And so do you, Jane. Your hair is perfect, and the gown … Oh, we are so fortunate in having the chance to dress like this."

Madame Benoit tucked a fold in on her shoulder. "You ladies have been a pleasure to make the gowns for. I just wish I could have a picture of you both wearing them. It would grace the finest salons in London." She did sound fairly regretful and Elizabeth knew that this lady indeed would have wished for a top society wedding in London, so that her gowns might be admired more widely.

"Madame, your gowns are so lovely that we will be wearing them on every possible occasion in the future. You can be assured that they will be admired every time and bring you much business." Elizabeth reassured her, despite her own nerves.

"Jane! Lizzy!" her mother's strident voice echoed up the stairs. "Are you ready yet? Oh, my poor nerves! Jane! Lizzy."

Elizabeth sat down suddenly. "You go down, Jane. That will leave me time for Madame to finish my hair, while you are admired from every angle."

Jane laughed, and a little colour returned to her cheeks. "I think you might be right, Lizzy, although I would prefer us to do this together."

"We will be together in the church, Jane. That will have to be enough."

Elizabeth watched her sister affectionately as she nodded and left the room.

"We will not be long." Madame began to weave the flowers into her hair as she worked.

Elizabeth turned and looked into the glass, watching as she was transformed into a beautiful stranger, or so it seemed.

"There!" Madame seemed satisfied and Elizabeth smiled at her own reflection. At least she recognised the smile.

She wondered if Mr. Darcy would appreciate her appearance. He had said,

"I have only met one woman in my life whom I am certain has no interest in my fortune, and that is you."

Would her costly gown and appearance make him wonder if she had tried to trap him for his fortune? She hoped not, even though a part of her knew that the thought of future security played a part in her acceptance of this arrangement.

But she consoled herself by confirming that she would never have agreed had she not loved him.

She took a deep breath. She must get through this day. *I am happy*, she told herself. *If this is not perfect, then it is the best I can expect, and I will make the most of it.* At least she would have the privilege of being permitted to be close to Mr. Darcy for the rest of her life. It was an extraordinary benefit, and she knew she would never regret saying yes.

"Hurry, Lizzy! The coaches are here!" her mother's voice ended her peace for the day, and she rose to her feet and thanked Madame and her assistant.

Making her way down the stairs, she felt as if it was not her who was doing this, it was a stranger who looked like her, and she wondered if she would feel this way as she stood and made her vows.

She was smiling wryly at the thought as she

turned the corner of the stairs and saw her parents in the hall, waiting for her.

There was an unexpected moment of silence and for a panicked moment Elizabeth wondered if there had been a terrible faux-pas and she was all wrong.

Then her father spoke. "You look absolutely beautiful, Lizzy. I could not imagine anything more lovely."

"Thank you, Papa." Elizabeth blinked the moisture from her eyes.

"Yes, you are very beautiful, Lizzy." Her mother sounded almost surprised, and Elizabeth waited for the inevitable comparison with Jane's superior beauty. To her astonishment, it didn't come, and that was, to Elizabeth, the greatest compliment of all.

She felt better as she went through to the parlour and heard Kitty's sighs of envy. "Don't worry, Kitty, I shall have several gowns that I will not need soon." She winked at her sister and Kitty sank into excited silence.

Mary drew breath, and Elizabeth turned to her. "Please, Mary, I understand and I will not suggest you receive a gown unless you tell me you would like one." Her sister silenced, Elizabeth could turn to Jane.

"Mr. Bingley will not be able to take his eyes

from you the whole time," she teased. "You must make sure he does not forget his words!"

Jane laughed and relaxed a little. "And Mr. Darcy will wonder who is standing beside him, Lizzy! I have never seen you so exquisitely beautiful."

Elizabeth could feel herself colouring. "Thank you. It is a good feeling, to think myself more than tolerable." Both of them laughed, and then their father was hurrying them to the open carriage provided by Mr. Bingley.

Other carriages stood behind to convey the rest of the family, and Elizabeth knew that Mr. Darcy had probably provided her father with the funds so that he could purchase the services needed to provide a suitable wedding without the shame of needing his future son-in-law to pay.

She smiled at the scenery as they made their way to the church. The carriage was decorated with flowers and she and Jane were together for the last time as single women.

Time seemed to jump again, and they were arriving at the church. Jane clutched at Elizabeth's arm.

"Oh my goodness, Lizzy, I feel quite faint with excitement."

Elizabeth looked at her sister. "Come now, Jane, you do not want to shame Mr. Bingley. He is a fine gentleman, and you know you will be very happy."

"Oh, yes, I know. But all those people will be looking at us."

"They are our friends, Jane. There is no one there who wishes us ill, no one." Elizabeth spoke firmly and bit back her regret that Miss Bingley and Mrs. Hurst would be there. She also resented that Mr. Collins had assumed an invite, but she could not invite Charlotte without her husband, of course.

"You are right, Lizzy, as always. I will be all right." Jane's voice was firmer and she sat up straighter.

"Good, because we have arrived." Mr. Bennet climbed down first, and handed each of his daughters down carefully. "I am the proudest of men today, girls."

CHAPTER 24

$\mathcal{M}$r. Fitzwilliam Darcy stood, ramrod straight, in front of the altar of the small village church. He stood beside his chosen bride and barely noticed Charles Bingley and Jane beside them.

He kept his gaze firmly to the front, his jaw clenched until the mist cleared from his eyes. Not for anything would he admit the sudden moisture that had appeared when he saw his Elizabeth at the door. Such a vision of loveliness as he had never seen before, and had never imagined would be his.

He heard her small gasp, and tore his gaze away from the great stained glass window and looked down at her.

"Is it wrong, sir? Am I not …?" her whisper

tore at him. Not for anything would he have hurt her.

He smiled. "You are so beautiful, I was almost overcome."

She bit her lip. "Tolerable, sir?"

He struggled not to laugh. This was the Elizabeth he loved, the Elizabeth who was able to discover his inner needs and meet them with a word.

He managed a small smile. "More than."

He could still barely believe she had agreed to marry him, but now it was real and it was now. He still stared at her, the fine tendril of hair in front of her delicate ear, the elegant line of her throat sweeping along her shoulder under the gown.

A movement in front of them caught his attention. The clergyman had stepped up and stood in front of them.

"Dearly beloved, we are gathered together here in the sight of God, and in the face of this congregation, to join together this man and this woman — and this man and this woman — in holy Matrimony; which is an honourable estate, instituted of God in the time of man's innocency, signifying unto us the mystical union that is betwixt Christ and his Church …"

Mr. Darcy concentrated on the beauty of the words that would bring them together. Behind them he heard the rustling of many people. He knew Georgiana was there, with Richard looking out for her. He knew few of the others more than superficially; Bingley's friends, and the Collinses, along with friends and family of the Bennets.

They were all the sort of people he used to disdain, feel himself above them. Until Elizabeth had taught him the error of his ways.

He pulled himself back to the present. He wanted to remember this moment, this day, forever.

The clergyman spoke to him first.

"Fitzwilliam Richard, wilt thou have this woman to thy wedded wife, to live together after God's ordinance in the holy estate of Matrimony? Wilt thou love her, comfort her, honour, and keep her in sickness and in health; and, forsaking all others, keep thee only unto her, so long as ye both shall live? "

"I will." Mr. Darcy made sure his voice rang out, clear and confident. He wanted all the world, and particularly Elizabeth, to know he meant every word of the promise he was about to make.

When she gave her consent, her voice was quieter, but clear and confident.

He felt the heat between them as he faced her and took her right hand in his. Then, led by the vicar, he gave her his vows.

"I, Fitzwilliam Richard, take thee Elizabeth Charlotte to my wedded wife, to have and to hold from this day forward, for better for worse, for richer for poorer, in sickness and in health, to love and to cherish, till death us do part, according to God's holy ordinance; and thereto I plight thee my troth."

He smiled at her, as if they were the only people present.

The next moment, she took his hand, as instructed by the clergyman and she gave her vows, clear and confident. But he noticed her trembling and felt his heart bound with a huge wish to protect her from all fear.

He thought his heart would burst with love as he placed his ring on her finger.

"With this ring I thee wed, with my body I thee worship, and with all my worldly goods I thee endow: In the Name of the Father, and of the Son, and of the Holy Ghost. Amen."

It was done, and he could relax, and listen to Bingley and Jane as they made their vows too.

They knelt in front of the clergyman as he led them in prayer. Then they stood as he pronounced each couple man and wife.

Mr. Darcy felt an ineffable sense of relief. She had kept her word. He had known she would, he trusted her. But at the back of his mind, he hadn't quite been as confident as he had tried to tell himself. But they were married now, and he could hope that in time, she might learn to love him and he could tell her how much he adored her.

The atmosphere lightened as they all walked out of the church. Everyone was cheerful and smiling, and he had his wife on his arm as they walked towards his carriage for the short journey to Longbourn and the wedding breakfast.

He watched his wife as they rode back to the house, a precious few minutes alone.

"You are the most beautiful lady I have ever seen, Mrs. Darcy," he said quietly. "I think I am the proudest man alive."

She went a rosy pink and looked down. "Thank you, sir," she whispered. "I will do my very best not to let you down and to keep to our arrangement."

He cursed under his breath. That damned arrangement, he wanted her to love him. He made himself take a deep breath. He must allow her time. Much would be new for her. While he would be back in his own home, with his own routine and familiar staff, everything would be new to her.

He leaned forward. "Elizabeth." He smiled. "I realise that everything is new to you from this day. Please tell me if I am expecting too much from you, if you need more time to become used to being Mrs. Darcy."

Her chin went up. She was a determined and independent spirit. "I am sure that I will be able to manage perfectly well, Mr. Darcy."

"Fitzwilliam." He smiled.

She bit her lip and went pink again. "Fitzwilliam." Her voice was quiet.

CHAPTER 25

*H*er home was already strange to her, different somehow, from when she had left it this morning, crowded with people, all pushing close to her, congratulating her and Mr. Darcy.

"Dearest Elizabeth, how beautiful you look!" Mrs. Gardiner kissed her on the cheek. "Your gown is exquisite."

Her husband shook Mr. Darcy's hand.

"Congratulations, sir. I can think of no better young lady to make you a fine wife."

"Thank you." Mr. Darcy bowed to him. "But I already know that."

Elizabeth was impressed with his presence. He seemed somehow to prevent anybody crowding her, seemed to know who she didn't really want to speak to for very long, and was instrumental in putting himself between her and Mr. Collins, enduring that clergyman's odious comments so that she could talk uninterrupted to Charlotte.

She knew his attention was on her and she relished it, not wanting to move out of his sight, as she would have done at the beginning of the year.

"Well, I must offer my congratulations." The sneering voice of Miss Bingley was in front of her. She steeled herself.

"Thank you, Miss Bingley." She curtsied politely, determined not to let the woman vex her.

"Of course, such an expensive gown cannot fail to make one feel more handsome. I suppose you have never worn one so fine before?"

"Indeed not. It is a wonderful feeling." Elizabeth smiled serenely. *I am Mrs. Darcy, she failed to capture him.* Her thoughts helped her not to feel belittled, and in a moment, her husband was beside her, taking her arm possessively.

"Miss Bingley, I am pleased that you were able to attend to support your brother's wedding. Don't Jane and Elizabeth look most admirable for brides on their wedding day?"

Miss Bingley curtsied to him, but looked simply furious, especially when he continued, "I think your sister is looking for you. I know she and Mr. Hurst wish to leave for London very shortly."

"Oh. Well, I suppose I should find her." Miss Bingley's tone was supremely sulky. "Goodbye, Miss Eliza."

"Mrs. Darcy!" He corrected her sharply, but she pretended not to hear, and threaded her way through the crowd of people.

"It doesn't matter, sir. Not today." Elizabeth murmured.

He looked down at her. "Thank you for being so generous of spirit, Elizabeth."

Soon they came upon Jane and Mr. Bingley, also surrounded by people congratulating them.

"Oh, Jane! You look so lovely." Elizabeth kissed her. "How does it feel to be Mrs. Bingley?"

Jane looked glowing. "The same, I expect, as it feels to be Mrs. Darcy."

Mr. Bingley looked proud and excited — and slightly disbelieving, too. "This is a splendid wedding breakfast that has been provided for us! Don't you agree, Darcy?"

"Indeed I do." Elizabeth's husband responded. "It will be a pity to leave when the day is over."

"So where are you staying tonight, Lizzy?" Jane asked. "It is such a long way to Pemberley."

Elizabeth looked at her husband.

He tucked her hand more possessively under his arm. "We are going to my — our —" he corrected himself, smiling at her, "establishment in London, as it is only a few hours. Then tomorrow we will travel towards Pemberley. I wish to spend our first weeks of married life there." She smiled back at him happily. It was what she wanted too.

~

*I*t was still quite early when they climbed into the coach to travel to London, and Elizabeth was happy about that, because she was tired and it was a journey of several hours. She looked around. "Is Georgiana coming with us?"

Mr. Darcy shook his head. "No, I have sent her back with Colonel Fitzwilliam and her maid. I think it more proper that we leave here as a couple."

"Thank you." Elizabeth's breath caught in her throat. Formal arrangement or not, it would be the first time she had been alone with a man when travelling.

She leaned out of the coach window and said her final goodbyes to her parents and Jane. Tears sprang to her eyes as she took in the enormity that she might not see them again for many months.

As the coach left the Longbourn estate, she sat back, determined to keep her features calm.

He looked at her sympathetically. "Goodbyes are always difficult," he said.

She stiffened, she would not show weakness. "And sometimes new beginnings, sir."

"Fitzwilliam," he said firmly. Then he smiled. "I know it is much more of a mouthful to say than you are used to. But I like hearing you say my name."

She bit her lip. "Fitzwilliam."

"Excellent — Elizabeth." He sat forward. "We have several hours to go, and it is just us. May I sit beside you, rather than opposite? It will mean you do not have to stare at me the whole time."

"Whatever you wish, sir — Fitzwilliam. It is your coach."

"I know that, Elizabeth. But if you would rather not, then I will respect that on this occasion."

She hesitated. "I have no objection, sir."

"Thank you." He slipped over to the other seat and they sat side by side, facing London.

For the first time, Elizabeth began to wonder how far the arrangement went as regards her marital duties. She wondered that it had never occurred to her in the past weeks.

But she had been so consumed with wedding preparations, she had accepted that she would be mistress of Pemberley, and the means by which

Mr. Darcy would protect himself from being ensnared by another woman. She had not thought further about her wifely obligations.

She stared out of the window, feeling her cheeks grow hot. She knew they must be stained red with embarrassment. He would need an heir for Pemberley — a legitimate child. And she was now his wife. She swallowed.

Would he wait until he admitted love for her? Or would he make love to her without words? Perhaps he would consummate their marriage in a physical way without love or gentleness. She didn't know.

She tried to control her breathing as she sat there. This must be why ladies were never alone in the company of a man, it was far too disturbing to the emotions.

He chuckled. "Please be composed, Elizabeth. You will find you can talk to me and be reassured I will never hurt you or cause you any distress."

He reached out and took her hand in his. His finger traced the ring on hers, heavy and unfamiliar. "I am pleased that you are wearing my ring, Mrs. Darcy. I am honoured that you accepted me."

She summoned up her courage — she was Elizabeth, after all — and turned to look at him.

"Thank you, sir — er, Fitzwilliam. I hope I shall not let you down, or cause you any trouble."

"I am convinced of that. Now, Elizabeth, I am sure you are tired. We have a time now when you can rest. When we are home, you will need to be strong again for dinner, before we can retire for the night."

He pulled her gently so that she could rest her head on his shoulder, but he did not embrace her, and after a few moments she was able to relax a little. She had no idea how she could sleep like that, though. The enormity of what she was doing made her heart race.

Not just the touch of a man … it was the touch of this man.

CHAPTER 26

$\mathcal{H}$ is establishment in London was large and imposing. Mr. Darcy took his wife in through the main entrance, proud of her apparent composure as she was greeted by the housekeeper.

He had obtained the help of Mrs. Gardiner to engage a personal maid for Elizabeth, and he told Elizabeth that she would be waiting upstairs in her bedchamber.

He smiled. "Mrs. Stephens will show you up so that you may compose yourself."

"Thank you." Her voice was quiet and he wondered what she was feeling.

He let her get ahead before he went up to his rooms to cleanse himself from the dust of the journey.

He glanced at the adjoining door between his room and hers. It was locked on his side, but she had no lock on her side of the door. He wondered when she would discover that.

Tonight he would go to her and his heart beat faster at the thought. He hoped ... But there was not time to consider that. First, there was dinner and politeness to endure.

His manservant brought in several tailcoats for him to choose from, and he dressed with care before going downstairs to the front drawing room, where he waited, his mind full of Elizabeth.

He remembered his emotions when he had seen her enter the church, ready to help him by giving him the rest of her life. Why would she do that? She'd said it was because the family were in such debt to him — surely it could not be that? Or at least, not just that?

He stood at the great window and stared out at the darkening street. He had not offered her his love, he wasn't sure she had been ready to hear it, and he could not have borne his love being spurned again.

So he'd offered this cold-hearted arrangement barely able to think straight while in such terrible fear of being compromised. It hadn't been a good idea, putting it like that.

But she'd accepted him, agreed to what he'd

asked. Did she have feelings for him? He could hardly hope for that, but her smile gave him some. He wondered how to tell her of his own feelings.

He saw Colonel Fitzwilliam alighting from his coach outside, and put his thoughts aside. Richard was a good friend, and he would make dinner easier, by partnering Georgiana and helping to put Elizabeth at her ease. He had seen the easy acquaintanceship between them at Rosings.

He went through to the hall to greet his cousin. When drinks had been served to them they waited for the ladies to come downstairs.

"Excellent ceremony, Darcy, don't you think?"

"Indeed."

"Do you quite believe that you are a settled, married man, then?" Richard teased him.

"Oh, yes. Although I still cannot believe my good fortune in Elizabeth agreeing to my proposal." Darcy thought that if only his cousin knew what sort of a proposal it had been, he would certainly not believe it.

Then came the sound of quiet voices in the hall, and a moment later Elizabeth and Georgiana entered the room.

Both men rose to their feet and the ladies curtsied in return to their bow.

Elizabeth was dressed in a silken gown which was a deep, dusky rose colour. She was breathtakingly beautiful to him. He approached her and lifted her hand to his lips.

"You look delightful, Elizabeth. I am pleased to see you look somewhat refreshed."

"Thank you," she said quietly, and he turned to his sister.

"Good evening, Georgiana. I hope you had a comfortable journey home?"

"Thank you, yes." She looked at Elizabeth. "We have been renewing our friendship upstairs."

"I am glad to hear it," he responded gravely, before turning to his wife and extending his arm to her.

"Let us go through to dinner."

Elizabeth took his arm and they went through to dine, followed by Georgiana and Colonel Fitzwilliam.

That dinner followed the usual routine, fine eating, good, leisurely conversation, and then the ladies were rising to withdraw while he sat with Richard over the port.

"I think you're going to be a very happy man, cousin." Colonel Fitzwilliam pushed his chair back and stretched out his legs. "I could see the way you were watching her."

"You embarrass me," Darcy grumbled at him, and the Colonel laughed.

"I can see as well as any other man."

"Well, let us not keep them waiting too long." Darcy drained his glass. "By the way, thank you for saying you will keep an eye on Georgiana for a few more weeks here. I am determined to give Elizabeth time to settle in before Georgiana comes back."

"Surely you're not worried that Georgiana will not be supportive?" Colonel Fitzwilliam sounded shocked.

"Definitely not! They will be close friends. But I want to be able to take her around and learn the geography of the park before she wishes to spend time in my sister's company."

"I see. Well, do not worry, my friend. I will pay Georgiana the closest attention."

Together the men went through to the drawing room to join the ladies.

He sat beside Elizabeth and engaged her in conversation, and they discussed the estate at Pemberley. She seemed eager to hear his opinion on the staff and how he oversaw the way the estate was run.

He noticed at one point her eyes went to Georgiana, and he followed her gaze and saw that she was deep in quiet conversation with Richard.

He was pleased that his sister was enjoying the company of his cousin and thought no more about it.

Finally, the evening was over. They all went to the hall to bid farewell to Colonel Fitzwilliam and he bowed to the ladies in turn before nodding at Darcy and taking his leave.

Elizabeth was watching Georgiana.

Mr. Darcy drew her attention. "I will attend to some correspondence in the library for a few moments while you ladies go upstairs." He bowed over her hand.

He turned to Georgiana. "Goodnight, Georgiana."

She curtsied. "Goodnight, Fitzwilliam."

CHAPTER 27

*I*t was time. Elizabeth could feel her heart hammering within her as she climbed the stairs to the bedchambers. Would he come to her?

He'd said goodnight to Georgiana and not to her, so he would come to her.

But perhaps that was because he thought that is what Georgiana would expect to hear, and he wouldn't come to her. After all, this was a formal arrangement in private, not a love match.

But he would need an heir, and she was his wife. She knew of many marriages made for expedience. She was sure he would come to her, his ring was strange on her hand, and her heart beat fast as her new maid assisted her to prepare for bed.

In the reflection of the glass she looked at the third door in the room.

There was one door which led to her own private bathroom. It was amazing to her; an elegant little room with its own copper bathtub sitting in the middle of the room, and a little washstand with a pitcher and jug.

The second door was to the hallway, and the third — she had tried it — did not open, but Rosina, her maid, had told her it led to the master's bedchamber.

When she was ready, she dismissed her maid and, putting a shawl around her shoulders, sat in the window seat overlooking the shadowed garden.

She would go into the garden tomorrow, she promised herself, and explore. She had a lot to think about, and she remembered parts of the day, and giving her vows. Mr. Darcy standing tall and straight beside her in church, promising to love her and to cherish her.

She touched her lips, wondering if he could possibly have meant the words he had spoken then. Or were they just words to him, a necessary part of obtaining a wife?

She jumped as there was a quiet knock on the third door and it opened slowly.

~

*S*he was up very early the next morning, despite feeling tired from the high emotion of the previous day. She dressed quickly without ringing for her maid, and slipped downstairs, looking around until she found a door to the gardens.

Then she was outside in the chill air, seeing the dew heavy on the grass. She stood on the step and took a very deep breath.

She was very glad it was a new day. The build-up to a wedding that everyone else thought to be a love-match; the strain of hiding her feelings from the man she loved but who never said he loved her; the long journey to London. And most of all, when Mr. Darcy came into her room last night.

Her heart beat fast as she remembered his tall, lean frame outlined in the doorway.

He'd joined her. He'd been gentle and passionate. But he hadn't kissed her. He had barely spoken a word. But afterwards she had gone to sleep in his arms, feeling very cherished.

And then she'd woken in the very early hours of the morning. She was alone, the bed cold.

And she'd lain awake and wept. Was this to be her life from now?

～

*B*ut her whole character was not disposed to be miserable and she determined that with a new day she would find pleasure in her new life. She would start right here.

Although the air was chill, there was a tiny sliver of sunlight at the end of the garden as the sun rose over the east wing of the house and Elizabeth made her way there, to the faint warmth of the sunlight.

She wandered around, tracing the tiny twigs to their end at dormant buds, looking over the shrubbery and peeking into a sweet little summer house.

At one point, she glanced back to the house, feeling as if she was being watched, but the many windows seemed to stare at her blankly, and she turned away again, walking along the gravelled path as the grass was so wet.

Only a few moments later she saw him striding towards her, his manner tousled as if he had hurried to clothe himself and join her.

She curtsied. "Good morning, Mr. Darcy."

He bowed. "Good morning, Elizabeth." He smiled. "Do you not yet feel able to call me by my given name?"

She felt herself blush. "You will excuse me. I had forgotten — Fitzwilliam."

"It is understandable." He offered her his arm and they turned and strolled back down the garden. "I had forgotten how much you enjoyed being outdoors, Elizabeth. I am pleased this house has a good-size garden — at least for London."

"It is a delightful garden, sir. And the morning air is crisp and clean."

"But it is quite chill at this time of year." He looked concerned. "I would not have you become unwell."

"You forget that I am strong and have lived much of my life outdoors." Elizabeth smiled. "I would not have you concerned for me, sir."

He raised an eyebrow at her, smiling wryly.

"I am sorry — Fitzwilliam." Elizabeth laughed. "I hope you will remind me as often as is necessary until I remember."

He chuckled, seeming relaxed. "With your permission, I shall do so."

They reached the end of the garden and turned back towards the house.

"We will go in for breakfast," Mr. Darcy announced. "Then we will take our leave of Georgiana and begin our journey to Pemberley."

"Of course." Elizabeth wondered if Georgiana would be sorry to see them leave. But after observing her last night in conversation with Colonel Fitzwilliam, she was quietly confident of her supposition that when Georgiana came to Pemberley, the good Colonel would not be far behind.

She was delighted, the amiable Colonel would be exactly the kind of husband that Georgiana needed, and being part of the family, Mr. Darcy could scarce credit him with improper intentions.

But she had also seen last night that her husband had not observed anything between the two. Elizabeth resolved to say nothing of the matter.

"How long do you think the journey to Pemberley will take, sir?" Elizabeth decided to think no more of it.

"I would normally expect to take three or four days, Elizabeth. But I think that the roads may be quite difficult, given the recent heavy rain in the north. We may need to take longer for the sake of the horses." Mr. Darcy stood back to allow Elizabeth through the door first. "I hope we might treat the journey as a way of getting to know each other better."

Elizabeth smiled uncertainly. Four days in the close confinement of a coach would really help her get to know him better. More precisely, so would the nights spent in the coaching inns along the way.

"Do not be anxious, Elizabeth." Her husband's voice was full of humour. "We will still be friends when we arrive at Pemberley, you can be assured of that."

"I am convinced of it." Elizabeth tried to sound as certain as her words, and he laughed as they made their way through the house.

"Excuse me, sir. I will go and make myself more presentable for breakfast." She curtsied to her husband.

He nodded. "I too, or I think my sister will feel us to be quite improper." He climbed the great staircase with her.

She gazed at the huge portraits on the wall. "Do you spend most of each season here … Fitzwilliam?"

He smiled at her use of his name. "So far I have not. I much prefer Pemberley at all times of the year, and I only spend a week or so here every few months." He stopped and looked at her.

"But I have been thinking as Georgiana gets older, that I should change my routine to give her more of a chance to move into society."

He bowed. "And, of course, as we are now married, the advantage for you of being in London for the whole season is inescapable."

"I would not have it that you changed your routine for me, sir." Elizabeth shook her head. "I can think of no more certain way to bring resentment than to demand a man changes his preferred habits for the sake of his wife."

He drew breath to speak, but she shook her head.

"And Georgiana is still very young to be out. It may be that with us both at Pemberley, she will be less lonely there, at least for a year or two."

He was quiet for a moment. "It might be that you are correct, but I would like to discuss it further in the future. I would not have you unhappy and not able to tell me, because you had made a too-hasty decision now."

She laughed, her hand on her door latch. "I think you do not yet know me as well as you think you do if you feel that I would not let you know if I was unhappy!"

She was amused as he tried and failed to keep a straight face. "Madam, I will see you at breakfast." He bowed and went into his own bedchamber.

CHAPTER 28

The coach was spacious and comfortable for the two of them, and Darcy had made sure the coachman knew not to hurry the horses on this first day. He knew that his steward would make sure that both coachmen, his valet, and Elizabeth's maid, would have good warm coats for sitting outside, but it would be a cold few days for them. And with the luggage for the journey too, it was a heavy load. He was happy that he had sent Elizabeth's trousseau to Pemberley direct from Longbourn.

He relaxed back as they came to the edge of the town and the houses and shops became sparser and the countryside encroached.

He watched her as she leaned to the window,

her lively interest in the passing scenery. He loved her so much.

He had thought long and hard before he went to her bedchamber last night. He knew she was nervous, and there was still the unspoken reticence between them. He was concerned about the formal arrangement by which he'd won her, but also the unacknowledged love he dare not speak of.

But they were married now. He could tell her, couldn't he? She would not give him such a stinging rebuke.

But as they sat in the coach he held his tongue. If his words were not what she wished to hear, then the rest of the journey would be difficult and uncomfortable.

But he had still gone to her. He told himself that she would be expecting him, that the longer he did not go, the harder it would be, and all manner of other reasons. But the real reason was that he could not stay away.

And now, he had the memory of that night, the joy of holding her in his arms as she slipped into sleep.

He smiled. "I am hoping to reach St. Albans in time for lunch, Elizabeth. Have you ever been there?"

She turned to look at him. "No, sir —

Fitzwilliam. Do you have a favourite place there to eat?"

"There are two places I find very good. If you have no preference from a previous visit, then I suggest we patronise The Swan. There is a comfortable private room, and the food is simple, but well-prepared."

"That seems perfect." She smiled and sat back against the cushions with a sigh.

The silence was companionable. He wanted her to feel comfortable when she was with him, without the need to fill all silences with inconsequential chatter. He already knew she was comfortable with silence, he just wanted her to know it was alright with him.

There was plenty of time for talk, plenty of time for everything. He was supremely happy.

❧

*A*s they drew up at The Swan, he gently roused her where she had fallen into a doze, leaning against his shoulder.

"I'm sorry, Elizabeth. We've reached St. Albans."

She sat up. "I'm so sorry. You shouldn't have let me fall asleep." She wriggled her shoulders.

"I have learned my first lesson," he said comfortably.

"Lesson?" She sounded surprised.

He nodded. "I'm very happy knowing that you can relax in my company and don't feel you have to make polite conversation."

She spluttered with laughter. "I never considered that you'd chosen me for my polite conversation!"

"But you are well able to be polite when circumstances necessitate."

She tossed her head. "Perhaps when we are alone in this coach I need to show you that I can be polite at all times."

"I would not wish that, Elizabeth. But now it's time for lunch." He alighted from the coach first and gave her his hand as she got out carefully, the elegant gown swirling around her ankles.

He felt pride in the way she looked and that she'd accepted his offer of a suitable trousseau.

He had to duck his head as he went through the low door, and she looked around her curiously. He waited while she looked around, and then signalled to the innkeeper who bowed them through to the private room he always used.

It had never been in use whenever he had stopped here and he wondered whether it was ever used by anyone else. Perhaps it was just too close to London for most people in a hurry to be ready to stop, but he liked it.

"Do the staff get a meal too?" Elizabeth sat at table.

He nodded. "It is partly why I choose a private room. Then they do not feel they must wait to serve us."

The innkeeper took their order and returned with the wine.

Elizabeth sipped. "Thank you for bringing me here, Fitzwilliam." Her eyes sparkled. "Are you able to tell me how we will spend the summer? I wish to be able to look forward to what is going to be happening."

He waited a moment before answering. "I am not settled on a course of action yet. I'm aware I am in a settled routine — but that is not a suitable one for a married man. I think that we must both change our habits and form a way of life that suits both of us."

"And Georgiana," she said quietly.

He inclined his head. "And Georgiana."

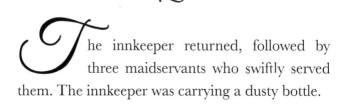

The innkeeper returned, followed by three maidservants who swiftly served them. The innkeeper was carrying a dusty bottle.

"Excuse me, sir, but I hear from your coachman that you married yesterday. I would like to offer you champagne from this bottle I have put away, sir, to show you and your lady my congratulations."

Darcy was shocked. Through the dust he could see the label of the high quality vineyard.

"I accept your congratulations with gratitude, man. But please tell me about the bottle you are holding, where and when you obtained it."

The man ducked his head. "Sir, I ordered it when the war with the French started and I decided I would open it when Napoleon was dead and we were at peace again and my boys were home safe from the war."

His face was creased with sorrow. "But the war is never-ending, and my boys are lost. I have no reason to celebrate as I wished." He straightened up. "But you are an illustrious customer, sir. And I am proud you patronise my humble inn."

Darcy caught his breath. His position of privilege and fortune was brought home to him again.

He rose to his feet respectfully. "Thank you for telling me. We would be proud to accept your champagne, sir, and we will drink to the memory of your sons."

"Thank you." The man's gratitude was

depressing, and Darcy wondered if many before him had refused it and offended the man.

Then they were alone, and Elizabeth's eyes were bright with unshed tears as she looked at him.

"Oh, that poor man!"

Darcy nodded his head. "He has been here for many years. I do not think the inn makes a very comfortable living and he must be too busy to grieve his private sorrows."

He was lost in a reverie for the first part of the meal and ate mechanically.

Elizabeth drew him out of it when the first course had been taken away. "Have you stayed in St. Alban's at all, sir? Is there much to see?"

He pulled himself together. "No. It is too near London to be worth a night stop. But there is a pleasant walk by the river we will take after lunch. I like to rest the horses for a couple of hours if I am not in a hurry."

"I am impressed at your care for them, sir." Her voice was soft and she did not sound as if she were censuring him.

He smiled. "I am proud of them. This is the first full-matched four that I have bred myself from animals that I selected and purchased for breeding."

She brightened. "Really? Tell me, how do you

breed to match the colour? On the farm, the foals are often full different from their dam."

He leaned forward. It was an interest of his. "Of course, the temperament and strength of the animal is most important, but then I select the foals for their colour. The others are fine animals too, and I use them locally." He smiled ruefully. "But I am proud enough of these to have brought them to Longbourn to draw our wedding carriage." He glanced humorously at her. "And why we are travelling at a leisurely pace to get them home."

She bit her lip and looked down. His heart nearly stopped, had he said something wrong?

Then she looked up at him through her eyelashes and her eyes were sparkling. "I knew there must be an ulterior motive for not hurrying to Pemberley!"

He frowned slightly, was she hiding her hurt with her teasing?

"I can send for another four to meet us halfway and the change of horses will cut the time by a day or more," he said anxiously.

She laughed openly. "I can see I shall have to work hard to teach you when I am offended and when I am merely acting offended to tease you!"

He smiled uncertainly. "I confess I am still not sure, Elizabeth."

"I was teasing, sir." Her eyes danced. "I will have to have a code word to use until you are aware of my mannerisms."

He shook his head. "I might then look for the code word and not trouble to learn the other signs."

"And now you are teasing me, sir!"

"Indeed I am, for you are forgetting yourself." He was enjoying himself.

"Oh, I think you do not like being called *sir*, Mr. Darcy!"

He changed the subject. He was not sure how to win this. "Have you finished lunch? We might take that walk along the river."

CHAPTER 29

*E*lizabeth's face was at the coach window again, waiting for the first sight of Pemberley as they came to the end of the trees. She was longing to see it again, to see if it was much changed from the summer, and she wondered if she would look at it differently now that she was mistress of that great estate.

And then it was there. "Oh, it's so beautiful," she sighed. She could sense him leaning forward beside her, watching too, and she turned to him.

"Is it always new to you?"

He smiled at her enthusiasm. "I never fail to look for that first glimpse. Never."

He reached for her hand and she felt that heat of desire that still filled her each moment. She'd been married nearly one week now, and it was still new, still exciting.

She turned to her husband, her hand still in his. "A new beginning, Fitzwilliam."

He smiled, relaxed. "A new beginning. Although I would venture to say that we have begun well. Do you not think so?"

She blushed, the best memories of the journey being the nights in a different inn each time. The lack of space in those inns meant that they spent the nights together, he did not have another bed to disappear to after she was asleep.

She'd slept much better as a consequence, knowing that she was safe in his arms.

"Elizabeth?" his voice was so gentle, she had to blink hard to keep the tears at bay. He was mostly silent, those nights. He had never said he loved her, never kissed her.

She wondered if she might conceive their children in those times, without any love acknowledged between them.

"What is the matter, Elizabeth?" he sounded almost devastated. "What can be wrong?"

"There is nothing wrong, sir." She could not tell him she wanted him to declare his love. It wasn't part of their agreement.

She drew a deep breath. Her job was to be a

good wife to him. She must not demand more of him that that.

"I have been looking forward to getting to Pemberley. I am just happy we are here now." She was good at keeping her real feelings hidden, she knew that.

He looked faintly unsure of her answer and she wondered how long it would be before she could no longer lie to him.

"Then I too am glad we are here now." As they drew up to the main steps, the housekeeper stood to welcome them, and Elizabeth remembered her name from her visit with the Gardiners from the summer.

She curtsied to them. "Welcome to Pemberley, Mrs. Darcy. Welcome home, sir."

"Good afternoon, Mrs. Reynolds." Elizabeth knew the housekeeper must be feeling unsure how the management of the house might change now it had a new mistress, but she must not be too accepting. "I am very glad to be here again."

It seemed very different to her as she looked around, being here as mistress of her new home, rather than as a curious visitor, or even as a dinner guest.

"Let me show you your bedchamber, Mrs. Darcy." The housekeeper curtsied again.

"Thank you."

Elizabeth bowed to Mr. Darcy and followed the woman up the great, sweeping staircase.

Her room was wonderful, and she stared for a long time out at the rolling parkland and the lake.

There was a door through to her husband's room, as there had been in London, and she smiled slightly as she set down her book on the table.

She would soon make this room hers. She would begin by picking flowers from the gardens, and she wondered if there were enough remaining from the summer to arrange some this very evening.

Rosina was unpacking the luggage from the coach and Elizabeth could see in the closet the gowns which had come ahead from Longbourn.

"You must be tired, Rosina. It was a long journey."

"I am all right, madam." The girl was anxious to please and Elizabeth said no more.

Then she was going downstairs to the drawing room to meet her husband for afternoon tea. Her new life had begun.

*T*hey sat over tea, and he leafed through a pile of papers and letters which had been waiting for him.

"With your permission, Elizabeth, I would like to speak to my steward before dinner, to discuss matters of the estate which have arisen while I have been away."

"Of course, sir. I will take the opportunity to pen letters to Georgiana and to Jane."

He smiled, his eyebrow raised.

"Oh, I am sorry — Fitzwilliam." She was taking much too long to get in the habit of this, she was fortunate that he was still good-humoured about it, and she wondered how she had ever thought him proud and disagreeable.

"What are you thinking of?" he sounded interested, and she was suddenly flustered.

She cast around in her mind. "I am thinking how much I shall have to say to Georgiana and Jane."

He seemed to accept that, even though she had written lengthy letters the previous evening, and she sipped at her tea.

A few moments later, a footman entered silently and bowed to Mr. Darcy. He held out a letter.

"An express post, sir."

"Thank you."

Elizabeth watched him as he frowned slightly at the writing on the letter, then broke the seal and began reading swiftly.

"Damnation!" he was on his feet and striding up and down.

"Sir?" Elizabeth was startled. She had never heard him utter any curse, even as mild a one as this.

He groaned. "I am sorry. I forgot myself. Please forgive me, Elizabeth." He dropped into the seat next to her, running his hands distractedly through his hair.

CHAPTER 30

S he sat quietly beside him. She must wait until he decided to tell her what the matter was.

Her eyes fell on the open letter. The writing was feminine, young and unpractised. But it was not Georgiana's writing.

She looked away, wondering what could possibly have happened. She hoped he wouldn't have to leave here, leave her behind, so soon after their marriage.

He was on his feet again, pacing up and down, unable to stay still.

What could it be? Elizabeth knew she should sit quietly, obediently waiting until he decided to tell her what was happening. But she didn't want to wait.

"You will forgive me, sir. But might I be of assistance to you in whatever has happened?"

He looked at her, almost as if he didn't know her.

"I am sorry, Elizabeth. It is not good news for the plans I had formed for our time here these first weeks."

She looked at him anxiously. "I hope nothing has happened to Georgiana?"

He shook his head. "No. This letter does not concern her. Here." He picked up the sheets and gave them to her to read.

> *Rosings Park*
> *Dear Cousin Fitzwilliam,*
> *I am so sorry to write this to you, but I*
> > *am in need of urgent assistance and I*
> > *am writing to you and Cousin*
> > *Richard, because I cannot think who*
> > *else to ask for help.*

Elizabeth turned to the end of the letter to confirm her guess as to who had written.

> *Please come and help me as soon as*
> > *you can.*
> *Your affectionate cousin,*
> *Anne*

Elizabeth turned back to the letter and read it as fast as she could. She thought of the cold, lonely life of Anne de Bourgh as she read.

> *Mother has had an apoplectic seizure, we believe. The physician says he will call daily, and the servants have carried Mother up to her room where she lies, unable to move, apart from one hand which she waves in her agitation. She seems to be unable to speak, but cries out in rage because we cannot understand her attempts to form words.*
>
> *The physician says that he is not sure whether she will recover any ability to speak or be able to leave her bed. But he states that as she is of a strong constitution she may live through this.*
>
> *It is proving very difficult, the servants are looking at me as if I do not know how to manage this house, and I have great difficulty in instructing them what to do.*
>
> *Mr. Collins is not being much help, but Mrs. Collins has been a great assistance. She told her husband to sit with mother and read to her, and then*

she came down and instructed the
servants to listen to my orders.

Elizabeth felt her lips curve. Dear Charlotte, she would be a great help to Anne, but the situation must be difficult and they were so far away.

She turned the letter and scanned it again to see how long Anne had struggled after her mother was taken ill before she had given in and asked for her cousins' help. But she could not see it mentioned.

"Oh, poor Anne, and poor Lady Catherine!" Elizabeth jumped to her feet. "Can you be spared again from business here so soon? But we must go at once. She must feel so alone."

"Elizabeth." He captured her hands in his. "I cannot possibly ask you to travel that far after you have only just arrived. It is unthinkable." His eyes fell on the letter. "But I must go to Rosings." His lips tightened. "Colonel Fitzwilliam must not leave Georgiana in Town alone and there is no one closer that I might ask."

"Would Colonel Fitzwilliam ask his brother to attend?" Elizabeth ventured. "It is within one day's journey, and he could help until we were able to get there."

She stepped closer to him. "I feel very much

for Miss de Bourgh, and I would like to assist if I can."

He smiled down at her. "If you permit me to go alone, I can ride. I will take a groom with me who can bring back my horse when it is weary and I can then hire horses and change them as they become tired. I could be there a full three days sooner than if I travel by coach."

He must have seen her expression. "I am sorry, Elizabeth, but I hope you can be brave with this and wish me God-speed. I do not want Richard to leave Georgiana unsupervised."

"If that is your wish, sir." Elizabeth lifted her chin. She would not cause him worry for anything in the world. She forced a smile.

"Will you have time to dine first, sir?"

He looked distracted. "What? Oh, yes." He looked at the gathering darkness. "It is too late to start now. I would not make much progress in the dark. I will stay here tonight and leave at dawn."

She curtsied. "How can I assist in your preparations, sir?"

"Elizabeth." He lifted her face to his. "Thank you for being so understanding." She wondered for a heart-stopping moment if he would kiss her. But no.

He stepped back. "I will see my servant about what to take — it cannot be much. I would ask that you arrange for a trunk to be packed for me and sent by post coach — perhaps this evening — with my manservant. It will catch up with me there." He stopped and thought for a moment. "I will write to Richard and ask him to remain with Georgiana. As her guardian, he has that responsibility. And I will write to my cousin, the Earl, to ask him to send assistance to Anne." He frowned, thinking.

"And when you have arranged about the luggage, maybe you would be kind enough to write to Georgiana and Anne and explain what I am about." He smiled at her. "I know that you will be able to explain to them that I am engaged in preparations for the journey."

"Indeed I will do what you ask, sir." Elizabeth curtsied and rang for the housekeeper.

Later, they sat over a hurried dinner. Darcy was distracted and thoughtful. Elizabeth talked quietly about how the situation would be at Rosings.

"I hope it is in order, sir, but in my letter I have suggested to Miss de Bourgh that she enlists the help of Mrs. Collins to engage several nurses to assist her. I believe the house servants may be unskilled in such personal care as may be required and if they are, then Lady Catherine may not receive the high quality care she needs and might reasonably expect, given her position."

He glanced up and his expression softened. "It was well thought, Elizabeth, thank you."

She smiled. "I will insist on you obtaining a good night's rest, sir. And with your permission, I will arrange for a selection of cuts to be on offer for you to make a good breakfast. You will not then need to stop until your horse needs resting."

He nodded. "Thank you."

She sat quietly, thinking over what she needed to do to make his journey go well.

CHAPTER 31

They went through to the drawing room for coffee together, and she slipped to the piano and played for him; quiet, restful pieces to help him relax.

She watched him as he sat beside the fire, relaxed in the large library chair there, his eyes on her. Thoughtful, unfathomable, it made her slightly uncomfortable, as if he knew what she was planning.

She shook herself slightly. He could not possibly know what she was thinking.

He smiled. "Come, Elizabeth. It is quite late enough. Let's retire."

She got up, smoothing the skirt of her gown. She wondered if he would sleep in his room alone tonight, the first time he would have the opportunity since their wedding night.

If he did, she could not argue that it would not be advantageous for him to be well-rested before his long journey.

But she would also be disappointed — after all, with the plan he was proposing, she might not see him again for many weeks.

And riding from Derbyshire to Kent, on hired horses, was not the safest means of transport. Her heart failed her as she thought of the terrible possibility that she might lose him, might never see him again.

"What is it? What is the matter?" his voice was sharp with concern as he looked at her face.

She smoothed her features, she should not have thought that. "It is nothing, sir."

He stepped close to her. "Please let us be honest with each other, Elizabeth. We owe each other that much, at least."

He was right, of course. She lifted her chin. "I would not wish to worry you, sir. But I had a thought that with hired horses, you might have a fall." She shivered. "Come back to me safely, Fitzwilliam. Come back safe."

His face softened. "I will," he promised. "I will see you again as soon as I possibly can." He hesitated. "I am taking an experienced groom with me. He will select the horses with care from those available, and I will not be riding alone. Please do not be overly concerned." He kissed her hand. "I will write to you very often so that you might be reassured as to my well-being."

They turned for the stairs. "I hope you understand why I am doing this, Elizabeth." He walked beside her. "It will mean I can be at Rosings some days earlier than I otherwise could, and I do not wish to leave Anne any longer than necessary."

They stopped outside her bedchamber door. "Lady Catherine has an impeccable sense of timing, sir." She smiled.

"If we had stayed in London, I am quite sure she would still be in excellent health!"

He gave a shout of laughter before schooling his expression back to his impassive look. "You are very mischievous, Mrs. Darcy. I will not say it is an unworthy thought, because it is entirely true." He bowed again.

"Adieu, Elizabeth." And he turned and was gone to his room. She stared after him for a long moment, before entering her own bedroom.

Rosina was there to assist her in getting ready for bed, and she instructed her most firmly that she was to be woken at the same time as Mr. Darcy before she dismissed her.

She stood gazing out at the moonlit park for a

long, long look, storing up the memory to take with her tomorrow.

Then she turned and climbed into bed. She would have a busy day tomorrow, and she could do with the rest. But she was still sorry he had not come to her.

A moment later her wish was granted and she heard his knock at the door.

~

*S*he had only just settled to sleep after a night of wakefulness when Rosina entered the room with a pitcher of hot water for her to use.

She sat up and stretched as the pale dawn outlined the room. "Thank you, Rosina."

She was happy that her husband had been with her the early part of the night, but she'd sensed he was distant and wasn't surprised when he eased himself out of bed when he thought she was asleep. She lay there, her eyes shut, trying to keep her breathing slow and even.

There had been the lightest of touches on the side of her face. Had he kissed her? Or was it just his hand? She wished she knew and puzzling over it had kept her awake much of the rest of the night.

Once she was dressed, she hurried downstairs. He looked up, and smiled as he saw her.

"I thought you would rise early to see me begin my journey."

She curtsied. "I would not leave you to dine alone, sir. You know I enjoy my food." She must keep the atmosphere light.

He smiled appreciatively and waited for her to be seated before taking his own seat. "You are forgetting my name again, Elizabeth."

She made a small sound of annoyance. "I'm sorry, Fitzwilliam. I promise I will practice each day and when we meet again, I will be word-perfect." She wondered how long it would be before she saw him, and what he would say to her.

She had been quite certain that, on arriving at Pemberley, she would risk everything and tell him of her feelings for him. She could not bear to keep up the pretence of the formal arrangement for much longer, and now they were at Pemberley, there was ample room in which to avoid seeing him too much if he rejected her confidences.

But now everything was different, she would not worry him before his journey. So their relationship must wait and she hated that the deception must remain.

"Please give Miss de Bourgh my very best

wishes and ask her if I might be of assistance in any way."

He nodded, "I will indeed do that." His eyes rested on her — was that amusement she saw there? "And if she feels it will help, I might send for you to join me."

"Of course. I would welcome the chance to be of use to her."

He pushed his plate away and drained his coffee. "I am sorry that I must leave you now, but I have the opportunity to make a good distance today and I am sure the horses are anxious to be off."

She rose to her feet. "I will keep you in my thoughts these days, Fitzwilliam. I pray that everything goes well."

He took her hand and raised it to his lips. "I will also be thinking of you, Elizabeth. You must take the greatest of care, and I will write to you often."

She looked at the expression in his eyes — had he guessed?

She would divert his thoughts. "May I ask a favour, sir?"

He smiled. "Only if you remember my given name."

"Oh. May I ask a favour, Fitzwilliam?"

"Of course, Elizabeth."

"I will take the greatest of care if I might be permitted to explore the books in your library. I have the thought that I would like to map out a course of study to keep my mind active. I am sure there is much local history that it would benefit me to learn."

He was taken aback. She smiled serenely, she knew he had thought she would follow him, and now he was wondering if he had misjudged her.

"Of course you may, Elizabeth. And when I am back, I will show you the geography of what you have learned." As they made their way down the great stairs to the waiting horses, he walked very close to her.

"You may also find that you are visited by local ladies who are curious to meet the new mistress of Pemberley." He looked down at the snorting, impatient animals.

"I would not normally say this, but as I will not be here to advise you, you may discuss the various local families with Mrs. Reynolds. She is discreet and will not share your confidences or take advantage of this in the future." His face was stern.

"If I might suggest it, then you might be indisposed from your journey if a certain Mrs. Mills pays a call. I will explain later my reasons for this."

"I understand." Elizabeth was sure now that he had been certain she would follow him in the coach, and her request to use the library had put his mind completely off this supposition.

She smiled, he was now thinking of all he had not thought necessary to say to her.

"Please do not be concerned. I like Mrs. Reynolds very much, and I am sure she will take good care of me."

"I am happy to hear you say that." Mr. Darcy shrugged himself into his top coat and buttoned it up. He took his hat from the footman and then took her hands in his.

"I will write to you this evening to tell you how far I have travelled, Elizabeth. Please take care and I will see you as soon as I can."

She curtsied. "Safe journey, sir." It would be nearly a week before she saw him again, she knew that, even if she followed him within the hour. And she was not certain that she could prevail upon the staff as quickly as that.

CHAPTER 32

*H*e lifted her hand and kissed it. He seemed to hesitate. Then he made up his mind, and let go, stepping back.

His groom was holding the horse and he took up the reins and mounted swiftly. A third groom was on another horse, following to bring back the Pemberley animals when they had tired and others were hired. It was all happening too fast. She stepped forward, knowing her dismay was showing on her face.

He circled her. "Be strong, Mrs. Darcy. I know you are brave and courageous and I will make this absence up to you as soon as I may."

She nodded, and stood still as the groom who was going with him hastily mounted, and the three horses trotted away down the long gravelled road. She watched his tall, straight figure, his tall hat showing his status, the grooms behind him.

She waited there until he was out of sight, then she hurried back up the steps. "Mrs. Reynolds, Mrs. Reynolds!"

The housekeeper appeared at once. "Yes, Mrs. Darcy?"

Elizabeth's heart failed her slightly. "I have had enough breakfast. Please arrange for tea to be served to me in the orangery."

"Yes, Mrs. Darcy." The woman curtsied.

Elizabeth went through to the drawing room and selected some Pemberley notepaper and a pen. Then she went to the orangery, which she had seen on her visit in the summer.

The air was humid and warm, the tropical plants forming a great jungle around the small table at which she settled herself.

She began to write.

> *My dear husband,*
> *I have just seen you ride away to Rosings*
> *and I am writing now so that this*
> *letter will await you when you arrive,*
> *four or five days hence.*
> *I want to tell you how proud I am to be*

your wife, and see the care which you
take of me and those around you.
I hope that you are able to assist Miss de
Bourgh, and that Lady Catherine
might perhaps recover somewhat, or
at least be peaceful.

She read her words back and smiled. She could not imagine Lady Catherine would suffer her illness gracefully.

I am hopeful you have had a successful
journey and that you are not too
fatigued.
I will maintain correspondence with
Georgiana and reassure her of your
well-being.
Your affectionate wife,
Elizabeth Darcy

She sealed the letter and addressed it to him at Rosings.

When the maid appeared with the tea, she sent her to get Mrs. Reynolds. When the house-keeper arrived, she forced away her fear that she would be rebuffed and spoke confidently.

"Mrs. Reynolds, I have decided to go to

Rosings. I know Mr. Darcy has ridden because he wishes to get there as soon as possible, but I intend to follow and join him there. I will go in the coach we travelled here in."

"Yes, madam."

Elizabeth looked at her. No objections? Her suspicions were aroused again.

"I would like to see the steward, please. He can inform me of what needs to be done with regard to the travel arrangements." She thought again.

"And I will, of course, take my maid and two men in addition to the coachmen."

Mrs. Reynolds looked at her doubtfully. "Have you ever undertaken such a long journey alone, madam?"

"There is always a first time, Mrs. Reynolds. If Lady Catherine is to be indisposed for some time, I will be able to be of more use there than here."

"Yes, madam." She hesitated. "Might I make a suggestion, madam?"

"Provided it does not involve abandoning my plans, then please speak."

"I think it would be a good idea if you arranged to take the steward with you, Mrs. Darcy. He is a fine man, is Mr. Fields. He has been here for nearly ten years now. He would be able to take on the requirements of booking suitable accommodation at inns along the way and would assist the coachman with the change of horses."

Elizabeth looked at her. "It is a good suggestion, Mrs. Reynolds. But who would manage the estate while he is gone?"

The woman curtsied. "Mr. Darcy has taken Mr. Fields with him before, to visit estates using new ways of farming, and discuss management changes. On those occasions, the deputy steward is accustomed to managing the Pemberley estate."

"Very well." Elizabeth made up her mind. "Please inform him of the plans and ask him to come and see me."

"Yes, madam. Mr. Darcy usually calls him into the estate office. Would you wish to do the same?"

Elizabeth nodded. There was so much to learn here. But she was determined.

"While I am seeing him and discussing the journey, please tell Rosina to pack for me and for herself." She glanced at the sun.

It was hard to think of another week's journey, even though Mr. Darcy had made the one just done as easy as possible for her.

This would not be so comfortable. She would push for longer days, as they would be changing horses. So there would be no long stops to rest them.

Hardest of all, she would not have his

company while travelling, and while dining and at night.

She stiffened and sat up straight.

"I will begin after lunch, Mrs. Reynolds. Please arrange it. And first, please show me the estate office."

The woman curtsied. "Yes, Mrs. Darcy."

After lunch, Elizabeth climbed into the coach. She was tired before she began, and the weather had taken a chilly turn. Wrapped warmly in her heavy coat, she knew that without movement, her feet would soon be very cold.

She took Rosina into the coach with her, as was proper for a lady travelling alone. Hopefully, she would find the silence comfortable. She sat back, hoping she had remembered everything.

Mr. Fields looked in the door. "Everything is arranged, Mrs. Darcy. With your permission, we will leave now."

"Yes. Thank you." She liked him very much. He was calm and competent, and she was happy to leave everything in his hands.

But she was even more sure now that her husband had known what she would do, and the previous evening he probably arranged for everything to be done that was needed — the staff had been far too unsurprised.

But he had doubted his guess when she asked him about the library. She was glad about that. Now he would not worry about her being on the roads.

CHAPTER 33

Four days later, Mr. Darcy rode into Kent. He stopped and stared at the rolling downland and eased his back. It had been a fierce ride, but there were only a few hours left. He had made better time than he had thought, but nevertheless he wondered if Lady Catherine was still alive, and who, if anyone, had come down from London to help Cousin Anne.

He turned in the saddle. His deputy head groom was there, imperturbable as ever.

"We will stop at the next inn for lunch," Darcy said. "These horses will be all right then to continue to Rosings."

"Yes, sir."

He turned and they trotted down towards the hamlet nestled in the valley. The man with him was very competent, but he would still have preferred to have had his head groom with him.

But he would be needed to drive the coach if Elizabeth did decide to come to Kent without asking him. His lips curved in amusement. He'd been quite certain that that was her plan and he had spent several hours ensuring that the staff would take great care of her if she did that.

He'd been confused when she mentioned the library, but as he lay in bed at night and thought of her, he decided it was a ruse to convince him of her obedience in staying there.

No, he was quite certain she would arrive at Rosings within three days of his own arrival. He wondered if she thought he might be angry that she hadn't asked permission. Perhaps he should try and appear to be. After all, the wife of a gentleman should ask her husband's permission before making any such journey.

He smiled again as he pulled up outside the small inn. But he hadn't expressly forbidden her, chiefly because he did not want her to disobey him and he was sure she would.

He would be pleased to see her, and he did not know how long they might be required to stay here. It all depended on Lady Catherine's health and whether Anne was able to take charge of the staff here.

He ate some lunch, but he was not really hungry, and they were soon on their way again. It was a pleasant day for the time of year, Kent being much warmer than Derbyshire, and Darcy daydreamed a little.

It might be pleasant to have a little cottage down here, or maybe even in Cornwall, for the winters where the weather was much easier. But he knew he wouldn't, he loved Derbyshire much too much to consider it.

An hour later, they turned into Rosings and walked up the driveway, letting the horses cool down. At the main steps, he dismounted and indicated to the groom where the stables were.

Stiffly, he climbed the steps, wondering that no one was at the door to greet him. When he got there, he realised the housekeeper was waiting, looking disturbed, glancing back at the drawing room.

"Good afternoon, Mrs. Atkins. How are matters today?"

She curtsied, looking flustered. "I am so glad you are here, sir. I did not know what to do. There are two gentlemen here and I think Miss Anne is troubled by them."

Mr. Darcy took off to the drawing room at a run. He crashed through the door, anger rising within him. He should have ridden harder this morning.

His Cousin Anne was sitting stiffly in her chair in the dark and dismal room. She turned towards him with evident relief.

He turned to see two uniformed officers sitting there and he nearly lost control. Wickham rose to his feet, taking a couple of steps back.

The other man — a Captain — rose, his pale, pockmarked face looking stunned and angry.

"Who are you, sir? I have business with Miss de Bourgh!"

"I don't care what sort of business you have with the lady. What the devil do you mean by sitting here with her unchaperoned?"

"I am Captain Matthews of the Dragoon Guards, sir! I am obliged to the lady and therefore I have made her an offer. And, in return, what right do you have to be here?" He was angry and he pushed himself close to Mr. Darcy who was only just able to prevent himself from striking the man.

He drew himself up to his full height, considerably more than the other man, who seemed to shrink slightly. "I am Fitzwilliam Darcy, of Pemberley. And if you are obliged to Miss de Bourgh, perhaps you should be stripped of your commission for the disgrace, sir! And any man in company with Mr. Wickham is doubly disgraced in my view."

He sneered towards Mr. Wickham who was edging towards the door. Then he turned back to the hapless Matthews and pushed his face close to the other man's.

"You will return in the morning and see me when I have had a chance to speak to my cousin, and I shall see what is to be done." He took a step closer, and the other man retreated.

"And Mr. Wickham knows he is not welcome here." He turned away contemptuously. "So we will see the colour of your bravery when you have to return alone."

Captain Matthews tried to bluster up some bravado, but was soon hurrying out of the house, preceded by Mr. Wickham, who was hastening away as fast as he could.

Mr. Darcy returned to the drawing room where Anne had given way to tears. He returned to the door and called.

The housekeeper appeared. "Where is Mrs. Jenkinson?" he barked at her.

She curtsied nervously. "The officers demanded she leave the room, sir. She did not want to go, but they were insistent."

"I am sure they were," he said grimly. "Call

her back please. She needs to attend to Miss de Bourgh."

He turned back into the room and pulled out his linen handkerchief. Thank heaven he was married. He could go and offer comfort to his cousin without risk.

He knelt beside her chair. "Here you are, Anne," he said gently, and she took the handkerchief and tried to smile.

"Thank you, Cousin Fitzwilliam. I'm so sorry."

"There is nothing to be sorry about, dear cousin. The vultures are circling, and you should never have been left alone to deal with them."

"He wants Rosings, I think. I only let them in because Mr. Wickham was there. I knew his name."

"I know. Can you tell me? Is he obliged to you? Has he hurt you?"

She shook her head. "They came yesterday and the day before. But today was the first day they frightened Mrs. Jenkinson away. I think he was going to … to …" She stopped, quite unable to go on, and he was relieved to see her companion come into the room.

CHAPTER 34

*M*rs. Jenkinson hurried to Anne's side. "Oh, Miss de Bourgh, I'm so sorry to see you all aback. Let me help you freshen up." She drew the younger woman to her feet. "Let's go up to your room and compose yourself. What a good thing Mr. Darcy came when he did! What a good thing!" She continued muttering as she led Anne upstairs.

Mr. Darcy was left striding angrily about the room. Then he stopped at the windows, taking a deep breath. He must control himself. He needed to take control here, needed to find out what the situation was, and sort matters out.

He went to the hall. "Mrs. Atkins!" he called. When the woman appeared, he asked the questions he would have asked of Anne.

"How is Lady Catherine?"

The woman curtsied. "She is little changed, sir. She tries to get out of bed and she tries to make herself understood. Both attempts fail and it makes her very angry."

He could understand that. To suddenly lose control of her body and her household would make anyone very frustrated, but especially such a person as his aunt.

"So, who of the family have been here?" He would not make his displeasure known outside the family, but someone had some questions to answer, leaving Anne in such a vulnerable situation.

"Sir, the Earl came down for two days, but he had urgent business back in town, and returned to London. There has been no one here for two days."

He stared at her. How had Wickham known to pounce the moment Anne was unprotected?

"And who is with Lady Catherine now? Have nurses been obtained?"

The woman faltered under his angry gaze. "Yes, sir. She has one of them with her at all times."

He controlled himself with an effort. "I'm sorry, Mrs. Atkins. I am not angry with you, but with the circumstances that Miss de Bourgh has been placed in." He forced himself to speak of the other odious man.

"And have Mr. and Mrs. Collins been here?"

The woman curtsied. "Yes, sir. Mrs. Collins has been here for part of each day. She orders the food and the menus and directs me. Then she was assisting Miss de Bourgh with the care of Lady Catherine until the nurses were appointed."

He was pleased. At least it seemed as if Elizabeth's friend had tried to help, even if he disliked her husband.

"Thank you. Do I understand Lady Catherine is in bed?"

"Yes, sir."

He made a face. He could not go up and see her. He wondered if she would wish to see him anyway.

She had told him when he announced his betrothal to Elizabeth that she would never speak to him again. But he expected that she would change her mind now that help was needed to protect Rosings Park.

He turned away. "Please arrange for tea in the drawing room."

"Yes, sir."

He paced up and down the room, waiting. The whole place was dark and dismal still, full of memories of the iron will of his aunt.

For the sake of his cousin, he fervently wished her mother did not survive long. Having her there and frustratedly not able to make herself understood would be a nightmare for all concerned.

He stared out of the window. Rosings Park was a huge magnet. Men from all walks of life would view it hungrily for the wealth and status it offered. Now that Lady Catherine was unable to intervene he did not think his cousin would have a moment's rest until she was safely married.

He scowled. It was just as he himself had felt only those few short weeks ago. But Anne was a lady, and of sickly disposition.

He had had Elizabeth to help him. Anne had no one. He shifted his shoulders stiffly in his coat. God! He needed a bath.

When the tea arrived, he turned and acknowledged the footman. "Has my trunk arrived from Pemberley yet? And my servant?"

The man bowed. "I believe they arrived this morning, sir."

He nodded his dismissal. "Thank you."

His cousin arrived to join him for tea. "Thank you for coming so fast, Fitzwilliam. I was afraid I would be forced into marriage."

He crossed the room and bowed over her hand. "I am sorry you have been so alone."

She tipped her head up. "I will get over this

awful time. It is difficult because so many people feel I am not capable of making the simplest of decisions."

She sipped her tea. "Do you know, when you and Cousin Richard spoke to me the last time you stayed, it seemed to me the first time that anyone had tried to believe that I could make my wishes known at all. I should have refused to let Mother speak for me all this time."

He bowed his head gravely. "Your mother is a powerful personality. I believe she has done you a grave disservice." He paused. "And we are all to blame too, for accepting the fact without trying to remedy the situation."

He smiled. "Richard and I were planning on the way home from our visit how we would get you to London without your mother, so that you could be an ordinary young woman."

She smiled slightly. "Did you think that would be easy?"

"No." He shrugged regretfully. "I fear we reached the end of the journey without the first idea how to accomplish the feat."

"And now events have taken over." She turned to him and her eyes were shiny with unshed tears. "I am afraid, Fitzwilliam. I am afraid of being taken advantage of."

He felt sorry for her. "I will do what I can. Be

sure, Anne, I will never allow you to be in that position again."

He was resigned that he would need to stay at Rosings some time, and he fervently hoped Elizabeth was on her way. If she was not, then it would be many more days before she could be with him.

He would write tonight, and if she was still at Pemberley, then at least he could get her started on her way to him. But he hoped she was already well on the road here.

He wondered, would she have started out the same day? Yes, of course she would. So perhaps she would only be another two days or so.

"How is Elizabeth?" Anne's voice made him start.

"She is well, thank you."

"I am happy that you married her. I liked her very much, and I could see that you were most attentive to her."

He remembered. It was before his first proposal. The memory of Elizabeth's cold words to him still stung.

He pushed those thoughts away, and smiled.

"In order to arrive as soon as possible I rode rather than bring the coach. I rather suspect Elizabeth is following me without waiting for me to request that she join me. If not, then I would like to ask her to travel down in the coach." He looked at Anne. "I hope this is acceptable to you, Cousin Anne."

"How could it not be?" she stood and walked towards the window. "It means that perhaps you will be willing to stay here to assist me for more than a few days."

"Cousin Anne, I will stay as long as I am needed. If Elizabeth is with me, I am sure she will be a great comfort to you."

He saw her sway slightly. "May we sit down for a few minutes? I have one or two questions about the estate."

Anne returned to the sofa with apparent relief. Her companion was sitting there still; quiet and able to seem almost invisible.

Mr. Darcy pulled up a chair to be a little closer. Anne's soft voice was difficult to hear across the room.

"Anne, might I ask what the business was that called the Earl away? I am wondering how Mr. Wickham knew to bring his friend here the moment you were unprotected."

She looked up, surprised. "I did not consider that, Fitzwilliam." She frowned and turned to Mrs. Jenkinson.

"Do you remember what the business issue was?"

The woman shook her head silently. "I am sorry, Miss de Bourgh, I do not."

"Never mind." Darcy pondered for a moment.

"I cannot think why Mr. Wickham did not wish to propose for himself." Anne's thoughtful words drew his attention.

"He could not, because he is already married. But I will find out the arrangement he has made with the other officer. I'll wager he has an agreement for a substantial sum as soon as Rosings is out of your hands!" His voice was bitter.

"I know that I will be obliged to marry soon," Anne said. "Or I will never be safe."

"We can surround you with enough protection for now." Darcy was thinking fast. "But I fear in the future, you might think that it is the best thing to do."

He looked at her curiously. "I expect you have heard a lot of incautious talk in these rooms. Do you have any preferences as to where you would like to see Rosings? Within the closer or wider family? Or without it?"

Her head went up. "I would value your advice, sir. Although I know that many men will look at me as an obstacle to gaining the estate."

He could not deny it, he would not question her further.

"Perhaps when Elizabeth is here, it will be

easier to talk to another lady." He felt an uneasy feeling. "Until then, perhaps it would be as well not to discuss it."

He thought of something else. "It is now a week since your mother became indisposed. Does the physician still call?"

"Yes, he does. He visits each morning." She looked at him curiously. "Would you like me to send for him again so that you may see him today?"

Mr. Darcy shook his head. "I will see him tomorrow. Does your mother take adequate food? Or is she unable to eat?"

"She is always hungry!" Anne laughed. "But I am afraid her opinion is not improved. She often hits out when we try to feed her and makes such a noise."

"I am sorry you have had this to endure." He stood up.

"Anne, I am also sorry. Would you excuse me? I would relish a bath and a chance to ease the ache in my back from the ride." He glanced around.

"Afterwards, with your permission, I will see your steward. I think we need more staff to be abroad on the estate and to prevent you being troubled by unwanted visitors."

As he bowed over her hand, he felt anger

emanating from her companion, and wondered briefly as to the cause. He wished Elizabeth was here, she had an unerring sense when something was amiss.

Two days. In two days she might be here, and he would feel complete again.

CHAPTER 35

The coach ride seemed interminable. But then she'd started this journey the very day after arriving at Pemberley, so really, they were both merging into one. Elizabeth stretched and hoped that the weather would warm up soon. This chill as the evening set in was most debilitating.

They should soon be arriving at St. Albans. She smiled as she recalled the first stop for lunch on the journey up. She'd asked Mr. Fields to use The Swan for the night stop when he had said they would be at St. Albans and explained why she wished to stop there.

But she was very anxious to reach Rosings. Only one more day, only one more.

There she would find her husband, and already she missed him.

She felt her lips curve. But she was also looking forward to the opportunity to spend more than one night in a comfortable room. Then she shook her head. It was unlikely that the Rosings guest room would be up to date, comfortable or even necessarily aired properly.

It didn't matter, she thought. She'd sleep just as well in the stables, she was so tired.

～

*T*hey arrived in the yard at The Swan as dusk fell, and she saw Mr. Fields leap down and begin speaking to the innkeeper, gesticulating to ensure that not only she, but all the staff could be accommodated.

Then the coachman lowered the step and Elizabeth stepped out carefully.

The innkeeper bowed to her. "Welcome back, Mrs. Darcy. I will ensure you have a comfortable night."

"Thank you. I remembered your kindness to us when we lunched here last week, and wanted to return here when this journey proved necessary."

"Yes, ma'am. Mr. Darcy also stayed here … three … no, two nights ago."

So she wasn't that far behind him. And he was safe so far. He would have reached Rosings the noon after leaving here and she would reach it tomorrow afternoon. Only two days behind him, but a week without his presence.

She ached for him, for his touch. And she wondered what she would find at Rosings. It seemed likely that she would spend a number of weeks of her early married life there.

Her husband had told her of the talk he and Colonel Fitzwilliam had had with Anne de Bourgh. She could easily believe the young woman had been too afraid to assert herself while her mother was so domineering.

But she also felt very sympathetic for Lady Catherine. It must be terrible to be so incapacitated, even though the last time she had seen her, the woman had been most unpleasant to her. But she could forgive her, she had the health and youth that Lady Catherine did not, and that was enough.

❧

*S*he dined alone in the same small private room. She knew Mr. Fields was standing outside the door to make sure she was not disturbed.

She smiled as she sipped her wine. He was a good man. And he was far too well-prepared. Mr. Darcy knew she was on her way to him. She wondered if he would pretend to be surprised.

She didn't sleep as well as she thought she would. Although she was tired, there was quite a lot of noise and the sound of people passing in the corridor late into the night. At one point she heard the voice of a drunken man outside her bedchamber and was sure she heard the steward's voice upbraiding him and hurrying him away.

That meant he was guarding her, keeping her safe. After that she was better able to sleep.

She glanced at his face the next morning as she went to her carriage. He was supervising the servants carrying out her travelling luggage.

"Did I hear you last night outside my room, Mr. Fields?"

She saw his neck flush red. "I am sorry you were disturbed, Mrs. Darcy."

"No, I am sorry you have had a disturbed night, protecting me. Thank you, I am very grateful."

He ducked his head, embarrassed by her thanks, so she just nodded and climbed in quickly.

She was happy that they would soon be at Rosings. Perhaps if she told Mr. Darcy, he would allow the man some rest before sending him back to the north.

～

*S*he only stopped very briefly for a quick meal at lunchtime while the horses were changed, being anxious to arrive at Rosings as quickly as possible.

Finally, they were driving along the hedges bordering the great estate and the coach turned into the driveway, drawing closer to the magnificent house.

Mr. Fields got down and the coachman dropped the step.

Elizabeth stepped wearily out. She decided she never wanted to see that coach in her life again — or perhaps for at least a week.

She looked up the steps and at the top a tall man hurried out of the door. Mr. Darcy. Her heart did a strange jump and she began to climb the steps.

He came down to meet her and she stopped when he reached her. He took her hand and brought it to his lips.

"Elizabeth." He was smiling. "That was a very fast journey."

She raised her eyes. "Your staff, especially Mr.

Fields, made it all very easy." She paused. "It was almost as if they were expecting me to travel."

He looked as if he was trying not to laugh, and he tucked her hand into his arm and escorted her up the steps.

"But then you diverted me with your question about the library. I was then concerned if I had not told you about the pitfalls of the local ladies and the social life."

He looked at her. "I have missed your company, Elizabeth. I am happy you are here, but you look very tired."

"I admit it will be pleasant to have a day when I am not sitting in a coach." She allowed him to lead her into the hall. "But I am sure it was not as uncomfortable as riding hard the length of England."

"Indeed." He had stopped walking to allow them to finish their conversation.

"And how is Lady Catherine? And Miss de Bourgh?"

His expression was grave. "There is not much change regarding my aunt. And Anne is pleased I am here to protect her." He hesitated. "I have much to tell you. Perhaps after you have greeted my cousin and had some tea, we might walk in the gardens."

"That is a good idea." She glanced up at him.

"Is there anything you wish me to avoid talking about to your cousin?"

He shook his head. "No. But might I ask you to notice particularly any part Anne's companion plays while you are there?" he had dropped his voice and she wondered at his comment.

CHAPTER 36

*H*e escorted her through to the drawing room, and left her with a bow. Anne de Bourgh sat on the same sofa where she had been on those visits Elizabeth had made to the house all those months ago, her companion sitting quietly beside her.

But it was different now. Anne rose to her feet.

"Mrs. Darcy, you are here! It is lovely to see you." Elizabeth curtsied, and Anne did also. But she sat down quite quickly.

"Thank you so much for allowing your husband to come down ahead of you," Anne said. "It has … helped a great deal."

Elizabeth smiled and waited to answer while several maids arranged a table and set a tray of tea beside them.

"I am so sorry about Lady Catherine's indisposition, Miss de Bourgh. It must be such a distressing time."

"It is quite difficult, Mrs. Darcy." Anne nodded at the woman beside her, who leaned forward and began to pour the tea.

"Please call me Elizabeth." She smiled. "It will be very nice to have the chance to become better acquainted."

"Thank you, Elizabeth. And I am Anne. I'm happy that we are now cousins."

Elizabeth took a sip of her tea. She wondered if Anne had wanted to marry Mr. Darcy as Lady Catherine had wanted. If she had, she was hiding it well.

"Tell me, Cousin Anne," she said, and saw the other smile at her words.

"How has it been, nursing your mother? Is she aware of her situation?"

Anne nodded sadly. "Yes, she is. It might be less distressing for us all if she were not. But she becomes exceedingly frustrated at her inability to form words and she shouts and hits out when we do not know what she wants." She put down her cup and saucer.

"It was kind of you to write to me, and I did as you suggested and asked Mrs. Collins for help. We engaged some nurses to sit with her and care for her, but we have already had to replace two of them, as she has made their lives very difficult."

Elizabeth nodded. "It is a very sad situation to be in, for her and for those of you around her." She took a deep breath. "I know that she wished to cut me out because she believes I stole Mr. Darcy away from you, but do you think she would allow me to visit her in her room?"

Anne made a helpless movement. "There is no way of knowing, Elizabeth. But I had already told her that I did not wish to marry Mr. Darcy just because it was her plan. So she was already angry with me."

Elizabeth looked sadly at Anne. It was surprising to her that Anne was able to talk so sensibly and had yet been so much under her mother's influence as to have people think her insensible.

"It is too early to make much in the way of plans, I know. But it seems to me that things can never quite go back to what they were before Lady Catherine was taken ill." She felt the interest of Anne's companion suddenly sharpen, but forced herself not to look at her. Was that what her husband wished to know?

"If she lives a lengthy period, she is still likely to be quite incapacitated. We must, perhaps, plan for this."

Anne nodded. "It is the most difficult of the possibilities." She drew a deep breath. "But it is the most likely. She has a powerful personality and she is eating well, and so remains strong."

Elizabeth looked around at the room, so redolent of its mistress, even though she was indisposed upstairs.

"It might be as well to see the physician and ask when we can perhaps assist her out into a bath chair. If the nurses walk her around the grounds in the fresh air, she might sleep better at night and can feel rather more in control of what is happening. She might also receive visitors." She smiled. "She could receive endless compliments as to her fortitude from Mr. Collins."

Anne looked up at her, her lips twitching. "Just as long as I do not have to stay in the room with him and listen."

Elizabeth laughed openly and finished her tea. She sat back with a sigh. "I confess it is the best tea I have taken in many days."

"I am happy to hear it." Anne sat back too.

"As am I." Mr. Darcy had come into the room. He bowed at the ladies.

Both stood and curtsied, but Anne obviously found it a struggle, and he bowed again. "Please do not weary yourself, Cousin Anne. I am not offended if you do not stand."

Anne sat back. "I confess I am very weary with all the changes here at Rosings."

"Perhaps I should leave you to rest," Elizabeth suggested.

"It feels as if I would then be exceptionally inhospitable," Anne said.

Elizabeth shook her head. "You have been most welcoming. If you will permit, I would like to walk in the gardens, and see what there is to see. It is much warmer than Derbyshire, and there may still be some late-flowering blooms."

"Of course. I hope you enjoy your stay here, Elizabeth."

"I'm sure I will."

"I will walk with you, Elizabeth." Her husband bowed.

❧

*M*r. Darcy walked beside her as they descended the steps from the great glass door from the drawing room, the manservant closing it behind them.

Elizabeth drew a large breath of air. "The whole house is still under the spell of Lady Catherine."

He nodded. "It is, although I am sure Cousin

Anne will make many changes if she is free to do so." His face was grave.

Elizabeth glanced at his face. "There are developments here that cause you concern, Fitzwilliam."

He looked down. "There are, and I fear for my cousin, somewhat."

She walked quietly beside him. He would tell her when he was ready, she knew that. As his wife, she was now part of this family, and she had a responsibility to do what she could.

He sighed. "It was a very hard, long ride to get here. I would not easily undertake it again." He gazed at the landscape. "And yet I am very glad that I did it. At the moment of my arrival I disturbed two officers with Miss de Bourgh. She was frightened and alone with them."

Elizabeth gasped. "Whatever were the staff thinking of?"

His face was grim. "Indeed. The one I did not know — a Captain Matthews — said he was obliged to Miss de Bourgh and he had made her an offer." He looked at her. "The other was Mr. Wickham."

She stared at him. "Mr. Wickham!"

"Yes, the very man," Mr. Darcy growled. "I was able to frighten them away, and discover that Matthews was not yet obliged to Miss de Bourgh, but obviously intended to be, probably that very afternoon. It was the third day they had called. The first day was the very day my cousin, the Earl of Matlock, had been called back to London urgently."

"But how did they know about that? And about Lady Catherine's illness?" Elizabeth wondered. She had a sudden thought.

"Oh! You suspect Anne's companion!"

"I am not sure. I value your intuition, Elizabeth, and over the next few days I would appreciate your opinion about her."

Elizabeth walked on slowly. "She certainly listens carefully. But I could sense her paying extra attention when we were talking about the future."

He nodded thoughtfully. "That is what I was thinking. I could sense her anger when I was telling Anne that I would ensure her security. I have begun making discreet enquiries, but I am hampered because she came from London several years ago." They turned the corner into the rose garden, silent and colourless at this time of year.

"I would not wish to remove Mrs. Jenkinson from Anne, she has been used to her company for such a long time. But while I can understand it of Lady Catherine, I find it strange that a woman employed to be Anne's companion should — discourage — or even hide, the fact that Anne is eminently more capable of taking part in activities around her and decisions about her future than any of us could suppose." His voice was hard and pitiless.

Elizabeth shivered at the thought he might one day be angry with her. She wouldn't like to face such implacability herself.

But he turned. "You are shivering, Elizabeth. Let us go in, your coat is not warm enough."

"Thank you, Fitzwilliam. It is not cold, but I feel cold because I am tired, I think." She smiled slightly. "Admitting that makes me feel very feeble."

She stopped. "But that reminds me. Your steward, Mr. Fields. I heard him at the inn last night outside my bedchamber, protecting me from a drunken man. I fear he may be very tired if he has been standing guard at night and travelling with the coachman all this way."

Mr. Darcy clasped her hand. "Thank you for telling me. I need him to assist me in taking proper charge of this estate. The staff here have become complacent. But I will ensure he has a day or two to rest first." He seemed to realise what he was doing and dropped his grasp of her hand, taking a step back.

CHAPTER 37

"I will take you indoors to find the housekeeper. Her name is Mrs. Atkins and she will have you shown to your bedchamber. When you have rested, I will see you at dinner."

She inclined her head and they went back to the house. She understood his sudden retreat into formality even though she didn't like it. There was much to do here, and little time to become used to being a married couple.

She climbed the stairs behind the housekeeper, who opened the fourth door along the spacious corridor.

"Thank you, Mrs. Atkins." Elizabeth realised how tired she was when she didn't query the fact that this room was obviously ill-prepared. Her maid, Rosina was still unpacking, looking flustered.

"Thank you, Rosina. As long as I have a gown for dinner, then the rest can wait." Elizabeth headed for the bed, pulling her bonnet ribbon undone. She took off her bonnet with a sigh of relief and sat on the chair, reaching to unlace her shoes.

Her maid curtsied at the door and left the room, closing the door quietly behind her.

Elizabeth looked at the bed. It didn't matter to her that it was ill made up, she was tired enough not to care.

She shook her head, and as she was alone, took off the light muslin cap denoting her status as a married woman. She still wasn't used to wearing it, and didn't see why she should when she was alone.

Lying on the bed, she pulled a light blanket over her and was asleep in moments.

❧

*S*he awoke after an hour, feeling refreshed. Dusk was already falling, but she knew it wasn't late. She stretched and got up. After tidying herself, she headed along the corridor towards the stairs to see what was afoot.

But she was halted by a terrible commotion from further along. A loud screeching of rage and the raised voices of people trying to sound reassuring at the tops of their voices.

Lady Catherine. Elizabeth couldn't ignore the commotion. She checked her cap was back on and patted her hair to check it was neat. Then she made her way towards the noise.

At the door she could see the old lady sitting in bed propped up against a mound of pillows, her arm and leg were flailing and she was tipping sideways.

"Lady Catherine, please calm yourself!" One nurse was holding the old lady's flailing wrist, while the other was trying to push her back into the centre of the bed.

None of them saw Elizabeth in the doorway, and the second nurse leaned over the bed and hissed at her.

"You're just a disagreeable old lady who cannot complain any more. So be quiet and stop hitting out. Let us do as we will."

"I beg your pardon?" Elizabeth saw red at such unkindness and marched into the room. The nurse jumped back with a little shriek of horror and stared at the other nurse, who put her head down and lowered her voice as she attempted to soothe Lady Catherine.

Elizabeth glared at the nurse. "What have you to say for yourself, then?"

The nurse curtsied. "Madam, I am very sorry, I just … just …" her voice petered out in confusion and she stood still, her head bowed.

Elizabeth drew a deep breath. It was not her place to do this.

"I think you may need a few moments in the fresh air to recover yourself." She nodded at the nurse, dismissing her. The nurse glanced at the other a moment, then left the room.

Elizabeth turned to the other, who'd stood back, looking nervous.

"I believe you were attempting to help Lady Catherine to a more upright position, is that correct?"

"Madam, take care!" the nurse spoke a moment too late, and Lady Catherine wrenched her hand from the nurse's grasp and struck Elizabeth a stinging blow across her face.

"Oh!" Elizabeth staggered back, her hand to her burning cheek.

"Madam!" the nurse sounded horrified and hurried to her side. "Here, madam, we have cold compresses. Let me put one on your face."

"No, thank you. It is well. Let us secure Lady Catherine so that she is not at risk of falling."

Elizabeth returned to the bedside, keeping a

wary eye on the old lady's hand. "Lady Catherine, let us assist you to get comfortable."

Lady Catherine stared at Elizabeth's face and as Elizabeth felt the fiery burning of it within, the other could almost certainly see the scarlet handprint she had inflicted. She set up such a wailing noise as to make conversation impossible.

Elizabeth signed to the nurse and together they lifted the old lady sideways and Elizabeth wedged a pillow under the lady's limp right shoulder and arm.

As she struggled to arrange the limp and swollen arm in a comfortable pose, she glanced up and saw a shadow in the doorway.

Mr. Darcy was standing almost hidden. Her shock at seeing him here, outside his aunt's very bedchamber, was compounded by the thunderous look on his face.

As the nurse tucked in the sheets around his aunt, her back to the door, Elizabeth stood back slightly, to increased angry shouts from Lady Catherine.

Mr. Darcy took a couple of steps into the room. "Mrs. Darcy! What are you doing, madam?"

"I …" Elizabeth stood back further.

"If you need assistance, then you must send

…" he stopped, obviously not willing to continue in front of the nurse.

Then it seemed he noticed her face. He took a swift step forward. "Did she strike you?" his anger was palpable and she quailed at his closeness.

"No, sir. I mean, she struck out at those around her. I do not imagine it was at me personally."

All this conversation was said with the background of the screeches of rage of Lady Catherine.

He glanced at his aunt. "We must leave this room."

"Yes, sir." Elizabeth didn't demur. She turned to the nurse.

"I will ensure you have some assistance directly."

She followed her husband out of the room and he shut the door firmly, muting the noise somewhat. Then he strode off down the corridor, his expression still cold.

She followed him with some trepidation, she didn't recall having seen him this angry before. He hurried down the stairs without a word and she felt anger rising within her. She was his wife, why was she expected to follow him like a naughty child?

She halted halfway down the stairs, wondering

whether she should turn and go back up to her room. But he stopped and turned.

"I wish to speak to you in the library, please, Mrs. Darcy." He'd moderated his voice, he didn't sound so cold, and she hesitated a moment, then recommenced making her way down towards him. If he was going to berate her for stopping Lady Catherine being abused by the nurse, and then from falling out of bed, then he might be surprised that she would not take the rebuke in silence.

He shut the door to the library behind them as she made her way over to the great windows. The rest of the room was too dim and dusty for her to want to be in there.

CHAPTER 38

*S*he looked around. No one would have thought this room was part of a great estate. What had the staff been doing these last few years?

He caught the direction of her glance and grimaced.

"Indeed. There is much to be done here. I believe there to have been lax control for the last few years and now all is chaos and confusion."

"Indeed, sir." Elizabeth wasn't deceived by the general words. He was going to rebuke her for what had happened in his aunt's bedchamber.

But she was ready with her counter-attack. He should never, *never* have been there. Protocol was absolute, how could he have even considered it?

She realised he was silent, waiting for her to

speak. She pressed her lips together, she would not.

He stepped closer. "Could you explain to me what happened?"

She glanced up at him. "I think you might know what happened, Mr. Darcy."

He frowned. "I came across one of the nurses in the hall. She looked somewhat upset." His eyes narrowed. "She told me you had sent her from the room to get some fresh air. Is that correct?"

"Yes, sir." Elizabeth was very conscious that he wasn't calling her Elizabeth, or rebuking her for not using his given name.

"May I ask why?"

Her chin went up. "Yes. I was drawn to Lady Catherine's bedchamber by the noise — as were you. I was not observed, and I saw the nurse being abusive to Lady Catherine." She turned away from him. "It is not my place to discipline or sack staff here, so I removed her from the situation." She paused, he did not speak, so she continued.

"As Lady Catherine seemed about to fall out of her bed and with only the one nurse there, it seemed advisable to assist in ensuring the safety of your aunt."

A muscle was jumping in his cheek. He was still angry, but she could not imagine that he would say that she had done anything wrong.

"And when did she strike you?"

She shrugged. "It is of no importance."

His expression darkened. "I will be the judge of that, please."

"The real question is how we protect the staff we employ from being abused by Lady Catherine, as well as how we protect her from being abused in return. It is a difficult situation, Mr. Darcy."

He looked frustrated. "I asked you a question, Elizabeth." He sounded as frustrated as he looked.

She capitulated at the sound of her name. "It was when I went to assist in moving her into the centre of the bed. I do not think she thought of who I was, she was just very angry and frustrated that she could not control the situation."

"Is it very painful? Should I call the physician?"

She stared at him. "Of course not, sir! It is a minor thing, to be forgotten."

He began to pace up and down. "Very well." He swung around to face her. "What were you thinking of, Elizabeth? What could have possessed you — you, — who has such a good sense of propriety, to dismiss a nurse from the room and then take her place? How do you possibly feel you can have any authority now over the staff?"

She took a step back from his palpable anger.

She felt angry at his apparent lack of understanding.

"You were not there, sir! Was I supposed to pretend not to see abuse of your aunt — a helpless, sick woman, and just pass by? Was I then supposed to let her fall out of bed?"

She spun round and walked away from him. She stood at the empty, dark fireplace. No wonder the room was so cold.

He was silent, allowing her time to think. But she did not want to think he was reasonable, or that he was right. She swung around again.

"And you came to her bedchamber! A gentleman! How can that be protocol?"

He shook his head. "It is not. Having been informed that you were there, I needed to assure myself of your safety, so I was forced to put myself in that situation."

So he could make it her error, and she turned away from him to hide her chagrin. She could not win.

"I am very sorry, sir, that you feel I have failed in my position as your wife. I still do not feel that I erred in caring for your aunt, but I understand you think differently."

There was a silence after that and she waited. But she knew she would not win this battle of wills, she was too tired after her journey, and a nameless weariness was within her. Perhaps it was the depressing environment.

She turned to face him. He was standing, waiting. She wondered why.

"Come here, Elizabeth."

Her chin went up again. She would not be treated as a naughty child if that was his intention. But it wasn't.

"Thank you for explaining the challenge you encountered this afternoon. I would like to explain how I feel you could act if a similar situation should arise again."

She looked down, suddenly furious. "Thank you, sir." She could sound obedient if that was what he wanted.

"If you see something like that again, then make sure the staff can see you watching their behaviour. Then they will perform their duties correctly and you will not be put in the position of doing a servant's work."

"Yes, sir."

He sounded resigned. "I believe Lady Catherine has been unable to see for some time that the household was not being maintained as well as she thought. The housekeeper has become slack and has not supervised the maids properly. Their diligence is not as it should be." He waited for her response, but she kept her head down.

"I think my cousin might require your assistance to gain control of the staff and ensure they do their work properly."

When Elizabeth did not reply again, he raised his hand and lifted her face to his. She was horrified when she automatically flinched, and he looked shocked.

"I'm sorry, Elizabeth. Did being struck affect you so?"

She blinked, she would not give way to tears in front of him. "I suppose it was the memory of that."

"Be assured I will never, *never* strike you, Elizabeth. I am sorry I need to say that."

"You do not need to. I know I am safe with you, I do not know why it happened."

He grimaced. "I should have been more thoughtful."

His hand dropped, and she was sorry to lose his touch.

"I think, as Mrs. Darcy, you could help Anne with the household management better than I could," he continued.

"I would like to speak to you both after dinner about the best course of action and then I wish you to be with her while she speaks to the housekeeper."

Her head went up. She knew what to do. "I

think I can speak to Anne myself. I know what is expected of me, Mr. Darcy."

His expression closed off. "Very well. You will need her to arrange for many more maids and footmen. Staff already here need to be aware that unless they begin to work properly, they will not be retained."

"Yes, thank you, Mr. Darcy. I said I know what to do." Elizabeth wished to march out of the door, but she knew she could not.

"Indeed." His voice was colder still. "Then I will merely say that I have already instructed that your maid move your things to the bedchamber adjacent to mine. It is more fitting."

Her lips tightened. She was angry, too. "Yes, sir."

CHAPTER 39

*A*s soon as he was out of her sight, he hurried up the stairs to his own bedchamber, slamming the door behind him. He paced up and down, trying to get control of his temper.

She had to learn to act in accordance with her status. How could she have let him down so?

He stared at the writing table. He had sat there the night she had first refused him, and he'd written to her, to explain the true circumstances surrounding Mr. Wickham, and then he'd waited out there in the grove, to give it to her.

But things had changed now. She'd agreed to become his wife, to protect him from the unwanted advances that were causing him such discomfort. It was a formal arrangement as far as she was aware. She didn't know how much he loved her, how much he'd wanted to punish his aunt this afternoon for striking her — it must have been a great shock to her constitution.

He must remember the circumstances of her background. He'd been raised to the knowledge of his station in life, knowing how to behave. She had been brought up in that chaotic household, by that silly, selfish woman.

He shook his head. It was just surprising how well-mannered Elizabeth was. He must make more allowances for her, he must allow her time to become accustomed to her role.

He stared out of the window towards that infamous grove. It was a great misfortune that they would need to spend the early part of their marriage here. He had wanted to shower Elizabeth with his attention, help her learn to care for — maybe even to love — him.

He swallowed thickly. And now they had had this disagreement. Perhaps he should have been more careful, not shown his anger.

But he needed her help here. It was not his place to manage household staff, and the housekeeper had not learned to respect Cousin Anne.

Anne needed Elizabeth's help. Only then could he be free to find out exactly what Wickham and Matthews had been doing here, and, more importantly, who among the household staff was in league with them.

He must go down now, before dinner, and speak to Mr. Fields. He would be very glad of the assistance of his own steward. He would be a great help to him to get the outside staff and stewardship of the estate back under control for Anne.

And Anne must marry. He was convinced of that. She needed the support of a husband in order to manage Rosings and keep it in her control.

It was a great pity Cousin Richard did not want Rosings. He would be very good as Anne's husband, and he needed the financial security. Darcy ran his hands through his hair. He wondered who the lady was that he suspected Richard was hoping to wed.

He wondered whether there was another cousin who was suitable and who could control the situation.

He gave up the thoughts and went to find his steward. As he left his room, he could see that inside the bedchamber next door, a couple of maids were cleaning it, and Elizabeth's maid was hanging gowns in the closet. He smiled grimly, the staff were perhaps realising that life here was going to be very different from now on.

~

*O*utside, he took a great breath of the crisp, cold air. It was good to get out of that house. Within a few minutes, Mr. Fields appeared from the back of the house.

He fell into step beside Mr. Darcy and waited for him to speak.

"Well, Mr. Fields? How do you find things?"

"It is not too bad, sir. The steward has been here for many years, and although directions from the house have been irregular of late, he is able to manage fairly well."

Darcy breathed a sigh of relief. If the estate management was in order, he could direct his attentions elsewhere.

"Continue, if you please."

"Yes, sir. The main difficulty seems to be a shortage of gardeners. Lady Catherine has been saying there is not enough money to pay for extra gardeners and he has not been permitted to replace those who have left because of age or infirmity."

"I believe there are adequate funds. I will have to look into matters first. How many staff is he short, by your estimation?"

Mr. Fields swept the landscape with a prac-tised eye. "I would think maybe ten, sir. During this season, it would also be well to have an extra team working on securing the Park boundaries. I have seen that there is a considerable amount of repair work outstanding."

Mr. Darcy made a face. "I will authorise that you assist the steward to engage for the repair work at least. What is the steward's name?"

"Dawson, sir."

"All right, get that underway tomorrow, Mr. Fields. And so you think Mr. Dawson is a capable manager of his staff?"

"I do, sir. The deficiencies are not with the man, but with the resources."

"Good. I understand you are probably very tired. I want you to take some hours off each day to rest."

"I am quite all right, sir."

"I thought you would say that." Mr. Darcy smiled. "I am indebted to you for ensuring Mrs. Darcy's safety on the journey here."

The man touched his hat and left him to return to the steward's office, and Darcy headed back to the house to prepare for dinner.

*T*hey sat at table that evening, the many candles flickering on the tarnished silverware. He was silent much of the time, his eyes on his wife.

He thought she looked pale, and the mark was still livid on her face behind her attempts to mask it with more powder than usual. His heart softened. She wouldn't make a fuss, but she must have been struck with a great deal of force.

His aunt's chair at the head of the table was empty, a brooding presence that forbade them from lively conversation. But Elizabeth made polite and cheerful conversation with Anne, who was much brighter than he'd seen her before.

He was glad Elizabeth was here, her presence cheered everyone in the room. Except Mrs. Jenkinson. He glanced at his cousin's companion. She was gloomily taking her soup and he could not see that she was needed at table any longer.

He must talk to Elizabeth and she could encourage Anne to begin distancing herself from her past needs.

He felt tired and depressed. There was so much to do, and the disagreement with Elizabeth had distanced him from feeling that they were standing together against everything. If she were wholeheartedly beside him, he would feel invincible.

He would go to her tonight, try and show her he was sorry. If he could rest with her in his arms, he could face tomorrow more easily.

CHAPTER 40

*E*lizabeth sat in front of the glass the next morning as Rosina did her hair. She examined her face, the mark was beginning to fade now. In another day it would have gone.

She made a face at herself. The memories of yesterday would take longer to leave her. Her husband had come to her last night and she had slept in his arms, feeling comforted. But his anger yesterday had been new to her and she felt unsettled because of it.

His pride and arrogance had been what she thought of him at first and she thought nothing of him. Then, when she was visiting Derbyshire with Aunt and Uncle Gardiner, he had been kind and solicitous and she had harboured dreams of winning his love.

Now she was his wife — without having his love. She had accepted him because the chance to be with him was all she had wanted. If she couldn't have his love, then she would accept this arrangement.

Living this way was going to be difficult. Would he ever love her? She didn't know. It couldn't happen here, and they were likely to be here for very many weeks.

She sighed, and caught Rosina glancing at her. She stiffened, she must be strong, must not show how much his opinion affected her. Today she would have to get Anne alone and talk to her about the staff and management of the house.

She had been unable to do so last night when they went through to the drawing room, leaving Mr. Darcy alone with the port, because Mrs. Jenkinson was there, sitting close to Anne. She seemed very defensive and Elizabeth wondered if she knew of their suspicions.

Elizabeth made her way down thoughtfully for breakfast. The sun shining in through the windows gave her an idea.

She ate some breakfast, watching Mr. Darcy covertly as he read the newspaper. Then when Anne appeared, she made light conversation with her for a while.

As she finished her cup of tea, she made her suggestion.

"I was thinking, Cousin Anne, as it is such a pleasant day, perhaps we could drive out this morning. You might show me the extent of the Park and then we may call on Mrs. Collins."

She felt her husband's gaze lift and settle on her, but she didn't look at him.

Anne smiled. "I would like to do that, Elizabeth. I have not been out of doors for what seems a long time now."

"Then that is settled." Elizabeth decided to have more tea after all. "Should we visit your mother before we go?"

"The physician calls each morning about this hour. I would be most grateful if you feel you may accompany me then."

"Of course I will. I was wondering whether you had considered what I said yesterday about discussing with him getting your mother up and out of her room?"

Anne made another helpless gesture. "How would that be done though, Elizabeth? I cannot think that she will ever be able to stand, much less be able to come downstairs."

Elizabeth didn't look at Mr. Darcy, although she could sense he wanted to speak.

"There was a friend of my mother's at

Meryton not long ago. They obtained a bath chair and the outside servants came in and carried it, with her inside, up and down the stairs each day. Then her maid was able to wheel her around the gardens when the weather was good. The fresh air helped her to sleep better, and she could receive visitors which eased the burden on the family."

Anne's expression cleared. "That is a good idea, then, Elizabeth. I have felt for too long, perhaps, that Mother might pass soon and I have perhaps been waiting for it to happen."

Elizabeth impulsively leaned forward and touched Anne's hand. "It has been so difficult for you. And she may at any time, recover more, or become less well. But we might at least ask the physician."

Anne nodded. "I welcome your advice and support, Cousin Elizabeth. I'm so glad you are here."

Mr. Darcy's paper rustled as he put it down. "I am happy with your plans for this morning, Cousin Anne, and Elizabeth. May I ask you to enquire of the physician whether there are any further treatments from London which might be appropriate, and have this in the hearing of Lady Catherine? She might be angry that we have not appeared to do anything to be making her well again, and if she hears it at the hands of the doctor, then it might make her less angry."

Anne turned to him. "I will try and do as you ask, Mr. Darcy. But Mother is often shouting and angry. I do not know if she is even aware of who he is when he calls."

"I understand," he said. "May I ask if we can meet here after he has called, before you go out? I might have some suggestions to make by then."

Both ladies looked at him, surprised, and Elizabeth waited for Anne to answer, as was correct.

Then she turned to Anne. "Perhaps it would be as well to go up first, and take a seat upstairs while we wait for him. Then you will have a chance to rest before his call."

"Thank you. You think of everything for my comfort." They both stood and curtsied for Mr. Darcy, who stood and bowed farewell.

As they climbed the stairs slowly, Elizabeth saw her husband leave the house by the main door.

❧

Two hours later, she and Anne were sitting in the small open carriage, with only the coachman upfront.

Elizabeth was sure she could now talk freely to

Anne without Mrs. Jenkinson there and she felt a great relief to be out of Lady Catherine's room.

"So the physician thinks your mother would benefit from being downstairs, and she will be in no danger from the exertion."

"I know." Anne sounded doubtful. "I am afraid for the staff, however. She will hit out at whatever they try, and I do not want anyone to get hurt."

"I agree with your concerns, and we'll have to think of some way of protecting them." Elizabeth watched the landscape unfurling in front of them. "But I wish to talk about what you want now, Anne. I think that for too long you have been — perhaps over-protected — by your mother and even possibly your companion. You know that no visitor had any idea as to what your wishes were until recently."

Anne turned and looked at her, and there were tears in her eyes.

"Has Mr. Darcy told you of when he and Cousin Richard insisted on talking to me alone, that day, and how angry Mother was?"

Elizabeth nodded. "Yes, he did. Of course, he did not divulge your confidences, but he told me that you had been able to express yourself for possibly the first time for many years."

"I am grateful to them for doing that, but I

feel guilty that her anger at us may have caused her apoplexy and that it is all my fault."

Elizabeth took her hand. "You must not feel that way. It was most assuredly not the cause, or the illness would have come upon her that very moment, I am sure."

"I hope you are right, Elizabeth. I hope so very much."

"I am certain." Elizabeth decided to change the subject. "Mrs. Jenkinson has been with you for many years, has she not?"

Anne made a face. "Not so very long. I had a lovely companion before, but she had to leave me because Mother didn't like her. I don't know where Mother found Mrs. Jenkinson, but she is not as happy as Jennifer was." She sighed. "I was going to insist that she was changed for someone I could choose, but I have not been well enough so much lately and I could not find the energy."

Elizabeth nodded and changed the subject. Surely Mr. Darcy would know that from his regular visits to the family. But she would remind him. She wondered if there was anything significant in Anne being unwell since Mrs. Jenkinson arrived and scolded herself. She must not think of such high drama when there might well be a perfectly ordinary explanation.

CHAPTER 41

*H*e sat at the writing desk in his bedchamber, scowling. He should be able to sit in the library, but the disorder within offended his spirits and at least this room was kept in adequate order.

Well, things should improve shortly. After Elizabeth and Anne returned this afternoon, they were going to speak with the housekeeper. He had arranged with them that he would happen to be passing through the room, so that she would see there was no way to divide their settled opinion.

He wondered if Mrs. Atkins knew what was going to happen to the house, and smiled grimly. It might not be spring yet, but a thorough spring clean was about to happen. Every room should always be ready for use, warm and well-lit.

He remembered Mr. Fields telling him that the Rosings steward had been told there was not the money to engage enough gardeners. He was certain that was only Lady Catherine's own opinion. There was certainly enough money. She would not be able to use more than she was allowed each year from the estate.

He needed to write to the Earl and ask him to visit, although he would rather it was Richard. But *he* must stay with Georgiana. He and the Earl could see the attorney together and discover the state of the Park finances.

It must be just that his aunt was getting old to think such a thing. The thought of his aunt put him in mind of the bath chair, and he decided to go and see Mr. Fields. He could entrust him to see to the purchase. As he came out of his bedchamber, he was surprised to see Mrs. Jenkinson outside the door.

He frowned and she quickly began shuffling past. He stood and watched her. He must find out where her room was. If it was beside Anne's, that might mean her presence was unsurprising. But if she had a room in the attics with the servants, then there was no reason for her to be here.

He turned and went back into his room. He would ensure that there was nothing to be found. He laughed at himself for the melodrama of his thoughts, shook his head, and went down to see Mr. Fields.

~

*W*hen he heard the carriage returning, he went out to meet it. As he assisted his wife and then his cousin to descend from it, he was pleased to see they both appeared tolerably cheerful and bright-eyed from the fresh air.

With a lady on each arm, he climbed the main steps slowly, at Anne's pace.

Soon they were seated in the dining room eating a light lunch. Elizabeth told him what had transpired at the Parsonage when they called to see Mrs. Collins.

"Mr. Collins is most curious as to what is happening here at Rosings," she said. "I think he was trying to receive an invitation to dine and discover the news."

"Never." Mr. Darcy was terse. "You may see Mrs. Collins all you will. But Mr. Collins will not dine here while I am staying."

Anne looked at him curiously. Elizabeth laughed. "I was hoping that when the weather is fair and Lady Catherine is sitting out in her bath chair, we might invite him to sit and talk with her.

After all, we might say that he could meet her spiritual needs as she is unable to attend church."

He glared at her, before understanding that she was teasing him. He gave in and smiling grudgingly.

"It will be interesting to see who declines the arrangement first. Well, if I have to return to Town overnight at all, you ladies may invite him and Mrs. Collins on that evening."

～

*L*ater, he walked quietly with Elizabeth around the shadowed grounds. She told him of Anne's feelings about Mrs. Jenkinson, then hesitated.

"I wonder, sir, how Anne was suddenly so unwell as to be too tired to have her changed."

He glanced at her. "I too, find my suspicions about the woman are sharpening. But I do not wish to lose her before I know what she is about." He rubbed his face thoughtfully. "Unless you feel Anne might be in any sort of danger."

Elizabeth shook her head slowly. "I do not know, sir. But if Mrs. Jenkinson was conniving with Lady Catherine, she will be feeling insecure." She looked around. "However, I cannot believe that she would have a position here for several years without making a move before now. I confess I am unsure."

He nodded. "I received a letter today from London. There is nothing useful discovered as yet, but I am hopeful of a new line of enquiry." He wondered whether to tell her what he had also discovered from his search of the Park accounts, but decided it would be best kept to himself at present.

He considered his position. Elizabeth was being perfectly amiable and polite, but she seemed to be without that spark of liveliness which he loved so much about her. She was still formal and cool towards him.

He ached for them to be away from this place, to have a chance at a reconciliation and to move their marriage forward.

"I want to thank you, Elizabeth, for what you have done today. I think Mrs. Atkins is under no illusions that things will be different from now on, and new servants in the house will soon make everything feel better here."

"It is nothing," she said quietly.

"That is not the case," he replied. "I appreciate what you are doing very much." He paused. "I was told you spent an hour with Lady Catherine this afternoon, holding her hand and talking about the gardens to her. I understand she was quiet and listened to you without becoming distressed."

"I believe her temper will improve if she has some companionship each day." Elizabeth's tone was calm. "And that will be easier when she can be downstairs."

"And what is your view of her health?" Mr. Darcy was curious. "I cannot believe she would choose this life."

"The only way for her to choose differently would be to refuse all food." Elizabeth turned away slightly. "She is not choosing that path. She eats well."

"Elizabeth, are you well? I do not feel that you are your usual self this evening."

She glanced up. He was shocked to see her eyes were shiny with unshed tears. "I am well, Mr. Darcy. Thank you for your concern. I may be a little tired, that is all." Her voice brooked no further discussion on the matter, and she turned back towards the house.

He fell into step beside her. The moment was over and he wondered despondently when he would have the opportunity to talk with her again.

CHAPTER 42

*E*lizabeth woke to find she was alone in the bed. This was becoming usual. They had been at Rosings nearly two weeks now and she was finding herself having to work harder and harder to hide her low spirits from her husband and Cousin Anne.

She rubbed her face, wondering if she was perhaps developing a cold. But she was not often ill, and she must put on a cheerful face and help Anne with all that was to be done in the house.

She glanced out of the window as she went to sit in front of the glass, and saw her husband returning from an early ride. It was a good thing. The chance to go out early in the morning and take a walk and get some fresh air had helped her often in the past.

As Rosina began to brush her hair and help her dress, Elizabeth considered it. She knew her position in society had changed now. As Mrs. Darcy, she could not go wandering as she had all her life. But walking in the gardens would be permitted. Tomorrow, she promised herself. Tomorrow if she woke early enough, she would dress and slip out for a brisk walk and that would help her feel more cheerful. Strolling with Anne was most pleasant, but she could not walk fast, nor was it seemly to stride out when in company.

When she was composed, she walked down to the breakfast room and joined her husband. Anne wasn't there. He stood to greet her and bowed.

"Good morning, sir." She curtsied.

"Good morning, Elizabeth," he said gravely, waiting for her to be seated before he resumed his breakfast.

She wondered despondently when he'd begun forgetting to remind her to use his given name. That tiny change meant there was still something amiss between them.

Perhaps she should say something. He wouldn't mind, would he? But he was leaning forward to speak to her and the moment passed. He spoke in a low voice, so the footman wouldn't hear.

"I am happy that Anne is not here yet. Might

we somehow propose that she spends some time with her companion this morning, so that you are free to assist me in a small task in the house without raising the suspicions of either of them?"

Elizabeth nodded. "I understand," she murmured, as she turned back to the door to greet Anne with a bright smile.

~

*T*wo hours later, she waved off the carriage. Anne and her companion were driving to Westerham to choose some new ribbons.

"I'd like to sit with Lady Catherine and re-trim some of her caps," Elizabeth had said to Anne. "I think she might be persuaded to enjoy making a choice between several ribbons."

Mr. Darcy had smiled and nodded. "But if Cousin Anne could manage with just Mrs. Jenkinson, I would welcome the chance to discuss a private matter with you."

"Of course, Cousin Fitzwilliam." Anne had blushed slightly. "I will do that with pleasure."

As the carriage turned away, Elizabeth mounted the steps to the house. Mr. Darcy was waiting for her in the hall.

"Thank you for agreeing to this," he said as he

led her up the stairs to the main bedrooms. She was puzzled.

"Where are we going, sir?"

He raised his fingers to his lips and she nodded and followed him silently. As they passed her bedchamber, Rosina came out of the room holding a copper water jug. She curtsied at Elizabeth.

Elizabeth looked between them, puzzled.

"This way." Mr. Darcy walked deeper along the corridor.

Elizabeth looked back. Rosina was standing in the doorway, holding the jug and looking anxious.

"Just what is …"

"Shh!" he said in a low voice and stopped. He turned the door handle and beckoned her in.

He spoke in a hurried, low voice. "The staff are all downstairs, doing out the library. I have hopes that none will be here for a short while." He had hurried to a writing desk and was beginning to look through some letters.

"Your maid is watching out. She will drop the jug and make some sound to alert us if she sees anyone coming." He was searching methodically, but without wasting a moment.

"I cannot trust Mrs. Atkins with this knowledge, because she and Mrs. Jenkinson have been here together for so long. But your maid is not part of the Rosings staff." He began to read a letter, and skimmed through to the last page. "Ah! This one!" he placed it to one side and stacked the papers as they had been, and then checked more from another pile.

"Sir! I must ask what you are doing!" Elizabeth wondered how she would feel if he was going through her letters.

"I must find out what Mrs. Jenkinson is about, Elizabeth. I am collecting evidence."

"No, I cannot countenance this, sir! It is abhorrent!"

He stopped what he was doing and stared at her in amazement. He shook his head. "One moment." He looked at the back of a letter and placed it with the one from the first pile. Finally, he made all tidy as it had been, slipping the two letters in his pocket.

"Now we have finished." As he closed the door, he was very close to her.

"You must thank Rosina for standing watch for us and ensure she understands the very great importance of remaining silent."

His gaze was piercing. "Then I will spend five minutes with you outside in the rose garden if you would care to prepare yourself for a walk."

Then he was gone, striding fast to the stairs. Elizabeth shook her head after him. She wished he had taken her into his confidence before the fact. But the deed was done.

"Rosina, Mr. Darcy wishes me to remind you of his thanks for doing this task. Please make sure you do not tell anyone."

"Yes, Madam. Of course."

"Thank you. Now I need my coat and hat."

~

*I*n the rose garden, he walked beside her. "I am sorry you feel that you could not approve of what I had to do this morning."

"I imagined how I would feel if I discovered you had been looking at my personal letters, sir."

He looked shocked. "I would never do that, Elizabeth! Never!"

She shrugged a little. "I never imagined you would do what you did this morning."

"I want to get the information to confirm what I think I know from another source. If I ask the constable to investigate, it will all come out before I am ready."

"I understand, sir." Elizabeth did understand. But she would not say that she did approve, for she did not.

He told her no more, and she felt her resentment increasing. He would use her for what he needed, but would not confide in her the things he had found out. They walked on in silence.

After several turns of the garden he seemed to pull himself out of his thoughts.

"I am very pleased at how the household is now run, Elizabeth. I think you are the cause of it and I know that Anne is most grateful. As am I."

"It was necessary." Elizabeth didn't need his thanks, and she was not inclined to fawn over him, expecting praise, if that was what he thought.

But her heart was heavy. She wished he would look at her with the warm regard he used to. She knew he had never expressed love towards her before their marriage, but she had felt then that he had regard for her. Now he was distant — not cold — but distant.

"May I go indoors, please? I feel a little cold."

"Of course." He turned beside her and they returned to the house.

CHAPTER 43

*A*t lunch, she admired the ribbons which Anne had bought, and they made a guess as to who would be correct in choosing which would be the choice of Lady Catherine.

"We will see who is right this afternoon. I will sit with her in the drawing room and sew her cap." Elizabeth declared.

"And I'll watch you. It is a skill I would like to learn," Anne said.

The post arrived and Mr. Darcy slit open a letter.

"Ah!" He read it quickly, then thrust it in his pocket and rose from the table.

"Please excuse me." He backed away. "You will please excuse me." And he hurried out.

Anne looked at Elizabeth. "What is that about?"

"I don't know." Elizabeth realised she sounded rather vexed, and spoke again with an effort to be pleasant. "But we are occupied this afternoon. We need not be concerned with Mr. Darcy's cares."

Anne look thoughtful. "I am so happy you are staying here. But I am sensible of the fact that it would not be the choice of either of you, but for assisting me."

Elizabeth reached for her hand. "This is what families do for each other. Rosings is a big place to learn to run when you have not been accustomed to it."

As she spoke she realised that she had been forgetting the huge debt she and her family owed to her husband. He had single-handedly rescued them from ruin. And it had not been his duty, for he had not been part of her family then.

She owed him more than an indifferent acceptance of his wish to help his cousin. As she prepared to receive Lady Catherine in her bath chair and sit with her a while, she vowed to be more agreeable, to return to her previous manner. She should not be cold towards him, he did not deserve that. She owed him more than she could ever repay, and she must trust him.

A few minutes later he came back into the room. He was holding his hat and whip. He bowed to them.

"I apologise, Elizabeth, Cousin Anne. I must go to town on urgent business that cannot be delayed. I hope to be away no more than two or three days."

They had risen to their feet. Elizabeth tried not to let the dismay in her face show.

"I hope you have a safe journey, sir." She curtsied.

"Yes, Cousin Fitzwilliam. Have a safe journey. I am sorry the circumstances here have kept you from your business so long." Anne looked from his face to Elizabeth's.

"It is nothing, Cousin Anne. I know that you will be all right here with Elizabeth, and I will be back as soon as I can be." He spoke to Anne, but his eyes were on Elizabeth.

She stayed on her feet. "If you will excuse me, Anne, I will see Mr. Darcy on his way."

"Of course." Anne sat down to wait.

They walked towards the door.

"I am sorry I have to go and I cannot take you with me." He did sound really regretful, Elizabeth decided. Perhaps he had seen the dismayed expression she had tried to hide.

"I am sorry too. But Cousin Anne needs someone here who can be on their guard."

He nodded. "Nevertheless, I would not leave you unless the matter was urgent. Please take care, and do not overtax yourself."

At the bottom of the steps, he turned to her and raised her hand to his lips.

"I will return as soon as I can, Elizabeth."

She forced a smile. "I pray that you have a safe and successful journey — Fitzwilliam."

His look was all she could have wished for, a dawning hope, and his smile was warm.

"I will return very soon." He turned and mounted his horse.

Elizabeth smiled foolishly after his retreating form. Perhaps things could be different when he returned. She climbed slowly back up the steps. She had been most remiss in failing to heal the breach between them as soon as she was able.

She reminded herself of the debt she owed him, of the promise she'd made to herself and in public at her wedding. She shook her head. She would not fail him again.

*I*n the hall, she saw Lady Catherine's bath chair being carried down the stairs with that lady inside it, her body held straight by bolsters and cushions.

"Good afternoon, Lady Catherine!" she called out cheerfully. "We have been looking forward to seeing you. Miss de Bourgh has been to Westerham this morning to buy a selection of ribbons for you to choose from. Then I will trim a cap for you."

A grumbling noise from that lady told her she'd been understood. But there was none of the screeching of rage and frustration — at least not at this moment.

She smiled. Lady Catherine was much improved now that she was downstairs for at least part of each day and Elizabeth tried to ensure she was involved in as many choices as she could arrange.

Her outbursts were still frequent, but she seemed in general, to be rather more accepting of assistance than she had been. Elizabeth was very happy at the change in her.

But before they could move into the drawing room and join Anne, the housekeeper hurried through to the front door.

"A coach, madam. And a gentleman, riding!"

Elizabeth and Lady Catherine stared at each other for a moment. Then Elizabeth took charge.

"I will find out who it is, Lady Catherine. Please go through to the drawing room, and let Miss de Bourgh know we have guests."

The nurse nodded. She would pass the message on.

Elizabeth went to the window and looked out. She thought she recognised the demeanour of the rider, and peered out more closely. Colonel Fitzwilliam! She smiled happily and went out to greet him, wondering who was in the coach.

She was soon informed by seeing her sister-in-law's face at the coach window and delightedly went forward and greeted Georgiana as she stepped down, followed by her maid.

"Oh, Georgiana! How wonderful to see you!" she embraced her sister-in-law, who looked gratified at the greeting. Then she turned to the gentleman.

"Colonel Fitzwilliam!" she curtsied in response to his bow. "It is very good to see you again."

He bowed again. "I am equally pleased to see you again, Mrs. Darcy." He hesitated, and smiled. "Or might I address you as Cousin Elizabeth?"

She felt her cheeks warm up a little. "If you wish, I would not refuse it."

"Excellent!" he beamed at her. "Let us go

indoors and see what Darcy has to say as regards the situation here. There have been so many letters from him that I determined to come down and speak to him face to face as to what is required." He turned and offered his arm to Georgiana.

"And Miss Darcy enjoined me that she may accompany me. She misses your company very much."

Elizabeth smiled at Georgiana. "I am delighted you are here. And I am sure you and Cousin Anne will become fast friends." The smile left her face.

"But I am desolated to say that Mr. Darcy has left for London, not twenty minutes ago. I am surprised that you did not see him on the road."

Colonel Fitzwilliam made a small sound of annoyance. "If he was riding alone, he would have taken the narrow path which cuts five miles from the road. It is a great pity. Did he say how long he was to be away?"

"He told me that he hoped to return in two or three days. I hope you can bear the wait with patience, sir." She dipped her head mischievously. "I am sure your aunt will be delighted to see you."

"Ah, yes." The Colonel gave his hat and whip to the footman waiting in the hallway. "How is Lady Catherine?"

"She is greatly improved in spirits, sir. She is much more content now we have arranged it that she comes downstairs for part of each day." She tucked her arm into Georgiana's.

"We should go in. I would not like to stretch her Ladyship's patience too thinly."

CHAPTER 44

r. Darcy rode over the track to the
other side of the ridge and settled
himself in for a ride of several hours.

He took encouragement from Elizabeth's face
as he had left her. She had bid him farewell and
used his given name, the first time for many days.

He must get to London and conclude his business as soon as he could. He must see Georgiana
and update Cousin Richard — and the Earl
as well.

Then he would return to Rosings. It would be
the first time he would be returning willingly, and
it was because Elizabeth was there. His wife. Her
beauty in his mind, he slowed the horse to a trot
and turned down to rejoin the road.

He hoped Georgiana would not mind too much when he left her again after so short a stay.

～

*I*t was quite late in the evening when he turned into the stable yard at his London home. A groom ran to take the horse and Darcy hurried up the back steps, wondering if Richard was dining here with Georgiana this evening.

The housekeeper appeared as he handed his hat and crop to the footman. "Mr. Darcy! We did not expect you!"

"I know. It was a sudden decision, Mrs. Stephens. Tell me, is Miss Darcy dining in this evening?"

She shook her head. "She left this morning with Colonel Fitzwilliam to go to Rosings to see you there."

"What?" He strode into the drawing room. The housekeeper followed him.

"It seemed to be a hasty decision, sir. I know they decided yesterday and sent you a letter, but perhaps it did not reach you in time."

"No, it did not." He stood against the fire-place. "Send the butler in to get me a drink. And ask the kitchen to provide me something to eat."

"Yes, sir." As she turned away, he added.

"Something simple and quick. Nothing too involved. Thank you."

The butler appeared noiselessly beside him, a whisky on a tray.

"Thank you." He drained it and put the glass back on the tray. "Another."

He dined alone, the candlelight flickering on the polished table, the servants moving quietly and efficiently around the room.

He thought of the company around the table at Rosings. Elizabeth was there, and now too were Georgiana and Richard. He wished he was there too.

"Thank you." He pushed away his plate. "Bring me coffee in the library, if you please."

He strode through to that room. The darkly polished wood gleaming in the candlelight and the fire leaping in the hearth pleased him. This was what a home should be, warm and welcoming. He sat at his writing desk and drew out the letters he had taken from Mrs. Jenkinson's room.

He perused them again. He had been proved right, and berated himself for not seeing the resemblance before. But this meant that the plans had been in force for several years. All this time, the net had been closing around Cousin Anne, and he had been remiss in not seeing it.

His heart went cold at the thought of what might have happened had he not ridden to Rosings and chanced upon Matthews and Wickham before Anne was compromised.

But she was safe now. The whole family knew that she was to be protected. Anne did not know anything just yet, she wasn't even aware that he had had his steward follow her carriage when she went shopping this morning, to ensure Mrs. Jenkinson had no chance of causing any disruption to his plans.

He strode up and down the room. He was pleased Elizabeth had told him that Anne was not attached to Mrs. Jenkinson. This would make it easier when she was exposed for what — and who — she was.

He wondered how she had won over Lady Catherine. But now that lady was incapacitated, she might never be able to speak of it, and explain.

He pondered over the next day. He would first call upon the Earl. It would have been good to have had Cousin Richard there too, Cousin David had never been as amiable as Richard. However, it could not be helped.

Then he had an appointment with the Brigadier and the Colonel of the Dragoon Guards at eleven next morning. He had the appointment he had received that morning folded in his pocket.

He smiled grimly. Captain Matthews would wonder what had befallen him. He would be called in to see them and Darcy looked forward to finding out the connection to Wickham, and seeing his downfall.

Then he must take luncheon with the Colonel and the Brigadier.

It would depend on what was discovered from Matthews regarding Wickham as to whether he would be able to get back to Rosings after that, and he longed to go.

But it was likely to be another day. He would have to see a magistrate and find out how to secure his cousin's safety. Perhaps the officers tomorrow could advise him.

Of course, she would never be really safe unless she married. He must speak to David about that, first thing in the morning. It was a great pity Richard was unwilling to consider it.

～

*E*lizabeth. He found his mind had returned to her, his memory explored her face, her eyes as she'd looked up at him.

He remembered her voice as she'd wished him

a safe and successful journey. Then she'd said his name. *Fitzwilliam.* The very sound of it on her lips had made his heart race.

If he hadn't known the Brigadier was willing to see him, as well as the Colonel, he might have been tempted to write and postpone the appointment. Then tonight he could have gone to her. His wife. Elizabeth.

CHAPTER 45

*E*lizabeth got up the next morning surprised she was still feeling low. She should be happy. She had friends here, and belonged. And although her husband was not here, he might be back tomorrow or the next day and she was sure he had understood what she had indicated to him when she bade him farewell the previous day. She hugged the pillow to her, smiling. She remembered the look in his eyes, the warmth which had been absent for these last weeks.

Unaccountably, she felt tears fill her eyes, and she felt very lonely.

But her maid had entered with a jug of water which she was pouring into the washbowl and Elizabeth must get up and begin her day.

She swung her legs over the edge of the bed and plastered a smile on her face.

"Good morning, Rosina."

"Good morning, madam." The girl curtsied and went to the closet. "The blue gown, Mrs. Darcy?"

"Yes, that will suffice very well." Elizabeth didn't feel very interested in her clothes. Mr. Darcy was not here, she didn't really mind how she looked.

Rosina held the towel ready as Elizabeth washed, and then brushed out her hair for her.

Elizabeth sighed as she descended the stairs. It wasn't like her, she had no appetite for breakfast today. But she must be cheerful, Anne relied on her good spirits a great deal, and she must ensure that Anne and Georgiana were able to relax with each other.

Dinner last night had been stiff and rather formal, and today she must somehow lighten the atmosphere. She drew a deep breath and entered the breakfast room.

Colonel Fitzwilliam sprang to his feet and bowed. She smiled, here at least was a friendly, amiable face. She curtsied.

"Good morning, sir. You are up early and ready for your day."

"Indeed I am, Cousin Elizabeth." He waited

for her to be seated. "But I wonder if you might remember to call me Richard. After all, we are cousins now."

"I will endeavour to do so, Cousin Richard. But I confess I will need reminding. I find my habits hard to change."

She poured a cup of tea and took a piece of bread onto her plate. She wondered if she could eat it.

The Colonel didn't appear to notice. "I cannot tell you how pleased I was yesterday to see my aunt downstairs and appearing to take pleasure in your conversation and needlework."

Elizabeth smiled. "She has much improved, sir. When she becomes frustrated, I try and talk to her, but if she becomes very distressed, she has to return to her room. It seems to be working much better than Mr. Darcy had anticipated."

"It most certainly is. Mr. Darcy has written to me, sharing what you have been doing for her. He is full of admiration at your efforts."

Elizabeth felt her cheeks grow warm. "Thank you."

"I am hoping," he said, draining his cup. "That you might be able to assist me in discovering more about the estate and how it works today. Then I can hope to know more before Mr.

Darcy returns and I will be able to help him more ably."

"I would do my best, sir, but I think Cousin Anne may well be of more assistance. She is more knowledgeable about the estate than any of us thought."

"It is a good idea." He nodded, and they both got to their feet as Anne and Georgiana came in, laughing together.

Elizabeth watched as they sat down and began their breakfast. She watched as Colonel Fitzwilliam tried to stop looking at Georgiana all the time, and she saw how Georgiana was shy with him.

She smiled to herself as she nibbled at the bread. It had surprised her that her husband didn't appear to have noticed, but she acknowledged that they were being very careful.

Of course, as her guardian, Cousin Richard would be very conscious of not taking advantage of his ward, and he would not wish to lose Mr. Darcy's friendship. Georgiana was only just seventeen, they might need to wait several years.

Elizabeth thought that there should be no need to wait too long. It was obvious to her that both of them felt the same, and she considered there was no possibility that it was just a passing fancy on her young sister-in-law's part.

She smiled slightly. Her husband was blind to it.

There was some discussion around the table. Finally it was decided that Colonel Fitzwilliam would begin to go through the accounts with Anne, and Elizabeth and Georgiana would take a walk towards Hunsford and call on Mrs. Collins.

~

*S*o, how are you, my dearest sister?" Elizabeth tucked her arm into Georgiana's as they strolled off down the lane.

"Oh, I am well, Elizabeth. I have had a wonderful time in London, but I am extra happy to be here. The house in London is not very alive when I am the only person there."

"And I am glad to see you here, too, Georgiana. We have not had enough time together to become good friends yet."

Elizabeth wondered whether to tease her slightly about Colonel Fitzwilliam, but decided against it. She was sure the girl felt herself to be able to hide her feelings from everyone.

They continued their conversation as they walked along, and Elizabeth pointed out the places she'd explored so far.

"It is most unfortunate that this happened so

soon after your wedding day," Georgiana said. "I know Fitzwilliam was most desirous that your first few weeks be at Pemberley. He must have been so disappointed."

"I think he was." Elizabeth mused. "But it was necessary, and I hope we will be able to make a difference here."

"Oh, you already have!" Georgiana was earnest in her praise. "Cousin Richard was warning me on the way down that the house was gloomy and cold and not very well-kept. But I found it is wonderful and bustling with life. It must be all down to you!"

"Not really. But it has been satisfying to see everything beginning to be more pleasant — including Lady Catherine."

"Yes," Georgiana breathed. "My brother wrote and told me how she had struck you. I am surprised you went back to her and were so kind to her."

"Oh, no!" Elizabeth shook her head. "Lady Catherine was very frustrated and could not make herself be understood. She struck out and I happened to be there. It was not at all deliberate, and not aimed at me personally."

"You are most generous, Elizabeth. I hope one day I can be just like you."

"No, Georgiana. I want you to grow up and

be the best Georgiana you can be. You do not want to be me. You must be yourself, the best you that you can be. Then you will be happy."

Georgiana sighed.

Elizabeth smiled. "Now I must warn you about Mr. Collins. He is quite — well, I must confess I find him odious and insincere. But Mrs. Collins was a great friend of mine and I do wish to see her. I am sorry that we will undoubtedly have to suffer the attentions of Mr. Collins too."

"I am content, Elizabeth, because you wish to see your friend. But I thank you for the warning." Georgiana walked up the path beside Elizabeth.

CHAPTER 46

M r. Darcy was enraged when he was held in London several days longer than he wished to be by this infernal business.

He sat each evening and wrote to Elizabeth, light and conversational letters that conveyed little, by design. He must wait until he saw her to tell her of his discoveries.

He hesitated before signing the first letter.

Your affectionate husband,
Fitzwilliam

He sealed the letter, wondering if she would write to him in return. But if she expected him home, she would not think she needed to write.

But he did get a letter, by return post, and hurried to the privacy of his library to read it.

He turned the pages over and over in his hands, smelling the fragrance that reminded him of her.

> *I am sorry that you are detained in Town for another day, Fitzwilliam. I will wait with as much patience as I can muster until you have returned to Rosings.*
>
> *I believe you must have been surprised on arrival in town to discover that Colonel Fitzwilliam and Miss Darcy had journeyed here to see you.*
>
> *We were also surprised at their arrival, which was within the hour of your leaving. However, it is delightful to have them here, and I have prevailed upon them to stay and await your return.*

He reread the letter several times, gleaning whatever information he could.

Another two days perhaps, then he might be free to return.

The Brigadier had been most obliging and Darcy was glad of his connections. He had even written to the magistrate for him, to ask for his particular attention, and Mr. Darcy was grateful for that, despite the delay to his plans.

It seemed that as the plot had not concluded successfully, there was little recourse by the courts that could be done in that regard. The money, however, might have been different had Lady Catherine been in a position to speak of the matter.

But Mr. Darcy could ensure that the plotters knew they had been found out, and lived to regret it. Here the friendship of the Brigadier had been instrumental.

Mr. Darcy smiled grimly. He must ask Elizabeth to ensure regular invitations to him and his wife to Pemberley. He was a useful man to know.

Captain Matthews was already suffering loss of status and regard within the Dragoons, and orders had been dispatched to the Colonel of Wickham's regiment in Newcastle.

He would be in no doubt as to where his difficulties originated, although Darcy had asked that the punishment not be so severe as to affect Mrs. Wickham — for Elizabeth's sake he would not do that.

He scowled, he was still sure that Wickham would take advantage of the connection. Ten thousand pounds! No wonder the plot had been laid so carefully, and such precautions taken. And that was just the new plan. The old plan had been Rosings itself. Now Wickham was married, he couldn't force Anne to marry him, so he'd bribed Matthews for the promise of ten thousand.

It was as he sat there with Elizabeth's letter that he realised the threads stretched back further than he'd thought.

He had thought last week that Mrs. Jenkinson's face had seemed familiar. Why had he not connected her with that other face from last year? Why had he not thought Mrs. Younge familiar when he first saw her?

His only excuse was his anger at that time. He shook his head and got to his feet. He must go upstairs and prepare for the day. In two hours he'd be with the Earl and Countess. He must explain in full to his cousin what he had found, and discuss with him the possible remedies.

But he already knew what it was. Anne must marry. The Earl would say it must be Cousin Richard. That would keep Rosings within the family and see him settled with a good fortune.

And Anne was becoming more confident, more able to be a good wife and mistress of Rosings. Mr. Darcy resolved to encourage the union. He was sure Richard could be persuaded. Whoever he had partiality for, nothing was in the open so it must be in its very early stages. He surely could be detached from whoever he favoured.

He frowned again as he climbed into the carriage to go to the Earl's London home. He knew he had been mistaken in the feelings of Bingley and Miss Jane Bennet, so might he be missing something here? But he could not think who she might be.

He smiled slightly. He would ask Elizabeth when he saw her. She was cognisant of such things.

He wondered if Cousin Anne had any partiality to Richard — or anyone else. He could not imagine she had met very many young men.

The carriage drew up outside the Earl's grand residence and Darcy stepped down, staring up at the entrance.

He was so tired. He wanted nothing else than to get back to Rosings and find his wife. Then he wanted to take her back to Pemberley and stay there quietly with her for a long, long time.

He climbed the steps.

*H*e drained the second whisky after an hour in the Earl's library.

"So there you have it, Cousin David. I have ensured that Wickham and Matthews are now no longer a danger to Cousin Anne. I intend to return there tomorrow and I will tell Anne that Mrs. Jenkinson must go." He glared at his empty glass. "I do not know what inducement she used with Lady Catherine to obtain such a remuneration. She has had a great sum from the estate over these two years — and I believe the housekeeper may have to be let go, too."

The Earl stirred in his chair. "Do not have another whisky, Darcy. You should be keeping your wits about you."

He turned to the footman. "Coffee for us both."

Then he sighed and turned to Mr. Darcy. "I am most sincerely grateful for all your efforts on behalf of Cousin Anne. Grateful, yes. But also amazed. I cannot believe that you have unearthed such a story from a single incident."

He waved his glass at Mr. Darcy. "It is impressive. I trust the Brigadier was equally impressed."

Mr. Darcy bowed slightly. "He is a useful man to know."

"Oh, indeed. I will be adding him to my wife's

calling list." He nodded at the footman who'd placed the coffee tray on the side table.

"In fact, the Dragoon Guards are a respectable division. With suitable patronage, it might be worth considering for Nicholas or James."

Mr. Darcy nodded. David and Fitzwilliam had been the old Earl's only two sons for many years, before the now-dowager Countess had produced two more sons late in life.

"It would be an excellent chance for either of them," he agreed. "Remind me, sir, how old they are now?"

"Oh, they are in their mid-twenties now, I think. I don't recall exactly." David waved his hand dismissively. "There was ten years between Richard and Nicholas, so that would be about right, wouldn't it? No." He frowned. "Early twenties, I suppose."

Darcy smiled. "It is not important, except that they should make some future for themselves soon." He stood and walked to the fireplace.

"But I suppose it might be as well to discover the risks of engagement with France before we put them in harm's way."

"That is a good point." The Earl stared into his coffee cup, frowning slightly.

"But let us turn to Cousin Anne. Unless you

intend to stay there with your wife for many months, we must consider how to make Anne secure."

Mr. Darcy frowned. "I agree. Unpalatable as it seems, we must encourage Anne to marry very soon. It must be someone who is capable of supporting her and of managing Rosings for the future. And it should be someone in the family."

David nodded. "Richard, I believe, is the ideal man for that. He can buy out his commission easily enough."

Darcy agreed. He did not tell David that Richard had his heart elsewhere. Surely, now Richard had seen how Anne had progressed, she must seem a good match for him?

CHAPTER 47

*A*nother morning. Elizabeth struggled out of bed, wondering why she felt this fog of exhaustion every day now. All she wanted to do was pull the covers back over herself and stay in bed.

But she must not. She was needed today again, as she had been yesterday and the day before. She sighed, and rubbed her face. The day had to begin.

She sat in front of the glass as Rosina did her hair. Perhaps she needed some fresh air and some exercise and that would clear her head.

She pondered on the day ahead. Colonel Fitzwilliam and Anne seemed to be deeply involved in estate matters, they spent several hours each day examining the books and talked at meal-times over what they had achieved.

And because of this, Georgiana seemed quiet and unhappy. Elizabeth was trying to keep her entertained and occupied. They sat at the piano often, playing duets; and going for walks in the garden.

But she was also required at the side of Lady Catherine, who was never quiet unless Elizabeth were there, cajoling her and encouraging her.

She was also assisting Anne with instructing the housekeeper as to the requirements of the day.

The woman was polite and respectful on the surface, but Elizabeth considered that the work set was not being done to her satisfaction.

But she struggled on. It was not up to her to change staff, and Anne seemed so engaged in the bookkeeping that she hadn't noticed what was amiss. She sighed. She wondered when Fitzwilliam would be back, she could hardly wait until he returned and assumed some of this aching responsibility from her shoulders.

She descended the stairs reluctantly. Perhaps he would return today, even though yesterday's letter had made no such intimation.

On the bottom step, she paused. She could not face breakfast and the start of polite conversations. She turned the other way and went outside. A brisk walk was what she needed, a long vigorous walk.

The brisk chill of the early-morning breeze set her back as she went down the steps, and she thought for a moment of going back in for a warmer coat. But then she'd meet Georgiana, or Cousin Richard, and be drawn into conversation.

She wouldn't be able to explain why she wanted to go outside, so she put her head down against the wind and strode out towards the trees, where she hoped the wind would be less.

It wasn't many minutes before she realised that her notion of going for a walk had been a mistake. She felt tired and a little faint. She put out her hand to support herself against a tree for a moment while she took some deep breaths.

"Cousin Elizabeth! Are you unwell?" Colonel Fitzwilliam's concerned voice was almost the most welcome sound she wished to hear. She pushed herself upright.

"Thank you, I am just a little breathless with the wind. It is colder than I anticipated." She reached for his arm to support her.

"But what were you doing out here, Cousin Elizabeth? You have not even a warm coat!"

"I made a mistake, sir. It was a silly notion I

had of partaking of some fresh air." She felt herself sway and concentrated on standing still.

His arm was steady and strong. He sheltered her from the direction the wind came from. "Let me assist you into the house."

"Thank you." She forced herself to stand upright from where she had unaccountably found herself leaning against him.

That was when they both noticed the rider. He'd rounded the house and had seen them. Regardless of the immaculate gardens, he spurred the horse and trotted towards them.

Fitzwilliam! He had come back early! She was so pleased to see him, but suddenly realised the situation may not look as innocent as it was. She let go of Cousin Richard's arm and tried to smile as he reined in the horse and dismounted.

He looked between them, unsmiling, and she knew it was up to her.

"I am so pleased you are home, sir. I'm sorry. I came out for a walk unprepared for the cold." She curtsied her greeting.

He bowed in return, and offered his arm to her. She took it and the Colonel took the reins of the horse and began to lead it beside them.

"I think Cousin Elizabeth is unwell, Darcy. I saw her from the breakfast room window and came out to assist."

"I thank you." Mr. Darcy still didn't smile, but he slowed down slightly and Elizabeth was thankful for that at least.

In the house, they went through to the breakfast room. Georgiana greeted her brother with pleasure, and then turned to Elizabeth.

"Are you unwell, Elizabeth? You looked so uncertain out there. I was glad that Cousin Richard was here to go out to you."

"I am well enough, Georgiana. Thank you for your enquiries." Elizabeth smiled and sat down. While she wanted nothing more than to go to her bedchamber and hide, she knew she could not do that.

Instead she turned to her husband. "You must have made a very early start, sir, to be here for breakfast."

He bowed slightly. "Indeed. I started before dawn was full begun."

"Then I hope you are ready for breakfast." She reached for the teapot. She handed him his cup and took her own. "May I serve you, sir?"

He nodded at her and she loaded up his plate with a good portion. That made her realise that there was no way she could manage even a slice of toast just yet.

Perhaps he would think she had already partaken. The coldness in his eyes concerned her.

It must have been a shock to him to have seen her leaning against his cousin.

The disappointment made her eyes sting, and she blinked hard, her face lowered. The scrape of the chairs told her that the men were rising and she looked up.

"Good morning, Cousin Anne." She made herself smile.

The men bowed and waited for Anne to be seated. She came alone to the table now, Mrs. Jenkinson no longer came with her.

Elizabeth saw her husband's eyes flicker to the empty seat and thought he showed some satisfaction.

She forced herself to be involved on the conversation, she didn't want Georgiana or the Colonel to comment that she had not eaten.

She smiled as she saw the effort that Georgiana was making to show her brother how pleased she was to see him. The Colonel kept glancing at her and then away, quickly.

After they had all finished their meal, all seemed to be waiting for Mr. Darcy to take control of the situation. He leaned back.

"So how have you all been employing your time while I have been detained in London?" his smile didn't reach his eyes.

"Cousin Anne has been showing me the management of Rosings." Colonel Fitzwilliam smiled at his cousin. "I think I am in a fair way to understanding what has been happening. This morning we were going to examine the servants' records for the grounds and estate."

Mr. Darcy bowed. "It would be advantageous, then, to continue with that if it is agreeable to you." He looked approvingly at Anne, who nodded.

"We can do that. Mrs. Jenkinson has been assisting us, bringing the ledgers that we need."

Elizabeth saw her husband start slightly. But he concealed it well.

"Then pray continue with it."

"Elizabeth and I have been assisting Lady Catherine partake in a little more social engagement." Georgiana looked at Elizabeth. "Is that not correct?"

"Indeed. I am most pleased at the improvement in her temper. She likes you playing for her very much."

"Good." Mr. Darcy looked at his sister. "Might I ask that you entertain our aunt this morning? I would like to talk to Elizabeth."

"Of course, sir."

Elizabeth felt her heart beat a little faster.

Would he be understanding and put behind them what he might have misunderstood this morning? Or might he tell her what he had discovered in London?

She soon discovered it was not either of those things.

CHAPTER 48

*I*n the library he waited with her in silence as they watched Colonel Fitzwilliam escort Cousin Anne to the estate office, followed by Mrs. Jenkinson.

She stayed silent too, unwilling to seem to be too defensive.

"Good." He turned towards her, but his expression was neutral and his eyes were cold.

"Please call for two maids to assist you and go up to your bedchamber. I must speak to my steward and then I will join you."

"Yes, sir." She was mightily puzzled, but she would not give him the satisfaction of asking what he was about.

After very few moments he appeared in her bedchamber as the maids waited in the hall.

"I need you to go to Mrs. Jenkinson's bedchamber. Mr. Fields is bringing up several trunks. You must supervise the maids as they pack up all the belongings for Mr. Fields to take downstairs." He raised his hand to prevent her objections. "I know that you will wish to argue with me, but pray do as you are told. I have discussed this with the Earl and with the magistrate and there is no objection to this plan." He stared pitilessly at her. "In fact, I am doing far more for her than the law requires. Please be about your task. I will ensure you are not disturbed."

He left the room and hurried off downstairs.

Elizabeth marshalled her thoughts. She turned to her own maid. "Please come with me too, Rosina." In the hallway, she beckoned the maids to follow her and swept along to the room she remembered as Mrs. Jenkinson's.

She gave them their instructions and as she did so, Mr. Fields appeared with the Rosings steward and several large trunks.

"Thank you, Mr. Fields."

He bowed his head at her. "Mrs. Darcy."

When they had gone, she found a chair that might not be in the way of the maids as they efficiently packed the trunks, filled them with the contents of a life lived here for several years.

She wondered how Anne would feel once she

discovered that Mrs. Jenkinson was to be sent packing. And she wondered what Mr. Darcy had found out about the woman to justify speaking to a magistrate and this summary dismissal.

She hoped he would tell her. But if not, he owed it to Cousin Anne to ensure that she knew.

Her attention was drawn back to the room when one of the maids gasped. She was carrying a pile of books to the trunk and one of them had fallen. Out from between the pages had fallen a number of banknotes.

Elizabeth hid her gasp too. It was more money than she had ever seen in one place, and as the maid scrambled to pick it up, she wondered what she should do.

"Put it over there on the table," she instructed. "Rosina, please go and ask Mr. Darcy to attend here if he is not with anyone else." She thought quickly. "If he is in company of anyone else, do not speak to him, but return here."

She turned back to the maids. "Check the other books as you pack them, please."

If the money belonged to Mrs. Jenkinson, then she must make sure she received it in full. But how could she have that much? Why, it must be above twenty pounds, an extraordinary amount to have saved.

As she watched them finishing the work, she

wondered how much a companion at a place like Rosings would be paid.

If Mr. Darcy had not saved her from Lydia's ruin, it was likely that on the death of her father, she herself might have had to become such a companion, and she was quite sure that her worth would not be so much as twenty pounds above her board.

For the first time she considered the room. Because it was next to Anne's, it was a superior room for a servant. Elizabeth wondered at the woman's power to get such a quality room and such an income as to be able to save such sums of money.

Mr. Fields returned, and Mr. Darcy too. Elizabeth showed him the money, now swelled to thirty-seven pounds. "It seems a very large sum, sir."

"Indeed." His jaw was set. "But it cannot be proven to be stolen. Place it in the trunk. I will tell her where it is."

Elizabeth caught the two maids exchanging a glance of incomprehension. It had clearly not entered their heads that the master would not declare it must have been unlawfully obtained.

Because it must have been. Even a gentleman such as Mr. Bennet would have been hard put to obtain such a sum. And to secrete it in her room and not the bank seemed most suspicious, even to Elizabeth's own generally trusting nature.

She watched the two stewards supervising the trunks being taken downstairs.

Mr. Darcy seemed to know what she was thinking. "Mr. Fields will stand guard over the trunks until Mrs. Jenkinson is in the carriage," he said.

"Thank you sir," she replied quietly, determined not to express all the questions whirling about her head.

He looked at her, and although there was no warmth in his gaze, she thought he was pleased with her obedience this morning.

She gripped the stair rail as a sudden wave of dizziness overtook her. She began to go downstairs. She needed to order tea and pastries, having had no breakfast.

As she sat with Georgiana and nibbled at the cake, he strode up and down the room, watching the door from the estate office.

Georgiana leaned towards her, "Is something concerning him?" she said quietly.

Elizabeth nodded. "I believe there is going to be somewhat of a disturbance in a moment. But I wish he had told Cousin Anne first. It will seem a great shock to her."

Georgiana looked puzzled, and Elizabeth

lowered her voice further. "We have packed up Mrs. Jenkinson's room. When she arrives from her task with Cousin Richard and Anne, I believe he will escort her to the carriage outside and banish her from the estate."

"Oh!" Georgiana gasped. "What has he discovered in town about her, I wonder?"

"What indeed?" Elizabeth mused. "Even I have seen things that have caused me some suspicion of her intentions, but I confess I do not know enough to feel as confident as Mr. Darcy obviously does."

CHAPTER 49

"*A*h!" Mr. Darcy had obviously seen something. "Elizabeth. Georgiana. Please could you come through to the hall? I would wish you to witness this — and maybe support Cousin Anne, if she needs it."

Elizabeth felt some anger. If he had thought Anne might be distressed, he should have spoken to her first, not made her receive the shock in public.

But she said nothing, instead going through to the hall with Georgiana. Anne came through from the office, her hand in Colonel Fitzwilliam's arm as she carefully negotiated the small step up. Elizabeth felt Georgiana's distress as well as Mr. Darcy's satisfaction. She could understand the one, but not the other. She pushed the thought aside to consider later.

Mrs. Jenkinson slipped into the hall behind the couple, and in the self-effacing manner of a good servant, she moved towards the stairs.

"Mrs. Jenkinson. Please come here." Mr. Darcy's voice was clear and stopped the woman in her tracks. She was good, though. Her face was politely enquiring.

"Yes, Mr. Darcy?"

He ignored that at first and turned to Anne. "Pray sit down with Mrs. Darcy, Miss de Bourgh."

Puzzled, Anne sat on the settle, and looked at Elizabeth, who was very glad to sit down again. She put her head close to Anne's and whispered to her.

"I am sorry we have had no notice of his intentions."

Mr. Darcy turned and faced Mrs Jenkinson. "You are not to go upstairs, Mrs. Jenkinson. We are dispensing with your services as companion here with immediate effect. Your belongings are all packed and waiting outside in the carriage."

As he spoke, her face showed incredulity, and when he got to the part about her belongings having been packed, she showed some consider-able emotion.

Beside Elizabeth, Anne clutched at her arm, and Elizabeth grasped her hand.

"But, sir, I am employed by Lady Catherine personally." Mrs. Jenkinson objected. "And I must deserve the time to pack my own belongings."

Mr. Darcy looked contemptuously at her. "Oh, yes, we should examine that contract of employment, should we not? A position of extraordinary generosity, giving you the life of a lady, an allowance of five times the expected amount, that has enabled you to save many tens of pounds." He stepped closer to the woman, who stood straight and fearless in front of him, to Elizabeth's surprise. "And a position that enabled you to use herbs and medicines to ensure Miss de Bourgh, the young lady in your charge, stayed feeling unwell and isolated in your care." His voice was full of suppressed rage. "A position that enabled you to call your cousin the moment Lady Catherine — the employer you must have bribed and abused — the moment she was incapacitated, so that your cousin could come down with another to compromise Miss de Bourgh and oblige her to marry, so that you and your family could get control of Rosings and all the fortune it represents." He spun on his heels and strode away from her. "You disgust me, Mrs. Jenkinson, you and your kind disgust me." He turned and faced her. "You are most fortunate that your ruse did not succeed and that I am a generous man. I do not know the full extent of the money you had secreted in your room, but the thirty-seven pounds we did discover is in the top of the large trunk. The rest will still be hidden in the items you had them in." He strode to the door. "The carriage is waiting to take you to London. It will deliver you to your sister. You are most fortunate that you are not sitting on the road outside with all your belongings." He went to the front door.

❧

"Goodbye, Mrs. Jenkinson. Tell Mrs. Younge that neither you, your sister, nor your cousin will escape the scrutiny of the constabulary if you attempt to prey upon another again."

As he mentioned the name Mrs. Younge, Georgiana gasped. Elizabeth wracked her brains to recall the name. Oh, yes. That was the woman who was looking after Georgiana in Ramsgate when Mr. Wickham desired to marry her. But nobody knew that Elizabeth knew that story, so she didn't look at her young sister-in-law.

But Colonel Fitzwilliam did. She saw his glance and was pleased. But he would have to pay

Georgiana some attention. Surely he could see her unhappiness?

They watched as Mrs. Jenkinson was driven away, her face a mask of disbelief.

Mr. Darcy came over to Anne, sitting next to Elizabeth, and bowed. "I am sorry to have made this such a spectacle, Cousin Anne. You must be most distressed." He offered her his arm, and she rose unsteadily to her feet.

"Thank you, Cousin Fitzwilliam." She said no more until they were sitting in the drawing room, and the footmen had been dispatched for fresh tea.

Elizabeth sat beside Anne, feeling that she was most likely at present to need her support.

"Are you composed, Cousin Anne?" she whispered.

Anne turned towards her. "I think what has distressed me the most is discovering that she was giving me medicines that made me feel unwell. It must be why I was unable to find the energy to ask my mother to dispense with her services."

"You could not have been expected to know." Mr. Darcy's voice was gentle and kind.

Elizabeth wished he would speak to her in that tone of voice too.

"I have spent many hours with the constable and the magistrate, endeavouring to get information from Mrs. Younge as to how she or her sister gained the knowledge to gain this appointment from Lady Catherine." Mr. Darcy shook his head. "I was unsuccessful, and Lady Catherine would be unlikely to want to tell us, even if she could. So we might never know. They are the daughters of an apothecary, so of course they were able to use their knowledge."

He went to the window. "Captain Matthews and Mr. Wickham will never obtain the opportunity to come here again without that knowledge being vouchsafed to us immediately." He smiled grimly. "But I do not think they will wish to."

Elizabeth hid a smile. The relish with which her husband spoke told her that his triumph over Mr. Wickham was very sweet. Poor Lydia.

"I must thank you, sir, for the very great efforts you have made to keep me safe. I think …" Anne shuddered. "I was in more danger than I realised."

There was some conversation within the room, everyone was stimulated by the scene they had just witnessed and were loud in their praise of Mr. Darcy.

Elizabeth watched him as he stood by the window, the conversation washing over him. He looked very tired, she thought. Tired and concerned. He had other news to give them, she thought. News he did not want to give.

She wished she could go to him, repair the breach between them, assure him of the innocence of what he had seen that morning. But she could not, at least not yet.

Anne touched her arm. "Elizabeth, might I talk to you privately a moment?"

"Of course." Elizabeth pulled her thoughts back to her cousin. "We might go to the small parlour. We would not be overheard there."

"Thank you." Anne rose to her feet. "Please would you excuse us?"

Elizabeth caught her husband's gaze on her as she followed Anne out of the room. An unfathomable gaze, she could not understand him. She wished she knew him better, that she might know more of what he was thinking.

CHAPTER 50

*S*oon they were sitting in the parlour, a room which did not yet feel as welcoming as the rest of the house was becoming.

"How can I be of assistance, Anne?" Elizabeth sat forward, so that she could take the other girl's hand in hers. She knew Anne was several years older than she was, but she felt that she was much older, somehow.

Anne sighed. "I am so grateful that you have been here these many weeks. But I know it cannot be for much longer." She looked down.

"I think Mr. Darcy is going to want to speak to me. He is going to tell me that, to be safe, I must marry."

Elizabeth had been expecting this. And, difficult as it was, she knew he would be right. Anne would never be safe until she was not a glittering prize waiting to be plucked. A huge fortune and a vast estate so near to London. Who would not wish to advance themselves?

"It is a difficult decision for you," she said. "What do you feel about the thought of marrying?"

Anne smiled. "Well, until recently, I thought my mother would force Mr. Darcy to fulfil her dream." She shrugged. "She pursued him relentlessly, even in front of me, but I always felt too ill to contradict her." She shivered. "And now I know why."

Elizabeth smiled. "I suppose these last few weeks when you have eaten with us, from the same dishes, there has not been the opportunity to make you feel so bad."

"No, it has been very nice, feeling so well." Her face changed, and she stopped smiling.

"But I think Mr. Darcy will try to decide for me who I should marry. I could sense him feeling satisfied this morning when I came into the hall on Cousin Richard's arm."

Elizabeth felt her throat tighten. She wanted Georgiana's happiness above all else. But she could not say so.

"And how do you feel about Cousin Richard?" she asked cautiously.

Anne shook her head. "It does not matter. I know his heart is given elsewhere. I would not cause such unhappiness."

Elizabeth looked at her with increased respect. "Has he told you so?"

"No. But it is obvious to me." Anne said. "And in any case …" She fell silent.

Elizabeth smiled and squeezed the hand in hers. "I'm very glad you have found someone. Is he family, too?"

Anne went a rosy pink. "You are very astute, Elizabeth." She hesitated. "I have not met many men, but I very much enjoy the company of Cousin Nicholas. Do you know him?"

"No, I don't think I have heard his name before. Does he visit here often?"

"No." Anne sighed. "Not very often. He and Cousin James come down about twice a year. They are much younger than Richard and David."

"Who is David?" Elizabeth needed to learn the names of her new family.

"I'm sorry. The old Earl died only two years ago. Cousin David is the new Earl. Then Richard is two years younger than him, and the two boys were born more than ten years later."

Elizabeth smiled. "Tell me about Nicholas."

Anne needed no other encouragement, but

Elizabeth soon realised that Cousin Nicholas may not know anything much about Anne at all. They had barely spoken. It seemed he was quiet and reserved, and Anne had not been in any position to seem the object of a possible alliance.

She smiled. "You sound quite excited, Anne. If Mr. Darcy speaks to you and encourages you to prefer Cousin Richard, you must speak out plainly and tell him you prefer his brother."

"I am not sure I will dare to cross him, Elizabeth. Will you stay with me when he speaks to me?"

"If you wish it, and Mr. Darcy consents, then I will, with all my heart. But you know, if you don't tell him, it might be difficult for Cousin Richard to withstand him, and I do not think you will be happy, marrying a man whose heart might be elsewhere."

"You are right, as always." Anne gave her a relieved smile. "I wish Pemberley was not so far away."

"We will travel to see you often, dear cousin." Elizabeth smiled. "Now we had better return to the company, or they will be wondering what we are about."

"That is true." Anne got to her feet slowly. Elizabeth watched her carefully.

"You are tired today, Anne. Perhaps you have been doing too much."

"It is not always easy to keep up with what Cousin Richard expects." Anne laughed. "He is most kind, but he cannot comprehend feeling unwell. I think it must be because he is never ill himself."

"True." Elizabeth laughed too. "Come on, let's return to the drawing room."

"It must be time for lunch. You must be hungry, Elizabeth. I noticed you had no breakfast."

Elizabeth looked sharply at Anne. She had not realised she had been observed.

"Please do not remark on it, Anne."

"Of course I will not."

As she followed her cousin back to join the rest of the company, Elizabeth suddenly understood what Anne would be thinking, having observed her not taking breakfast.

She stopped, thinking hard. Would Anne be right? Suddenly the suspicion firmed within her. *Goodness, it is true.*

She realised Anne had stopped and was looking back. She composed her features and hurried to catch up with her.

❧

*A*t lunch, she managed to eat a small amount, and by not taking too much and by eating slowly, what she ate was not remarked upon.

After coffee in the drawing room, the gentlemen retired to the library, now polished and dusted. The ladies remained in the drawing room.

After half an hour, Elizabeth got up. "I hope you two will excuse me. I am going to walk to the Parsonage to visit Mrs. Collins."

Georgiana looked up. "Do you wish for some company, Elizabeth?"

"No, do not trouble yourself, Georgiana. I would not disturb your conversation." She smiled. "I will take my maid if you think I should. But I would rather walk alone."

"You must do what you wish, Elizabeth. You have been so good to us, and a little colour in your cheeks will cheer us all up." Anne picked up the needlework she had begun.

"Georgiana, can you show me where I have erred in this stitching?"

Elizabeth smiled at them as she slipped into the hall and went upstairs to get her warm coat and a hat.

CHAPTER 51

*A*t Hunsford, Mrs. Collins welcomed her warmly and took her into the sitting room she regularly used.

"Mr. Collins happens to be visiting in the parish," she said. "It is a happy coincidence, for we will have time to talk freely."

"That is good, Charlotte." Elizabeth took off her coat and bonnet. "I would love to catch up with all your news."

"And I most definitely wish to catch up with yours. Tell me, how is Lady Catherine now?"

"She is improving daily in her spirits." Elizabeth settled into the chair. "But I am not convinced that she will recover much more in the way of movement and speech." She made a resigned face at Charlotte. "I think this fact occurs to her sometimes and she is much put out when it does."

Charlotte looked sad. "It must be very difficult for her, having to relinquish control to others when she has always wished to control not only herself but everyone around her."

"Yes." Elizabeth put down her cup. "And does Mr. Collins grieve the loss of the patronage of Lady Catherine de Bourgh?"

Charlotte looked pensive. "He does. But I remind him that the gift of this living was most generous and he must appreciate it." She smiled. "I can understand that we are not invited to dine so much. It was good of you to invite us when Mr. Darcy was away. Is he returned?"

"Yes." Elizabeth watched the housekeeper bring in the tea tray. "He returned this morning."

"I am happy for you, Elizabeth. It seemed all the responsibility of Rosings Park was on your shoulders."

"No, Charlotte; Colonel Fitzwilliam and Georgiana have been a great help, and Miss de Bourgh is much more able than her mother gave her credit for." She would not talk about this afternoon and what had transpired with Mrs. Jenkinson. It would be all around the parish the moment Mr. Collins knew about it.

A happy hour passed for Elizabeth and then

she got up and prepared to return to Rosings Park. Charlotte stood up too and came to the door to see her off.

"Elizabeth, I do not want to speak out of turn, but you do not seem very happy. It grieves me to see it." She put her hand on Elizabeth's arm. "We were good friends once. If I can assist at all, please know I will do all in my power to help you."

Elizabeth forced a smile. "Dear Charlotte. I am fine, thank you. I think I am just very tired, that is all."

"As you know, Elizabeth, I am not romantic. But even I have had to become used to the thought that the married state is not at all like I had believed. There are disappointments to be overcome and it seems to be the wife who has to do the adapting to her husband's wishes." She put her hand on Elizabeth's arm.

"Dear Elizabeth, I know you are so much more of a romantic than I am. I hope that your unhappiness is not disappointment. Things will settle down so much better for you when you can go to Pemberley and begin a normal married life, I am sure."

Elizabeth's throat constricted. Charlotte did not know that her marriage was a formal arrangement, without a declaration of love from her husband. But it was true she had hoped that he would learn to love her — after all, at his first proposal he had said so.

She forced a smile. "I am not disappointed, Charlotte, only that Mr. Darcy wished so much that our early weeks together would be spent at Pemberley. But when he was needed here, he did not hesitate. And that is as things should be." She embraced her friend and began to walk slowly back to Rosings.

Now she had the time to think on her discovery this morning — after Anne's words had drawn her attention to it. But it was still so early that she had not even considered that there might be adverse effects on her health and her emotions. This was why she had been feeling tired, this was why she hadn't been hungry.

But it was scarce eight weeks since they had married. She smiled to herself, her life was going to be changing more completely and far sooner than she had thought.

❧

She was walking very slowly along the track when she saw Colonel Fitzwilliam striding towards her.

"Cousin Elizabeth! I was walking to meet you. When Cousin Anne said you had gone to visit

Mrs. Collins alone, I thought I should come and ensure you are well."

She stopped and smiled a polite welcome. "Thank you, Cousin Richard. It was a very kind thought, but quite unnecessary, I assure you. I am very well."

He turned to walk beside her. "I have thought these last few days that you have looked very tired, Elizabeth. Much has been placed upon you, and the demands of my aunt and the rest of our company have all seemed to centre on you."

"I assure you it has not. Why, you yourself have taken on much. I know that Cousin Anne has been most grateful for your assistance." She glanced at him, watching for any sign that he might be changing his allegiance from Georgiana to Anne.

He looked very uncomfortable. He hesitated. "Darcy spoke to me after lunch. He seems to feel I must take on a far greater responsibility, and do it soon." He seemed most downcast.

Elizabeth stopped. She must say something, and surely now would be the best time.

"I hope you will forgive me for speaking plainly, sir. But I think it would be the biggest mistake of your life. You would be making not only yourself, but two young ladies very unhappy.

Not for a short time, either, but for the rest of all your lives."

He turned towards her, uncomprehending. "Two young ladies?"

Elizabeth smiled. "I have been watching these last few weeks, Cousin Richard. Forgive me if I think I have discerned where your heart lies. Although you have been most discreet." Elizabeth smiled. "And can you not tell that your feelings are returned?"

"She is too young." The Colonel looked wretched. "And I am her guardian. I should not have made my feelings so plain that you could discern them."

You have hidden them very well." Elizabeth hurried to reassure him. "But she is old enough to reciprocate, I think."

He groaned. "Darcy will never forgive me."

"I think maybe you might consider more the feelings of Georgiana. She has seemed very out of sorts this last week, while you have been helping Anne so much."

He looked most unhappy. "I know it, and it has hurt me very much seeing her face." He looked straight at her. "But you said *two* young ladies. I cannot imagine that I could make two ladies unhappy."

Elizabeth began to walk on. "Have you never

considered that Cousin Anne might have developed partiality to another, and that if she marries you, she can no longer harbour a dream of marrying in line with her heart?"

He took her arm and stopped her, turning her towards him. "Are you speaking in all seriousness, Elizabeth? I can scarce believe it." He shook his head. "No, you must be mistaken. Who is the gentleman she prefers? How has she had the opportunity to meet another?" His voice was disbelieving and hopeful at the same time.

Elizabeth shook her head and smiled. "It is not a confidence that I am authorised to reveal, sir. It is for you and Mr. Darcy to ask her, perhaps, and then to facilitate the arrangements."

He seemed to have had the weight of the world lifted from his shoulders. He took her hands and grasped them, bringing them to his lips and kissing them. "Oh, Elizabeth! You don't know how much you have lifted my spirits today."

"I am so pleased, Cousin Richard." Elizabeth gave him a smile of real happiness, "and I thank you for your kindness in coming to meet me."

They turned back towards Rosings.

Elizabeth's heart stopped.

Standing silent in the centre of the path, watching them, was her husband.

CHAPTER 52

*H*e was out of earshot, but she knew he had seen them talking and Cousin Richard kissing her hands.

Even from where he was, his ice-cold expression pierced her heart.

Having observed that he was seen, he walked towards them, disapproval etched in every step.

The Colonel stepped back a pace, and Elizabeth started walking towards her husband. It took every ounce of courage she had, but her anger was rising. How could he even think that she would do anything wrong, that she would jeopardise his position?

"Darcy! I am glad you have come." Cousin Richard's joviality sounded rather forced.

If Elizabeth hadn't been so anxious about

393

facing her husband, she might have been amused by Richard's reaction. But all her attention was focussed on him.

She stopped and curtsied. "Mr. Darcy."

He bowed. "Elizabeth." Then he turned and began to walk beside her.

"Fitzwilliam, I think Anne would appreciate your assistance." His voice was cold as he spoke to his cousin.

"Thank you, Darcy." The Colonel sounded uncomfortable.

He didn't look at Elizabeth as he spoke to her. "Thank you for your advice, Mrs. Darcy." He bowed and hurried on ahead of them. She watched him go. He would judge it best to explain himself to Mr. Darcy when Elizabeth wasn't there. But that didn't help her now.

But she wasn't going to try and explain anything away herself. She had nothing to be ashamed of at all. Let him start the conversation.

They continued in silence for some moments. His anger speeded his pace and despite her preference to walk fast, today she could not. She slowed down.

He looked around and slowed his pace to hers and she felt his increasing annoyance.

Her chin went up. Would things be easier or harder if she spoke first?

But the matter was taken out of her hands. He turned off the path and went to a small summer house nestled in the shrubbery close to the main house.

He reached out and opened the door. He held it for her, his face set.

"Thank you, sir." She went through to the pretty little summer house and selected a seat. She was very glad to sit down.

Mr. Darcy did not sit down, but the summer house was too small for him to pace around. He stood and looked at her. His look was enigmatic.

"Please explain." The cold words settled around her heart.

She looked out at the grounds, reminding herself that her marriage was an arrangement, no more than that. She should not feel that she'd lost his love, because it hadn't been there in the first place.

"I believe there is nothing to explain. I visited Mrs. Collins this afternoon, and, as the others have been concerned about me these last few days, Colonel Fitzwilliam decided to walk out to escort me home."

A pause. "And why would the others be concerned for you?"

She looked away. "I do not know, except they think perhaps that I am tired."

One eyebrow went up and she knew he was wondering why she should be so tired. But she wasn't going to tell him.

"May I know of what you were talking about so affectionately to my cousin?"

"Will you listen?" Elizabeth suppressed her rage. How dare he just assume things?

"What I saw looked most compromising. It might explain how you got into such a position."

She looked at him. She felt like refusing to say a word, but then the wrong things might happen. She could not abide for Georgiana to be unhappy a moment longer than she had already been.

"We were discussing the future of Rosings, sir. Colonel Fitzwilliam told me you'd had a conversation with him." She looked at her husband. How much to tell him?

"He did not say exactly what it was about, but I guessed." She took a deep breath. "I told him that I thought it would be a very great mistake."

She smiled, resigned to the way it had looked. "You happened upon us the moment I convinced him he would be wrong to go along with it."

He turned away and stared out of the window.

"Sometimes sacrifices have to be made, Mrs. Darcy. Rosings Park and Miss de Bourgh must be protected."

"But you were not willing to make that sacrifice yourself!" She flung at him.

His lips tightened. "I have Pemberley. I do not have need of Rosings too. Colonel Fitzwilliam is the most amiable of men, but as a younger son, he must marry well."

He swung round. "You are now Mrs. Darcy. You knew what you were doing when you married me, and to lead my cousin on to defy the proprieties is insupportable." He stared grimly out of the window.

She gasped at the implication. "You are as cold and unobservant as you ever were, sir! Even if you care so little for me, have you not noticed the unhappiness of your own sister?"

He jerked and glared at her. "What?"

"And that you have not even spoken to Cousin Anne! Her heart is elsewhere. But you wish to control everyone."

It was impossible. Elizabeth rose to her feet. "I must return to the house, sir." She thought she might have to push past him, but he stepped aside.

"If you intend to willfully misunderstand the import of my words, then I think this conversation should be postponed."

She walked carefully across the lawn, feeling her legs wobbly with shock at his anger. As she got to the back door, she glanced back. He was still standing in the doorway of the summerhouse, watching her.

She glanced at the clock as she went through the hall. She needed to be in the drawing room for tea in half an hour or so. She could escape to her bedchamber until then.

She hurried up the stairs and along the corridor. She shut the door behind her and leaned against it, closing her eyes. The memory of his cold, accusing look burned behind her eyelids, and they flew open.

She pushed herself upright and went to the window. The little summerhouse was empty now, the windows blank.

How could he think she and Cousin Richard were partial to each other? And that he could be so inattentive to Georgiana's unhappiness!

She sank into the nearest chair, her feet aching. And the biggest question of all. Why in heaven's name had she agreed to this marriage?

Ten minutes later, she still hadn't answered her own question. But she had decided that it must be business as usual. She owed him her loyalty, even if he was questioning it. She would act as his wife.

A few minutes later, after tidying her hair, she slipped downstairs as the footmen were carrying in trays of tea and cakes.

"Thank you," she said to them as she sat

down, her hands folded calmly in her lap to wait for the others. She fervently hoped that the first arrival would be neither Mr. Darcy nor Cousin Richard. She hid a small smile. That might take some explaining.

But she was fortunate. Georgiana came in. "I'm happy you're here." She curtsied. "May I sit next to you?"

"Of course." Elizabeth moved up a little. "So, did Lady Catherine come downstairs this afternoon?"

"For a short while." Georgiana smiled. "She was most put out that you were not here, and it was not possible to divert her attention for long. So she went back upstairs."

"I must make sure I am here tomorrow," Elizabeth mused. "Perhaps we can play for her, you and I."

Georgiana smiled. "You are very good to her."

"I can imagine very well what it must feel like to be in such a position as she finds herself."

She sensed her husband in the doorway, and glanced up. "Good afternoon, Mr. Darcy. Would you like me to pour your tea?"

He bowed acquiescence and came forward to take his cup. Then he sat in a chair further away and opened a book.

CHAPTER 53

*H*e stared at the open page, unable to read a word. He was still stunned at seeing her with Richard again. Twice in a single day. And now, here she sat, apparently without any concerns.

Cousin Anne appeared, and joined the conversation between the ladies. As he couldn't concentrate on the printed words, he listened to the conversation. He wondered how he had not noticed before how much the others relied on Elizabeth, how much they asked her advice — and how thoughtful and kind were her answers.

Cousin Richard entered the room and hesitated. His jaw set and determined, he bowed and joined the ladies.

Mr. Darcy still sat with his gaze firmly fixed on

the page. He listened as Elizabeth drew Richard into the conversation without embarrassment or showing any special regard.

The other ladies seemed to see nothing unusual in the conversation. They would have sat like this each day while he was away.

Had he been mistaken in what he had assumed today? Had his anger blinded him — made him see what he was most afraid of?

He watched the group unobtrusively. He saw Georgiana glancing at her cousins, but always ending by looking at Elizabeth as if she needed solace. He watched as Richard paid no particular attention to Anne or Georgiana, as if he dare not. So he would look at Elizabeth, then seem to remember that Darcy was there and his gaze would flicker away from Elizabeth uncomfortably.

Mr. Darcy could hardly bear to watch, and he forced himself again to his book. But his attention was drawn away again when his wife spoke.

"Would you all please excuse me? I missed seeing Lady Catherine downstairs this afternoon. I wish to call on her to assure her of my attention to her."

The others rose and acknowledged as she left the room. Mr. Darcy had also closed his book and risen to his feet. He bowed as she left.

How had he missed seeing how much she was doing? How much the others relied on her?

He had seen what happened that very afternoon when the nurse had arrived in the room with Lady Catherine; how immediately his aunt had showed her distress that Elizabeth was not there and how the other ladies were quite unable to calm her. It had not been many moments before the nurse and footmen had taken Lady Catherine back upstairs.

Anne had confided to him almost tearfully how much her aunt relied on Elizabeth's kindness and understanding and was tractable and interested in the company when in her presence.

He returned to his book and his thoughts. Her words had hurt him deeply when she accused him of wishing to control everyone around him. He wondered who Anne was partial to. That might make an early marriage possible.

But what had she meant about Georgiana's unhappiness? He'd been hurt by her accusations that he hadn't noticed. And if it was true, then he was doubly grieved, both at the accusation and at his sister's distress. He watched Georgiana. She sat quietly now that Elizabeth was gone upstairs.

Then she sighed and gave a sidelong glance at Cousin Richard and moved to the pianoforte. She sat and began to play.

He noticed that Richard did not move to sit beside the instrument and turn the pages as he had for Elizabeth last year. But that would have left Anne on her own. He could hardly do that.

The tunes Georgiana had chosen were plaintive and sad. Mr. Darcy put down his book and went to join his sister.

She looked surprised, but didn't stop playing.

"I am sorry I cannot turn the pages for you, dear sister. But you know I do not read the music."

She laughed. "I do not know any gentlemen who do, Fitzwilliam. You must watch me, and turn the page when I nod my head."

"Ah, that is how it is done." He sat there for some minutes, the sadness of the tune entering his heart.

"You play sad music today, Georgiana. Are you unhappy here? I am sorry if you have been feeling neglected."

She looked surprised. She hesitated for a moment. "I am not unhappy, sir." She stopped playing and selected a different piece of music. He knew she was not being honest with him, but he didn't know quite how to ask her what she wished to do.

He glanced over at the other couple. Anne

and Richard were listening, but neither seemed to be showing any partiality to the other.

The music faltered, and stopped. He glanced round. Georgiana was smiling.

"You stopped watching when to turn the page, Fitzwilliam." She closed the lid over the keys. "Excuse me." She stood and curtsied to him and left the room.

He cursed under his breath. Things seemed to have been going well until he arrived, and now everyone was on edge. And he had caused Elizabeth distress — accused her of something terrible.

He sat by the silent pianoforte, uncaring of what the others must be thinking.

No, it would not do. He must go to her, now, before dinner.

He pushed away his chair, and went back through to the drawing room.

"Excuse me." He bowed and left them, taking the stairs two at a time.

He went to his bedchamber first. He must compose his thoughts. He sat at his writing desk, preparing his words in his mind. He was very aware of his greater ability with words on the page than in conversation, and he did not wish to lose his temper again. It would mean he might hurt her once more and he would not do that. He clenched his fist. He must not do that.

He sighed and got heavily to his feet. This was a depressing house. The whole place always sapped any good spirits he may have had. It was an abominable place to have started their married life. He went downstairs.

He found the housekeeper. "Please send Mrs. Darcy's maid to her, and ask if she would do me the honour of joining me in the small lounge."

He noted with amusement the morose demeanour of the housekeeper. She had undoubtedly noted the precariousness of her position now that Mrs. Jenkinson had been dispensed with so unceremoniously.

He stood looking out of the window in the small drawing room for several minutes.

"Mr. Darcy." He heard his wife's voice in the doorway and turned. She curtsied and he bowed.

He smiled at her and indicated a chair.

When they were both well seated, he realised that all his planned words were disappearing from his mind.

"Thank you for coming down, Elizabeth."

She inclined her head and sat on the edge of a chair.

She did look rather pale, he noticed, and he wondered how distressed she had been by the emotions of the day.

"I want …" he jumped to his feet and went to

the window. This was going to be hard for him. "I need to apologise for my attitude to you this afternoon." He swallowed.

"I would … value your advice on how best to ensure the safety and happiness of Cousin Anne. And how to cure my sister's unhappiness."

He turned towards her. "I have been most remiss in not noticing what you seem to have discovered. I would wish them to be happy."

Her head tilted upwards. "I think that you must ask them, sir. I am not at liberty to betray confidences."

He bowed. He had not expected her to speak frankly. "But will you assist me? I think that they might speak out more willingly if you are there."

She looked down. He had to make himself wait, he wanted to draw her into his arms and embrace her. He wanted to tell her of his love, of his hope that his love could be returned. He must not.

"I will be with you when you speak to Cousin Anne, sir. We have talked and she knows that she must explain to you what her wishes are, and she said that she would like me to be there if you consented."

"Thank you." He had to be content with that. It was a beginning.

"And how did you find Lady Catherine just now? I know that she relies on you."

She smiled slightly. "She was pleased to see me, I think, sir. I stayed with her some minutes. It will be well when the weather is warmer and she might spend some time outdoors."

He did not want her to have too much responsibility and have it stretching out longer.

He spoke without thinking. "I would like you to return to London with me tomorrow afternoon. I believe that the situation here can be managed by Colonel Fitzwilliam until Anne is betrothed to whoever it is she is partial to. Georgiana might stay as a companion to Anne until then."

He looked at her expression as it closed off. What was he doing wrong? In London she could rest.

"We could perhaps return each weekend when you are rested."

She didn't look up at him. "I am sorry, sir. At present I do not feel able to travel."

"Are you unwell?"

"A little, sir. It is as much as I can do at present, to maintain what I do here. And I think it is valuable."

"I agree. But I think that it is so valuable that you are being taken advantage of. The others will do what is necessary while you are not here."

"I thank you for thinking of me for that, sir. But I do not feel well enough for a journey of that length at the moment. I beg you to reconsider."

He tried to keep his temper. "Are you saying this in order to stay with my cousin? You are well enough to fulfil many needs in this house, but not well enough to travel?"

She rose to her feet. "I think this conversation is at an end, sir! For the final time, I have no partiality to your cousin. I meant every word of the vows I spoke at our marriage!" Her hand was on the latch. "And he has no feelings towards me! I know where his heart lies — and you can see it if you look!"

She lifted the latch and was gone.

CHAPTER 54

*I*n her bedchamber, she sat on the edge of the chair and pillowed her head in her arms.

She wished she could show her anger to him, but even that energy seemed to be denied her. She let herself give way to tears of frustration.

How dare he accuse her of breaking her vows, even in her mind?

She was so angry she decided she would not tell him of her suspicions as to the reason why she was unwell. But she supposed she would survive the journey if he insisted.

If only the need here wasn't so great. She would much prefer Pemberley to London. But she knew she could not do that journey just yet.

She pushed herself up and looked outside at

the darkness. Night fell early this time of year. And soon she would have to get ready for dinner.

An empty, sick feeling filled her. How could she endure dinner? But how could she not attend?

There was a brief knock on the door and her maid entered and went to her closet to bring out a gown for her to change into.

She could not do this. Not just yet.

"No, Rosina. I will not be attending dinner tonight." She took a deep breath. "Please inform Miss de Bourgh that I am unwell and would she please excuse me tonight." She turned away. "I will go to bed early."

The maid curtsied. "Yes, Mrs. Darcy. Would you like your dinner brought up to you?"

Elizabeth felt sick. "No, thank you, Rosina. Just some water."

"Yes, madam." The maid curtsied again and left the room.

Elizabeth pushed herself to her feet and went to the glass. She began taking down her hair to brush it out.

She was tired, and an early night would help. But it would not solve her problems. She must face them all soon enough.

But she would take tonight and build up her defences again, strengthen her resolve and be the wife Mr. Darcy needed.

She reminded herself of what he had done to save her from ruin, to make Lydia as safe as she could be, married and not a disgraced woman who was alone in the world with nothing.

She owed him everything. Jane's marriage and happiness, none of that could have happened if he had not saved Lydia. She took a deep breath.

～

*T*here was a knock on the door. That would be Rosina with her glass of water. "Come in."

But it was not. Her heart failed as she saw her husband reflected in the glass.

"Oh!" she clutched her hand to her heart.

"Elizabeth." He came forward. "I heard your maid telling Cousin Anne that you were unwell, that you did not even want any dinner brought up. We must talk."

He looked around, there was another chair at the writing desk. He drew it over.

"Should I call the physician, Elizabeth? It seems you have appeared to be unwell for a number of days." He reached for her hand. "I am sorry I disbelieved you."

She took her hand back. It was the reason he had imputed for her feigning illness, rather than the fact of not believing her, that had distressed her.

"No. I thank you, Mr. Darcy. But I do not need a physician."

She would not tell him of her condition. "I am a little tired, that is all."

He was silent and after a moment or two, she raised her eyes to his face. He was looking at her with the warm regard she had loved before, and a lump rose to her throat. She looked away again, fast.

"Elizabeth," he said quietly. "After you left me earlier, I thought that I was probably relying on you to assist me with what is my responsibility. I should not do that if I regretted that the others of our party were doing the same."

He shifted slightly to sit further forward. "So I have spoken to Cousin Anne. She has told me of her partiality to Richard's younger brother, Nicholas."

Elizabeth looked up at him. "I hope you were kind to her, sir."

He nodded gravely. "I trust I was. I will write tomorrow to the Earl and ask him to speak to Nicholas. I will emphasise how improved we find Anne, and that it would be as well for him to bring that young man down as soon as possible."

He smiled at her. "The sooner they are betrothed the better for all of us."

Elizabeth sat back in her seat. She was much relieved, and Georgiana would not have to watch Colonel Fitzwilliam doing his duty and marrying Anne.

She saw Mr. Darcy was watching her. "I think you may be pleased with what else I have done, for I have been much engaged since we parted."

"Oh?" Elizabeth was puzzled.

"Since I wanted to spare you extra work persuading me to do what I must, I then went to find my Cousin Richard."

Her heart was in her throat. Would Mr. Darcy part him from Georgiana, say that he had betrayed his guardianship?

"Sir, I would beg ..." but he stopped her.

"Don't worry, Elizabeth." He reached for her hand again, and this time she permitted it to stay in his warm grasp. Maybe all would be well.

"Colonel Fitzwilliam told me an extraordinary tale. I find it difficult to believe that he could have hidden his feelings from me for so long. But I am convinced that he has been afraid to say anything so that I might not accuse him of taking some advantage of his guardianship." He looked around the room. "I find him to have been most honourable."

Elizabeth held her breath, and after a moment, he continued.

"But she is, of course, much too young, and he assures me that Georgiana is not aware of his feelings towards her."

Elizabeth could not help laughing, and he looked surprised.

"You think he deceives me?"

"No, sir. I think he deceives himself. You are correct, he is being entirely honourable, but I am sure he deceives himself."

"Even so, Georgiana must have the opportunity to meet other suitable gentlemen," Mr. Darcy said. "She cannot know her own feelings."

Elizabeth smiled. "I think you might be like many fathers of young women, sir. It is hard for them to believe their own may be quite grown up."

The smile left his face. "You think she is not too young?"

"She is too young to marry, sir. Of course she is. But I think she is very unhappy, and an acknowledgement of her feelings — and his — might ease her mind. An informal understanding, perhaps?"

"Perhaps." He seemed thoughtful. "Do you think it would be a suitable match? He is near twice her age."

"He is a kind and honourable man, sir. You know him well enough to know he is not in pursuit of her fortune, or he would have preferred Anne and Rosings Park."

He bowed his head in acknowledgment. "That is a consideration I had not understood so well."

He brought his chair closer. "Might I ask your assistance one more time in this matter? Will you speak to Georgiana and say that I understand and that this — understanding — is acceptable to me. I will tell Colonel Fitzwilliam."

"I will do that with great pleasure, sir."

It is a great relief to me." His hand tightened around hers. "Now there is just one more matter to sort out."

She looked at him, but she was too tired to argue any more. *Just let it be over soon.* "Sir?"

"Yes, Elizabeth. You told me downstairs that you meant every word of the vows you spoke at our marriage. Is that true?" His eyes darkened with emotion.

She looked away. "Yes, sir."

"Would it help you to know that I also stand by every promise I made then, too?" He drew her hand to his, his finger tracing the wedding band on hers. "I took you as my wife, *to have and to hold from this day forward, for better for worse, for richer for poorer, in sickness and in health, to love and to cherish*." His voice was thick with emotion. "Every word of that was true, Elizabeth. Every word."

She stared at him. "*To love and to cherish?*" her heart was racing.

"I love you, Elizabeth. I've loved you all this time. I'm so sorry I didn't tell you earlier. At first I thought you might not want to hear it. Then I was driven to ask for your help in keeping others at bay, and I still didn't think you wanted to hear it." He was still holding her hand, still rubbing the ring with his thumb.

"I wanted you come to love me without feeling pressured to say so." He made a resigned face. "And no sooner had we arrived at Pemberley than we heard Lady Catherine had become incapacitated and we had to travel here."

He leaned forward and drew her into his arms. "I love you so much, Elizabeth, and I have such high regard for everything you have achieved here." His embrace tightened, and he drew her to her feet.

"But I am disturbed that it seems to have been at the expense of your health. Please let me call the physician, even if it is merely to satisfy my own concerns."

At last she was safe and secure in his arms where she'd ached to be for so long. She rested her head against his chest, feeling as well as hearing his strong, steady heartbeat against her ear.

"When you proposed this arrangement, sir, I felt at first I should refuse. For how could I marry a man I loved so much, when he did not love me?"

He kissed the top of her head. "And why did you decide to agree?"

"I believe I told you at the time that I was so much in your debt, I must help you."

"Yes, you did." His voice was amused. "But I am sure that was not the only reason."

"No, I hoped that I could make you love me again if we were married."

"Elizabeth, you could never make me love you again, because I already loved you. I still love you and I must offer my profound apologies to you for having hurt you."

She leaned against him. "Please say you love me again. I might soon believe it."

He nuzzled her neck. "I love you, my dearest Elizabeth. I love you more than I can say. Please believe me."

"I believe you, Fitzwilliam. I love you."

*H*e sighed. "I do believe it is almost time for dinner. Do you think you could come down with me? It might give you the opportunity to speak to Georgiana so that she does not wait another day to be reassured."

She hesitated, but then shook her head. "I am most sorry, but I do not feel able tonight. Perhaps there is time for Georgiana to come here to my room for a few moments before dinner, and then we can talk further tomorrow."

"I am concerned for you, Elizabeth. You must eat, or you cannot get well again."

She smiled at him. "Tomorrow I am sure I will be well. I will rest after I have spoken to Georgiana, and then I hope you will be able to come to me tonight. We have much to talk about."

"If that is your wish." He put his finger under her chin and lifted her face to his. His lips brushed hers in a searing promise.

"I will see you later, Elizabeth, my love."

CHAPTER 55

She lay in bed, waiting for him. It had been lovely seeing Georgiana leaving the room with a smile of relief, and she was happy her husband had asked her to do it.

Georgiana revered her brother, but she would have been most embarrassed to talk about such things to him. But it was done, and Elizabeth hoped everyone was now be as happy as she felt.

But it was so cold. She was still wrapped in her shawl and had wrapped another around her feet before pulling the covers over her.

She hoped he would not think they were there as a barrier to him. She smiled. She would remove them when he came and be sure.

But everything was all right now and she could relax. Everything was all right …

~

She woke in the middle of the night. She was warm and curled up in his arms. She could scarce believe she had gone to sleep before he came, and especially that she had not woken as he joined her.

She smothered a laugh, almost wishing he had woken her then. His arms tightened around her.

"So you've decided to wake up, have you, Elizabeth, now it is the middle of the night?"

"I wish you had woken me, sir, I …"

"My given name, if you please. I love to hear you say it."

"Fitzwilliam. I was about to say I fear that I might have made you cold."

"You were indeed cold when I came upstairs, Elizabeth. But I think you are warmer now, are you not?" his arms tightened around her. "I'm here, Elizabeth. I'm here and I'm never going to let you go. You may go back to sleep feeling safe."

~

"Thank you, Fitzwilliam. But may I say something first? I think you wanted to know if there was a reason that I was tired."

"You may say it now or in the morning, Elizabeth, whatever will ease your mind."

She leaned in closer to him. "I just want to say that I think our lives are going to change completely sooner than I had thought. It is perhaps too early to tell you, but my health seems to be affected already, so I need to tell you that I believe you will have an heir to Pemberley about harvest time."

The room was only dimly lit, the flames from the fire had died down to a glow behind the screen, but she saw him lift himself up onto one elbow and look down on her.

"Elizabeth! Are you sure?" his voice was astonished and delighted all rolled into one. "I am … I am so …" his voice tailed off.

"I believe I am sure, but I do not want it too widely known just yet. There are still many weeks when we do not know how things will go."

She smiled into the darkness. "But I think others might begin to suspect now that I am finding it difficult to eat."

"I will call the physician tomorrow," he declared. "I must know that you are well."

"Dear Fitzwilliam, I am well. Do not be concerned." She reached up to his face. "But I will see the physician if you wish me to."

"Thank you." He seemed thoughtful. "London. We will stay in London where the best physicians are to be found."

She lifted her face to his. "Maybe nearer the time. But we might have the summer at Pemberley, if things are settled here, might we?"

There was a smile in his voice. "Whatever you want, Elizabeth, whatever you want."

He lowered his face to hers. "Oh, my love, I have waited for this moment for so long."

CHAPTER 56

*H*e walked out of the great doors onto the terrace overlooking the lake. The early morning light and the birdsong were a background to his contentment, and he surveyed the park.

This summer was proving the happiest of his life. He was at Pemberley, Elizabeth was at his side, and family matters no longer needed so much attention.

Matters of business were pressing, of course, but he was trying to arrange matters so that nothing would disturb him when Elizabeth and his new family might need him.

The months had flown by and not long remained now. He heard her step on the flagstones behind him and turned, offering his hand to assist her to the stone wall at the edge of the terrace.

She smiled serenely. "Good morning, Fitzwilliam. What a beautiful day."

He lifted her hand to his lips and kissed it. "And it is going to be very warm. I hope it is not too hot for you."

She laughed. "You worry too much. When it is very warm, I retreat indoors. Some of the rooms remain so beautifully cool, the afternoons are very pleasant."

He nodded. "It has been a good idea of yours to drive out in the early mornings before the sun rises too high."

She stared around her. "Yes, I have been storing up the memories to recall during the winter in London."

She seemed to look inwards for a moment, then smiled. "Your child is kicking hard this morning, Fitzwilliam."

He placed his hand gently on her swollen body. "Good morning, my child. Do not kick your mother too hard, hmm?"

She moved his hand to the other side, and he felt the sharp heel or elbow moving within her.

"Does it feel strange, Elizabeth?"

She laughed. "I am enjoying all the new feelings very much. And I am so happy that I feel so well now."

"And I am too. You had a difficult time at first, I think."

"It is all forgotten now. My only sadness will be saying goodbye to Pemberley later."

"It will be waiting for us next spring, and we will watch our child growing here."

She nodded, and he offered his arm as they turned to go in for breakfast. It would be the last they would eat here for many months.

Georgiana joined them, and he smiled. "Good morning, Georgiana, are you ready to begin the journey?"

She curtsied to him. "Yes, Fitzwilliam." Then she turned to Elizabeth.

"Good morning, Elizabeth."

Mr. Darcy sat drinking tea and watching his two favourite ladies in the world having a cheerful conversation.

He noticed that Georgiana was absolutely radiant. Of course, they were going to London and she would see far more of Colonel Fitzwilliam than she had this summer.

He was pleased with her, though. She had been ladylike and happy, exchanging letters almost daily with Cousin Richard, and behaving most decorously when he had visited every few weeks. And Richard had been most discreet too.

Darcy smiled reminiscently. Richard was just pleased at the understanding, and that he had not lost Darcy's friendship and his chance to see Georgiana.

Elizabeth had spoken to him last week about them. Now Georgiana was within a few months of being eighteen, he had agreed that he would speak to them and allow a formal betrothal.

He knew she would be ecstatic about it, and he was also sure that she would be happy with Richard.

"What?" Both ladies were looking at him. "I'm sorry, I wasn't listening."

Elizabeth laughed. "I thought so! I was saying I would love to stay another day here. I love Pemberley so much. Perhaps we could postpone starting our journey until tomorrow?"

He smiled. "Elizabeth, you know that for you I would do anything. But you said that yesterday — and the day before — and I agreed each time." He looked at her tenderly.

"I think we must leave today, my love. Everything has been rearranged twice, and Georgiana is most impatient to get to London."

She looked at him. "Those are not your real reasons, I think."

He smiled. "You are right. I would be happy to delay another month or more, invite Cousin Richard here so that Georgiana does not pine." He made a rueful face.

"But the physician tells me we must not delay too long. And you have agreed that now is a better time to travel than when it becomes more uncomfortable for you."

"I know you are right." She sighed. "And yet I would remain here all year. I am sure the baby will be happier and healthier in the country."

He knew he agreed with her. Yet the fear of losing her was too strong within him. He had to have the finest professionals in London within easy call, this first time.

She reached over to him. "I know your fears, and I am content that we go to London. I would ensure that you are as reassured as you can be that you have done all you can."

He was, as always, amazed at her courage and strength. Never once had she intimated to him that she might be afraid for her own life or for the baby. And it was she who would suffer through the birth, he was just a bystander.

He pushed away his fear. She would be all right. She must be. He smiled at her.

"The coach will tour the Park first so that you can say goodbye. And we will travel only a short period each day for you to rest in the inns in the afternoons."

"Yes. You are very good to me. I will be well."

"And, of course, you will be close to your family. They will wish to visit you and meet the new member of the family."

She smiled happily. "It will be good to see everyone again."

They got up from the table and the ladies went upstairs to freshen up before taking the coach.

He stood waiting for them in the hall, his mind running over all the possibilities. The list in his pocket of all the best physicians in every town on the route so that he knew who to summon if required. The extra trunk, packed with every possible necessity if it might be required. She need know nothing of this.

He looked up as they came down the stairs together, arm in arm. He was so happy that they had become such good friends.

The housekeeper came to wish them farewell, holding something behind her, and she curtsied at Elizabeth.

"Excuse me, madam, I have crafted a small something for the next heir to Pemberley. I hope it is acceptable to you." And she held out a small package.

"Oh, how very kind you are, Mrs. Reynolds." Elizabeth took the package. "May I peep inside now?"

The woman looked delighted. "Thank you, madam."

He watched, a little amused, as Elizabeth tore open the wrappings and took out a beautiful baby gown, delicately embroidered with details he couldn't see from where he was.

She exclaimed with delight. "Look, Georgiana! There are little scenes from the Park, and little birds around the hem." The ladies bent over the gown, examining it in detail. "Oh, thank you so much, Mrs. Reynolds. It must have taken you all summer to work this much detail. It is beautiful."

He could see Elizabeth had tears in her eyes, and the housekeeper looked gratified at her response.

He stepped forward. "Thank you, Mrs. Reynolds. It has been very kind of you to take so much trouble over your gift."

She curtsied, and hurried to the door, embarrassed by so much praise.

Elizabeth folded the wrappings around the baby gown carefully, and held it as she climbed into the coach.

"Wasn't that kind of Mrs. Reynolds?" she said

to Georgiana, and the two began to talk about the stitches used.

Mr. Darcy swung in and nodded to the coachman. He looked at his wife. "But it will be too small, surely, for the baby. It is very tiny."

She smiled at him. "It is the perfect size for a new baby, Fitzwilliam. New babies are smaller than you think. It is most beautiful, and if there were no family heirloom baptism gown, it would be suitable for that."

"Then let us use it. Mrs. Reynolds has served the family a long time. She would be delighted if you wrote and told her the baby had worn it at the baptism."

He reached for her hand. "Now you need to say goodbye to the estate. I would not have you miss the last views."

CHAPTER 57

*E*lizabeth stood at the window and looked out on the London scene. She had grown to love it here, although not as much as Pemberley, of course.

But the gracious house was already decorated with holly and filled with laughter.

Christmas had always been her favourite time, and now the nativity season held a special joy for her as a mother.

She heard the door open, and turned. The nursery maid was bringing her son to her. He bounced excitedly when he saw her, and she reached out and took him.

"Good morning, sweetheart. Did you have a good night, or were you troublesome?"

"He slept very well, madam." The nurse curtsied, and Elizabeth nodded.

She turned back to the window, watching for her husband. There he was, riding past and turning into the stable.

"There you are," she told her son. "Papa is home." She jiggled him in her arm. "Say Papa, Papa."

The baby cooed happily at her and she sat down and bounced him on her lap.

It was only a few minutes later when she heard a door banging and some footsteps outside.

"Here he is now." She looked up as the breakfast room door opened and her husband entered.

❧

"Good morning, Elizabeth." He bowed.

"Good morning, son." He stepped forwards and ruffled his son's hair.

"May I?" and he scooped the child up and swung him high over his head and the baby shrieked with laughter. It was their usual way of greeting and the swing had got higher and more exuberant as the boy had shown his confidence. Then he brought him down and settled him back on Elizabeth's lap.

But he didn't stay distant. He dropped to one

knee to be at the child's eye level. "So, Charles Richard Darcy, are you looking forward to Christmas dinner? Are you to be permitted to stay up late?"

Elizabeth enjoyed watching the developing bond between father and son. She laughed.

"We will have to see how well he takes a sleep this afternoon. He might be even-tempered enough to stay up for a while."

She touched her husband's arm. "It is very good of you to allow my family to come for Christmas."

"No. They are my family too, now. Of course they must come for Christmas. In future years, if we are at Pemberley, it may be too far for them. But this year, we are here, so they are all welcome."

She knew he meant it. All were invited — not the Wickhams, of course, but they were in Newcastle.

She sighed. "I believe everything is ready for them. I cannot remember a time when so many of the family were together, the Gardiners, the Bennets, the Bingleys, the Darcys, Cousin Richard, and Anne and Nicholas." She paused.

"I cannot wait to see Cousin Anne again. Nicholas is very good for her."

"I agree." Darcy was tickling his son who was

wriggling and laughing. He looked up, serious. "I was sad when Lady Catherine passed so suddenly last month, after all the work you had put in to help her be content with her life. But I cannot be sorry that it happened. Rosings Park can now truly be Anne and Nicholas's."

Elizabeth laughed. "Poor Mr. Collins has finally lost his patroness."

Mr. Darcy threw back his head and laughed. Then he looked at her, suddenly serious.

"But we have no need of any outside patroness, or anyone else. We have each other. You are the only one I need, Elizabeth, and you will be beside me forever. You've given me joy and happiness. And a son —" He paused and tickled the baby again.

The baby had a rich, contented chuckle just like his father's.

Elizabeth couldn't help but smile when she heard it from either of these two men in her life.

"And I am as indebted to you, too, sir, for the same. Your love is what I wake with each day, your presence is what gives me the joy I feel every moment."

Her lips curved. "And I am so happy that you are learning that when I tease you, it does not mean I love you any the less."

He reached for her and embraced her, their son between them. "And I love you for all of that too, Elizabeth. I am much blessed."

ABOUT THE AUTHOR

Harriet Knowles loves writing about Jane Austen's wonderful characters from Pride and Prejudice.

She is the author of several novels, including

Mr. Darcy's Stolen Love
and
Compromise and Obligation

Her next book is
The Darcy Plot

Printed in Great Britain
by Amazon